The Literate Thief

BOOK 2 in The Slaves of Erafor series

WALTER RHEIN

Perseid Press
P.O. Box 584
Centerville, MA 02632

Literate Thief

Published by arrangement with the author.

First Perseid Press trade paperback edition, 2018
First Perseid Press Kindle edition, 2018
First Perseid Press e-Pub edition, 2018

This is a work of fiction. All the characters and events portrayed in this book are fictional, and any resemblance to real people or incidents is purely coincidental.

Book design, Christopher Morris
Cover design, Roy Mauritsen
Cover art: Copyright © 2018 Perseid Press

Trade: ISBN-13: 978-1-948602-09-9
ePub: ISBN-13: 978-1-948602-10-5
Kindle: ISBN-13: 978-1-948602-08-2

Published in the United States of America

Related titles by Walter Rhein

READER OF ACHERON

LITERATE THIEF

Contents

The Literate Thief

BOOK 2 in The Slaves of Erafor series

Chapter 1: Dark Industry

Janus squinted against the penetrating light. He lifted his hand and turned his head in search of shadow. Orion had summoned him to this place beneath the world, and the subterranean pathways that had brought him were lit only by the dim luminescence of the guardian moss. After a few moments of pain, Janus's vision began to adapt, and the Seneschal took stock of his surroundings.

He stood at the doorway to a sterilized chamber. Blazing, artificial light flooded the room, revealing four bare walls unbroken by windows or adornments. Orion stood with his back to the entrance obscuring with his body a metallic slab overspilling with tubes and wires.

Janus was a well-muscled man, clothed in the uniform black of his station. He moved with the practiced grace of an accomplished swordsman. Even among the Seneschal, he had a reputation as a competent and contemplative man. Few among the residents of Edentown held higher positions, yet Janus suffered the presence of a master now.

The Seneschal attempted to discern the source of the chamber's illumination, to no avail. The blinding radiance was impenetrable. Janus turned in defeat, blinking away the afterimages that blackened his sight.

The room provoked a sense of vulnerability. The slippery, polished surface of the walls and floors glistened in a way the warrior found disturbing. Janus had done enough night work to understand the need for a chamber resistant to blood-spatter. Dark industry had conceived this place. The Seneschal's attention turned to a drain beneath the central slab.

Flooded to wash the filth away, he thought. *How efficient.*

Orion gave no acknowledgment of the Senechal's arrival, but Janus knew Orion was aware of his presence. Janus had never seen Orion surprised by anything. Orion was physically smaller than Janus, but his dominating presence was almost as oppressive as the blinding light. He wore a light blue apron over a gray shirt. Orion's hair was white, but the man was athletic, strong and stood with no bend in his back.

Janus found it difficult to peer past Orion to see what horror the table held. Then again, maybe his subconscious had guessed and his senses conspired to spare him the confirmation.

Orion spoke without offering any salutation or explanation as to why Janus had been summoned.

"I remember a time," Orion said, "when there were toilets available for public use. Pleasant structures designed to provide relief when you found yourself in need away from the comfort of your home." Orion tugged at a pair of rubber gloves that extended just past the fleshy part of his palm. His face screwed up in an expression of disgust. "The walls became stained with fecal matter. You could see fingerprints in the filth." Orion's nose wrinkled at the unpleasant thought. "They'd trace out figures . . . perhaps write their names. What place is there for a breed of sub-human that would perform such acts?"

Janus didn't answer. He was keenly aware that the familiar weight of the sword on his belt was missing. The Seneschal had been asked to surrender the weapon at a checkpoint some hundred yards back. It had been a ceremonial gesture, Janus was certain Orion had no fear of a man armed with a mere blade.

Orion was untouchable.

How old is he? What secrets does he keep?

In the brilliant light, Janus could not focus on the questions. As Orion moved, Janus's eyes continued to adapt, he caught glimpses of the bundle on the table. An opaque brown sheet covered an object of considerable bulk. Tubes of various sizes and colors ran out from beneath and connected to boxes and cylinders standing behind the slab. Janus stepped forward and caught a scent which caused him to choke back a gag.

"In my youth," Orion continued, "I used to gather young people together to share knowledge. Not my choice," he clarified, turning back to gaze directly at Janus for the first time; "the task was forced upon me."

Orion turned and grabbed the corner of the brown sheet that covered the slab. With a sharp motion, he pulled the obstructing canvas away.

Janus gasped at the revealed horror.

Upon the table was the body of a human being. The torso had been cloven down the middle and pried open with clamps. Four thick restraining straps held the poor creature down, with additional restraints at the ankles, wrists and neck. Every limb had large swaths of the skin peeled away. Hundreds of lines of white thread kept the chunks of flesh in suspended positions above or to the side of their natural location. The face was covered with a mask connected to the largest of the mysterious tubes.

Orion reached out to the body. With great care, he caressed the creature's shoulder. Beneath his light touch, the mutilated man on the slab twitched.

Janus stepped back in shock.

"He lives?" he said, surprised to hear the horror in his voice. Surely Orion heard it as well, and Janus feared his slip would have consequences.

But Orion continued, seemingly oblivious to the transgression.

"I used to teach," he said, "and you must understand the value of my lessons. For thousands of years, great men and women have toiled in obscurity, driven by a special sort of madness, dedicating the sum of their lives to the distillation of truth. This type of person exhibits a unique and special form of insanity. They are willing to forsake family, wealth, love, and the admiration of their peers for the hope of some abstract, fleeting instant of enlightenment. Can you imagine?" Orion looked up, and Janus had to correct his expression to something more appropriate than a reflection of the horror on the slab. Orion shrugged and looked back to his labors. "The scholar's sacrifice was collected in the form of minuscule droplets compiled and passed down for generations. This distillation went on for centuries, and by the time the knowledge was entrusted to me, they had amassed *gallons*!"

Blood stained Orion's rubber-encased fingers. Janus was no stranger to blood, but he did not endure stains on his clothing when necessity had passed. Orion seemed not to care.

"I would freely distribute this concentrated genius won by suffering." An edge entered Orion's voice. "Yet my charges had the temerity to come to my lectures intoxicated! You'd smell it upon them, see the displacement in their vacant eyes, and the whole enterprise was reduced through their disengagement. They mocked the sacrifice of the brave pioneers who had given everything."

Orion pushed aside bits of flesh in his subject's torso. He let out a long whistle.

"What is it?" Janus asked.

"Do you see that?" Orion pointed into the chest cavity. The tone of his voice had changed; curiosity replaced the consternation of his prior discourse.

Janus peered forward but could make no sense of what he saw. There seemed to be only a chaotic mass of internal organs and blood.

"The adrenal gland," Orion said. "The color is wrong and it's three times larger than it should be. This is a new manifestation, almost as if there has been a chemical change."

Orion pulled back his hands and stood for a moment, a pensive look on his face. Again, Janus found himself disconcerted. Orion's consciousness seemed to have flown, with only a husk of disanimate flesh remaining. Yet after a moment, Orion's full presence returned.

"The *Bliss* is responsible, of course; that's why they're so strong after years of use. If only there was some way to keep the benefits of strength while eliminating the additional aggression." Orion glanced at Janus. "Think how much more effective they'd be." He looked back at the body, "But something else seems to be have happened to this subject, something I haven't seen before."

Orion grew contemplative. He stepped back from the slab and walked over to a small basin with a pitcher of water. Janus was only too pleased to step away from the mutilated subject on the table as well.

As Orion washed his hands, he called over his shoulder. "It has been weeks since Cassius went out after Adam Lockhart. I think we can safely assume that he is dead."

"Lockhart?" Janus replied.

"No, Cassius."

Janus's head snapped up. "Surely he has only been delayed. Should we not hold out hope he will send word soon?"

"His messages stopped a week ago."

Janus tried to process the information. Cassius had been among the strongest of the Seneschal. "Who could have killed Cassius; surely not that feeble old man?" he asked.

Orion finished rinsing his hands and dried them with a towel. He approached Janus.

"Somebody has discovered ambition," he said, tilting his head in reflection. "The culprit is nameless now, but time will draw him out. Every idiot thinks he should have been higher born, that his shoulders can bear the burden of leadership. Watch the coward wither at the first glancing touch of the prize. The neck of a low-born usurper is crushed by the weight of a crown."

Orion smiled as if at some private joke.

Janus's eyes returned to the body. Following his gaze, Orion spoke. "It's easy to hide in the shadows and cast stones at a leader of men. But when the leader stands tall and absorbs all assaults while continuing in stoic competence, the true nature of the revolutionaries is revealed. They are dregs with but a fragmented grasp of the larger picture, and must be trained in obedience. Order is not a natural state; it must be forced—with violence, if necessary. If it is not so, the upstarts stumble haphazardly onto just enough strength to wreak havoc on the plans of greater men. I can think of no more selfish act than to disrupt the machinations of a functioning system merely because a single individual feels slighted by his lot."

"Certainly not," Janus agreed.

Orion gave Janus an appraising look. The moment endured, and Orion's straight white teeth glinted with predatory malice.

"Good," he said finally.

Janus sensed a dismissal and was tempted to take his leave, but the Seneschal's curiosity got the better of him.

"Who was he?" the warrior asked, making a casual gesture toward the dissected subject.

Orion turned with a confused and slightly perturbed expression, and then laughed. "Oh, a slave. He might live for another day, which would be advantageous since it is better to observe an operational system."

Janus went quiet. In almost a whisper, he asked, "Did he have a name?"

Orion scoffed. "Probably, if only for the sake of the master's convenience. You know how slaves are; unless you are specific about designating a task, they all plead confusion."

Janus nodded. He wanted to look away from the torment before him, but on impulse decided to hold his gaze. He stared at the mutilated human being strapped down on the table. He memorized what he saw for the purposes of later reflection. There was value in comprehending what Orion could do. Janus wasn't sure how he felt at the sight, but some part of the horrific image resonated to the core of his being.

Orion came to stand beside the Seneschal.

"Remember, my friend; as you climb, you encounter both assistance and opposition, but the peak is solely populated with those who would pull you down."

Janus felt the blood drain from his cheeks.

"Here's something to direct your meditation." Orion gestured at the table. "This one earned his fate. What must his transgression have been? You are a reflective man; I've always appreciated that about you."

"Was he one of those who painted with his own excrement?" Janus offered.

Orion snorted and shook his head.

"No . . . he's guilty of much, much worse. This one sought to rise above."

Chapter 2: The Master's Hold

The air was heavy with the smell of cold, wet earth. Patches of melting snow littered the landscape; defying the warmth of encroaching spring by persisting beneath bushes and in hollows of natural shadow. Dormant brown grass stretched to the horizon, still prostrate from the weight of winter's bulk. The landscape seemed newly born; the creatures that walked the surface did so on shaky legs, feeble with the strangeness of life.

Quillion, Kikkan, and Cole crouched behind a stony ridge overlooking a valley. The three sported thick beards grown for protection against freezing winds. These they would cut when, or if, they sought enlistment in a local militia. Quillion disliked the prospect of hiring out his arm for coin, but the way of the mercenary had an eternal compulsion.

Kikkan, the former slave, was by far the largest of the three. The heavy winter coat that wreathed his shoulders could not conceal his broad back or hide the implication of rippling muscle beneath. His clothing was a mixture of homespun and reclaimed articles discovered in abandoned buildings during his travels. On his back he wore a canvas pack, and the threaded end of a metal pipe jutted out over his right shoulder within easy reach of his hand.

Though not as massive as Kikkan, Quillion could also be called larger than average. He too had managed to bundle himself with scraps of cast-off fabric, and had adapted a wool blanket into a poncho. On his hip hung a sword in a scuffed and battered sheath, but this was an item of last resort. Quillion's greatest battle asset was his cunning and knack for strategy. He preferred gambits that were decided before his opponent even thought to draw a blade. Quillion's eyes sparkled with keen intelligence, darting back and forth across the landscape with an insatiable curiosity.

Cole was the smallest, though what he gave up in strength he more than reclaimed in speed and agility. He too was equipped with a sword that hung from his belt in a black leather sheath. Although the weapon was worn, the pommel gleamed with the polish of meticulous care. In repose, Cole's right hand seemed to quest for the grip. He rubbed his thumb and forefinger together absently, and the dead metal almost seemed to quiver in longing to answer its master's call.

The three companions observed a farmhouse nestled below in a quiet valley. The building had two stories with the typical combination of old and new construction that indicated an occupied residence. A meandering stream boasting boulders large enough to create flashes of white water passed through a cove of nearby trees, and several cows grazed in a fenced-in area where the valley widened.

In the silence of their observation, Quillion could sense Kikkan's rage.

Over the last several months, the three had traveled together in a sometimes uneasy alliance. They had met in Oshia at the battle which had claimed the life of Cassius of Edentown. The scholar known as Adam Lockhart had seemed delighted to witness the forging of their fellowship. Although

Kikkan considered the elder man a mentor, Quillion harbored doubts about Lockhart's motivations.

Quillion had observed in Kikkan a tendency toward uncompromising, emotionally-driven behavior. In light of the larger man's background, Quillion didn't begrudge Kikkan's adherence to a strict moral code. Quite the contrary – Quillion admired the survival tactic. Yet the northerner feared that sooner or later, the former slave's inflexibility would create problems. The prospect of going into battle with an unpredictable asset like Kikkan weighed on Quillion.

"The farmhouse is the residence of that old man," Kikkan said, nodding at the figures below, "with a small shed for his two slaves; a man and a woman."

Quillion had come to the same conclusion, but he wished to hear how Kikkan had arrived at his assessment.

"How do you know the man and the woman are slaves? Perhaps they own the property together, and the old man is the servant?"

Kikkan's jaw tightened and his eyes narrowed to murderous slits. He raised his hand to point.

"That one is the master," he said, indicating the somewhat stooped farmer meandering about the premises.

Quillion turned to observe as directed.

"Watch how he moves," Kikkan said.

Quillion watched.

The man was slow and deliberate. He seemed to favor his right leg, yet when he planted his foot on the ground, he twisted with a jerk that rent the earth beneath his heel.

"What am I looking for?" Quillion asked.

"Urgency," Kikkan hissed.

"I see none."

"That's how you know he's free," Kikkan replied. As he spoke, Kikkan reached behind him to pull forth the long metal pipe. Quillion happened to glance at the end of the weapon as it passed before his eyes. The threads that had been cut into the tip were stained with clotted blood and remnants of hair.

"Look," Cole said, speaking for the first time. He pointed, and both Kikkan and Quillion followed his gesture.

Two children appeared in the clearing before the house. The tittering sound of their banter echoed up to the three warriors squatting in the dirt. The appearance of the little ones seemed to paralyze Kikkan. The effect lasted only a moment. The large man shook his head.

"The presence of children changes nothing," Kikkan growled. "The slaves must be freed."

"Wait," Quillion hissed, reaching over to place a steadying hand on Kikkan's arm. The former slave cast a withering gaze at the audacious mercenary. Quillion released Kikkan, but the northerner continued with his point.

"We should leave this," he said. "We don't know the circumstance. It's not our battle."

"Slavery is my battle," Kikkan growled.

"But—"

Kikkan cut him off. "But nothing! It's easy for one such as you to find tolerance when you have never known the cut of a master's whip. I can't turn aside and sentence that life upon another. The master's heel scars the earth and even here I feel the cut of his boot upon my back. No, I shall oppose the abomination!" Kikkan stood and began striding down the valley wall, pipe in hand.

Quillion sighed as the big man made his way.

"We should stop him," Cole said when Kikkan was out of earshot.

Quillion glanced over at his friend and noticed the smaller swordsman's expression of contempt.

"I'm not sure we can anymore," Quillion admitted. "Kik-kan has grown strong since we first met. Free air and regular meals have put muscle on his frame I've not seen on another soul in all my days. Plus, he's no dullard to be taken down with a trick."

"Do you think the children belong to the slaves or the master?" Cole asked.

"I don't know."

Cole stood. He didn't look at Quillion, but he spoke with resolve. "If he intends to lay a finger on those children, he'll meet my blade. If that happens, you'd better back me up, be-cause he'll be coming after you when he's done with me. Use that little toy you got from Lockhart if you have to."

Cole started making his way in pursuit of Kikkan.

Quillion sighed, his hand reflexively going to the loaded .38 snub nose that he carried in his pocket. One of the first quests he and Cole had shared with Kikkan had been to re-turn to a farmhouse where Kikkan had discovered several boxes of ammunition. Quillion carried those boxes now. The prospect of using the archaic weapon on his traveling com-panion caused a wave of discomfort to pass over him. Quil-lion sensed there would be ample targets more deserving of his limited store of bullets than this man who had walked beside him as a friend. But fate was fickle and sometimes brought great tragedies to pass despite the will and labors of cunning mortals.

For a moment, Quillion considered sitting out the up-coming conflict, but he discarded the thought and stood, shaking his head in befuddlement. Lately, it seemed he spent more time playing catch-up to the schemes of others than putting his own plots into action.

What madness deluded men into thinking they might harvest honor from the fray? Quillion's focus was always on the slim chance of death that existed no matter how great the probability of victory. Prudence had kept Quillion alive. If others wished to tempt the eternal blade, Quillion had no qualms about guiding the cutting edge across their throats. Yet, here again, harm's way beckoned, and as Quillion made his way after his companions, he could dimly hear the muffled chortling of the underworld.

*

Kikkan neared the clearing, with Cole trailing a dozen yards behind. The old man, two slaves and the children saw him coming. At first, there was no response to Kikkan's approach. Then the two slaves sprang into motion and sent the children scurrying back into a small hut.

The old man stepped forward, keeping one arm behind his body.

"Is there something I can help you with, stranger?" he said. His voice was strong and cut the air with authority.

Kikkan locked eyes with the man and never slowed. "Do you claim ownership of those people behind you?" he said, gesturing with his pipe.

"Yes. I am the owner of this farm and everything on it." The old man retreated in the face of Kikkan's growing menace.

"Then today you will know disappointment, for while you claim the lives of slaves as your property, I claim the lives of all slave owners as mine!" Kikkan lifted his pipe.

The old man reacted with surprising spryness. He dropped into a crouch and pulled his arm from behind his back to reveal a black machete with a gleaming edge. He swung the weapon wildly.

Kikkan was so focused on his own assault that he didn't have time to react to the counter-attack. The tip of the blade dug into the former slave's leg just above the knee. Kikkan howled and lurched forward with his left hand to grab the farmer's wrist. The farmer jerked backward, causing the blade to saw against Kikkan's leg. The large warrior's muscles tightened at the electric jolt of pain, and he brought his right arm down in a violent chop, the pipe making a hollow whistling noise at it crashed through the air.

As always, the impact of metal against flesh was heralded by a dull thud. Kikkan felt the fight leave the farmer's arm instantly. The wrist, so recently tight with resistance, turned flaccid in Kikkan's fingers and slipped from his grasp.

The farmer's body fell in a heap just as Cole arrived. An unsettling silence ensued.

"Is it over?" Cole asked, and Kikkan couldn't quite interpret the tension that seemed to line Cole's eyes. A haze of pain, his injury, and their current proximity to death had sapped Kikkan's strength. The former slave nodded in somber agreement.

Their brief reprieve was shattered by a tortured scream.

"No!"

The word was drawn out in a hollow wail as the woman Kikkan had identified as a slave came sprinting to the body of the fallen man.

"What have you done?" she cried.

Kikkan made a shuffling step in retreat, only then realizing the machete still protruded from his leg. He pulled the weapon free and dropped to his knees as agony rolled over him.

"We better stop that bleeding," Cole said. Kikkan heard the sound of tearing cloth and was vaguely aware of Cole attending to his wound.

The woman dropped to her knees beside the body of her master. Tears lined her face.

"Cecilia!" came a sharp command from behind.

Kikkan looked round to see a man approaching.

"Cole," he managed to grunt, alerting his companion to the potential danger.

Cole gave a final tug on the crude bandage and stood as Quillion trotted over from his jog down the hill. Quillion had seen what had transpired and moved to take control.

"We wish no further conflict," Quillion stated. "My companion here," he gestured at Kikkan, "has freed you."

"Freed us?" the man asked.

Quillion experienced a sinking sensation. "Yes, freed you."

"Who presumed we wished to be freed?" the man snapped. He kneeled down in the dirt next to his master's body and began to comfort the sobbing woman.

Quillion glanced at Cole in confusion.

After a few seconds, the woman looked up with a tear-streaked face.

"He was kind to us," she snapped, "he allowed us to live together as a family and raise our children."

"Now you are free to live as you wish," Kikkan said.

"Where are we to go?" the man growled.

"Live here," Kikkan said. Take this property as your own, continue the life you have known, but labor for your own reward and not his."

"How are we supposed to do that when we are known in this community as slaves to this master?" the man said. "Do you think they will accept our crops at harvest without a lawful freeman to barter for a price? We will be hung as murderers and our children will be separated and sold."

"No!" the woman sobbed.

Quillion set his jaw. "Well," he said, directing the words at Kikkan, "now what?"

Kikkan returned Quillion's stare. "The transition to freedom is sometimes unpleasant, but the rewards justify the struggle," Kikkan spat.

"Will you assist them in this transition?" Quillion retorted. "Are they not your charges now?"

"Their freedom is their own, I must not interfere," Kikkan replied.

Quillion scoffed. "I don't think you've thought this out."

"No," Kikkan snapped, "it's *you* who have not thought it out. Slavery is not a clean business filled with eternal glory. It is vile! Slavery is a rot that exists in the mind and heart as much as in the iron shackles that bind ankle and wrist."

"Not all patients survive when the sickness is cut out?" Quillion snapped. "Is that what you're saying?"

"I am," Kikkan replied, his voice firm.

Quillion shook his head. He kneeled and took the machete from Kikkan's hand. The large man did not resist, but his eyes showed suspicion. Quillion stepped over to the newly freed slave. He handed him the weapon.

"Gather up your family and as many provisions as all of you can carry. Travel north to Acheron and say that you are free people and that your home was burned by raiders."

"But we are slaves," the man protested, his voice quivering, "they'll never believe –"

"Make them believe! At the gates of eternity, no just god will begrudge you this deception. You have no choice now; the sooner you understand, the greater your chance of survival. You are free. No matter how it happened, or whether or not you wanted it, this freedom has come to you. Your previous life has ended. Take a family name and go where your faces and background are not known. Go now, time is against you!"

The man hesitated, so Quillion gave the former slave a starting push. The woman stood and regarded Quillion with murder in her eyes, her body tense.

Quillion returned her stare unflinching.

"Remember your children, Cecilia," Quillion said, repeating the name the man had used. "No good can come from further bloodshed."

The defiance lingered in Cecilia's eyes and her hands trembled in the throes of indecision.

"That iron you feel in your spine is what will save you," Quillion said. "Your master's 'kindness' was an illusion; you've never needed his protection. I can see in your eyes you have all the strength you shall ever need. It's time for you to come to know that as well."

Somehow, the words penetrated, and Cecilia turned to join her husband. Quillion watched as the man set about making preparations. Then the northerner turned back to his companions. "Can you walk Kikkan?"

Kikkan nodded.

"Then we should go. We need to distance ourselves from this place."

Kikkan didn't protest. He stumbled to his feet and even accepted Quillion's shoulder when the stout mercenary offered support.

"Did it go as you had hoped?" Quillion asked. He didn't intend mockery, and regretted how the words sounded the instant they left his lips. But Kikkan surprised him as he had done so often.

"It was not what I expected," he replied, his voice soft, the defiance gone. "I have much to consider."

"As do I," Quillion replied, conceding the point. "As do I."

Chapter 3: Reunion

In early autumn of the previous year, a thief called Simyon sat at a restaurant known as the Vine. The Vine was located beside the main thoroughfare of San Borja, the second richest district of Edentown. Situated on the corner of Andennium and Colver Street, the Vine provided an excellent vantage point for people-watching. Vine patrons lounged in iron-wrought chairs, sipping fine coffee made from exotic beans. If not coffee, a wide variety of teas were available. Every one of the boiled herbs boasted a different medicinal property: be it a sleep aid, an energy magnifier, or something to boost sexual potency.

In truth, the last was the most popular. San Borja was widely known as a fine place for high class citizens to find young ladies willing to offer themselves as companionship for a discreet and exhilarating evening. The residents of San Borja were not as wretched as the creatures that existed in the provinces, and thus were adequate for taking sport.

Simyon, however, hadn't come for that.

He was a young and handsome man. Wealthy ladies had elected to contract his services on occasion. However, Simyon had long since concluded he should avoid such arrangements. Clients tended to work him hard. His female friends who were adept at turning tricks, laughed at the recounts of his labor. The fair ones could spin a coin from shadow while hardly interrupting an evening stroll. Simyon, however, was often ridden to a lather and then expected to tidy up in whatever time remained. Thus, the enterprise became too much like honest work. There were also inherent dangers, such as the unexpected arrival of the cuckolded spouse. Angry husbands were especially dangerous and unpredictable in close quarters. Most night-walkers carried a deterrent in a vial as protection. When broken, the vial released a cloud of sleeping gas. Simyon, however, had never been able to get the mixture right, and had been exposed without recourse more than once. He considered simple theft a far safer mode of obtaining sustenance.

Still, the young thief enjoyed observing the girls who worked the Vine. He was not blind to the spectacle of a well-formed body, and the artistry of a woman managing a fool was a joy to behold.

A dulcet voice interrupted his musings.

"Do you mind if I sit with you for a moment, sir?"

Simyon's face twisted into a wry smile as he turned to regard the female speaker. The voice was known to him. She had grown from whelp to woman on the streets at his side and then been torn away, though on occasion their paths did cross.

Valeria.

"Please," Simyon said, his words catching in his throat as he peered into her hazel eyes. "Please, by all means." He stood to pull an empty chair away from the table.

"You're too kind," Valeria said.

Simyon returned to his seat to assess his new table companion. She wore a form-fitting dress that left little to the imagination. A fashionable shawl around her shoulders provided some relief against the chill of the late autumn air. To all outward appearances, she was a young woman of considerable means, but Simyon knew the truth. She was as much a sewer rat as he. The two of them had run together for years; breaking homes, avoiding constables, and sustaining themselves however they could. Survival became easier as they matured, but at times, the outcome had not been at all certain. She was the closest thing he had to family.

"May I offer you some refreshment?" Simyon asked, motioning for the waiter with one arm.

"A tea would be wonderful," Valeria replied, pursing her full lips in a seductive smile.

"Goldenroot?" Simyon asked, smiling.

"That's quite presumptuous, sir," Valeria scolded, her cheeks flushed.

Simyon was impressed. She had gotten good at her trade if she could make him almost believe.

The waiter arrived and inclined his head in silent submission.

"Two black teas," Simyon declared with a wave. The waiter hurried off.

The sun was going down in the distance and the shadows were beginning to lengthen. Soon, the night dwellers would come alive and start looking for trouble, but for now, calm remained. Silence fell between the young man and woman. Two liars, who sat feigning comfort in the encroaching darkness, dressed in clothing that had cost them plenty; both in labor and dignity.

Labor was cheap; dignity, less so.

"So," Simyon said finally, "might this visit not interrupt your earnings for the night?"

Valeria laughed, her lips making a perfect 'O' that framed her shining white teeth and the flickering of her pink tongue. Simyon went quiet.

"Hardly. The best players don't come out for a few hours yet, and besides, the real money lies elsewhere."

"Oh? Where's the real money?"

Valeria tilted her head and smiled. "It's nice to see you . . ." She let the sentence trail into silence without uttering a name. They had learned all the tricks of camouflage years ago. For a moment, Simyon's mind danced with memories of chasing Valeria through the alleys and dark spots of Edentown into hidden places only they knew.

Quiet places where they could lie low and be alone.

Be careful of this woman, she's out of your league now. She's a girl no longer, remember that!

Valeria leaned back and smiled. She lounged easily in her chair, her delicate legs crossed and bouncing in the brisk air of the early night.

The tea came and the waiter backed away, not inquiring as to their need of further service.

Only then did Simyon realize he was staring at her. His gaze slid up and down her cheek, tracing every outline in the dim light. Simyon watched fascinated as the glimmer played off her skin and caressed her body. The sight captivated him, just as it always had. Why couldn't he turn away? He closed his eyes, breaking the spell, and wondered how she could have such power over him.

"Do you still have the bow?" he asked.

"Whatever do you mean?" There was a touch of reprimand in Valeria's tone.

Simyon smirked. The days of her bringing down rats in near darkness were so long ago. They had been replaced by the backs of wrinkled old monarchs pounding like slaves in a field. The sound of forced and falsified pleasure ringing out from Valeria's lips.

They never even knew the difference. She was an artist . . . of course they didn't.

"Tell me," Simyon said, lowering his voice, "is it true what they say?"

"And what do they say?"

A hint of flirtation remained in her voice.

"Wealthy men have a tender touch."

Valeria's eyes flashed. Not one in a thousand would have seen it, but to Simyon, the flash shone as clear as lightning.

He had struck a mark. Good, maybe there was something left inside the shallow husk after all. She used to give him the same look when he pulled on her pigtails.

"It seems you've done well enough for yourself," she replied, nodding at his clothing.

Did other men notice that she never answered a question?

"Well," Simyon sighed, "I'm still here. I haven't been swallowed up by the underworld yet."

"That's better than some."

"And you're here."

At this, her head tilted and the smile drew thin.

"Should I go?"

Simyon hesitated. He dropped his eyes.

"No, no, I don't want you to go."

It was as close to the truth as he was willing to share.

"Are you going to be nice?"

He didn't answer. He merely lifted up his tea and took a sip. "Who are you waiting for tonight?" He could change the subject, too.

She leaned back in her chair with a laugh and looked at the sky, her feet kicking out. Simyon was drawn by the curve of her ankles, the daintiness of her foot. She projected a stunning innocence – like an angel, like a newborn child.

Where had she learned *that*? On what model had she based her interpretation?

She had been more of a tomboy when they had lain together for the first time. She told him she loved him, and that she wanted them to be together always. He might have even said the same.

The tea scalded his tongue.

"He's very wealthy," Valeria said, not meeting Simyon's gaze. "He wears fine clothing and rides a mighty charger and is quick and agile with a sword."

"Flesh or steel?"

"Now, you said you'd be nice." Valeria pouted.

This girl could have every cent from me, Simyon thought. *She could get me to give it to her and make me think it my idea.*

The truth became clear. "You're making a regular thing of this one, aren't you?"

Valeria shrugged.

Simyon snorted. He looked away. He had to continue to look away to retain a minor bit of control. Why had the gods decided to make one such as she so cursedly beautiful? To distract himself, he continued with his line of thinking.

"You're trying to make him believe he loves you; am I right? You let him steal you away for an afternoon or a weekend. He fills your head with promises, tells you how he's going to leave his wife behind . . . How he's going to marry you and make the children you bear him his legitimate heirs . . ."

Simyon was talking just for the distraction, but he caught another faint blush and suddenly realized he had hit closer to the mark than he might have guessed.

"Has the subject of payment even come up?"

She didn't yield much as he searched her features for a response, but she showed enough. Awe settled in.

"My, my . . . that is the big time. How much are you investing?" He eyed her attire. "Are you sure . . . I mean really sure . . . it isn't you who is getting played this time?"

She smiled coyly and remained silent, her face again unreadable. They sat together on that cursed street, not a half-mile from the dock under which they had met.

Back when she had been cast aside.

Back when nobody wanted her.

Nobody but him.

Now she was here, right beside him, and a thousand miles away. Too good for his poor company. Hanging her hopes on the lies of some lecherous nobleman.

Simyon knew he too was lecherous, since above all he wanted her. His fingers twitched in anticipation. Sweat trickled down his forehead and his abdomen. Even his toes curled. He wanted her. He wanted to leap across the table and take her; take her in front of every man, woman, and child at the Vine. He wanted to take her so that all would know she was his and his alone forever.

"We could go, you know," he said.

"Where?"

Simyon dropped his voice. "To the underworld, the hidden cities beyond Brinewater; there are places for us, opportunity . . ."

Valeria laughed. "Join the sewer rats? Scurrying for food and constantly running from demons? I thought you'd die rather than submit to that fate."

"Things are different now." Simyon became aware of his own intensity and looked away.

Valeria sat in silence.

"Yes," she finally said, but the word was a hiss more than an affirmation.

Simyon looked up, an electric thrill coursing through his breast. Whatever emotion had begun to take life, Valeria slaughtered with her next words.

"Yes, wealthy men have a tender touch."

Simyon looked away.

He didn't have to watch her get up.

He didn't have to watch her leave.

She was gone. The second she had matured, he couldn't begin to keep the hordes away.

Every mangy dog wanted her; every sailor, every soldier, every nobleman's son.

How could she stay with a weakling thief?

How could he have driven all of them off?

He watched as she strutted down the cobbles. A man swooped in beside her. A man just like her description; tall, black robes, with a fine blade in the scabbard at his side.

Simyon watched as the mysterious figure placed his hand upon Valeria's back and guided her through the open door of a waiting carriage. The young thief's eyes narrowed as his full attention turned to his adversary. The man in black moved with fluid economy. He lifted himself into the carriage with a single balanced step that, considering his bulk, indicated an impressive athleticism.

An alarm sounded in Simyon's mind. If not for the blindness of emotion, he might have arrived at the conclusion that the man was a Seneschal. Cassius, the only Seneschal Simyon could recognize, had been absent many weeks. The man in the carriage was not Cassius, though perhaps others sought to encroach upon the legendary swordsman's territory. Under normal circumstances, any suspicion of Seneschal involvement meant the end of Simyon's ambitions. The dark ones were not to be trifled with.

Yet that was his Valeria. She always managed to taint his ability to make a pragmatic decision.

Simyon slid his hand down his leg to test the edge of the dagger hidden beneath his clothing.

After a moment, he stood, tossed a couple coins upon the table, and slipped into the anonymous currents of the faceless strangers who wandered Andennium.

The crowded road slowed the progress of her consort's carriage.

Simyon fingered the knife.

He had work to do that evening.

He too could separate a man from his most precious possession.

It was true what Valeria had said . . .

Simyon's touch was none too tender.

Chapter 4: Effective Engagement

Quillion stared past the shards in the window frame to the strange landscape beyond. Kikkan's injury had prevented them from traveling far, but in the last few miles, the terrain had evolved into something different from anything the three of them had encountered before. The decaying remains of ancient infrastructures appeared with increasing frequency. The farmhouses that existed in Acheron and further north were replaced by larger constructions that looked like lurking monoliths against the horizon: stone cubes without a window on three sides, and replete with shining teeth of broken glass to mark the fourth. Flat black stone spread out in a field before these buildings, crisscrossed with sprouting vegetation and the occasional standing or toppled column of delicate, rusted metal. In the distance, Quillion caught sight of artificial mountains rising up to scrape the sky; silent monuments of lost achievement and ancient hubris.

The three mercenaries picked a random structure for shelter. Minimal exploration revealed that the building had seen modern use, but dust and spider webs suggested the inhabitants had long since departed.

"Look." Quillion pried off the top of a metallic container sitting beside the window. He reached inside and held up a small white capsule for Kikkan and Cole to see. "*Bliss*."

Kikkan snorted. "Burn it."

Quillion dropped the pill back into the container and sighed. "*Bliss* can be extremely useful, Kikkan." Then to himself, "How strange to find this here."

"Those pills are potent," Kikkan said, interrupting his musing.

"I know," Quillion replied, "and that potency can incapacitate those who seek to harm us." He drew forth a small plastic bag which he filled with the contents of the container.

Kikkan opened his mouth to protest, and then stopped. "I don't have the strength to argue with you."

A crash interrupted their conversation. Kikkan and Quillion looked up to see that Cole had toppled a leaning bed frame. A cushion remained stuck to the weeping concrete.

"One side is a little damp," the lean warrior admitted, "but I think it will do for a night."

He pulled the mattress onto the bed frame with the damp side down. Quillion brought down two more frames and mattresses.

"We've slept on worse," he said, sliding the bag of *Bliss* into his pack, hoping it was sufficiently sealed to stave off the hungry.

The two mercenaries helped Kikkan onto a bed and Cole set to work attending the former slave's wound. Kikkan winced as Cole pulled away the field dressing they had applied back at the farmhouse. The lean swordsman dabbed at the injury with a rag to clear away the dried blood.

"The cut is not deep," Cole said. "When I saw the machete dangling from your leg, I feared the worst. But mainly I think the blade got caught up in the fabric of your pants."

"A fine thing, to let yourself get wounded by an old man," Quillion said.

Kikkan shrugged. "I let my anger blind me. I will not allow that again."

Quillion produced a flask and took a swig before offering the bottle to Kikkan.

"What is that?"

"Something I scavenged from a farmhouse in Nirdeen. It will numb your pain."

"Then I don't want it."

"Suit yourself." Quillion took another hit and then passed the vessel to Cole.

Cole hefted the flask for a moment while gazing at his wounded companion.

"Kikkan," he said finally, "I have used this fluid before and found that it helps prevent infection. May I have your permission to apply this to your injury?"

Kikkan's brow narrowed. "Will it dull my thinking?"

"Not if you don't drink it, but it will sting."

"You won't be able to properly cave in the head of the next slave owner you meet if you can't solidly plant your leg," Quillion added.

Cole and Kikkan shot Quillion withering looks. The stout swordsman merely shrugged. "It's true."

"It will help you heal faster," Cole continued.

Kikkan nodded. "Then do it."

Cole splashed the liquid onto Kikkan's leg. Kikkan sucked in air but he didn't flinch, and the burning quickly subsided. Cole wrapped the man's leg with as clean a bandage as he could find.

Quillion retrieved the flask from Cole and sat down heavily on the bed he had prepared for himself.

"While we have a moment," he said, taking another hit, "there are some things we should discuss."

Kikkan gritted his teeth. "I'm in no mood for a lecture."

"I don't intend to lecture you, but I think we'd have better success if there existed a clearer understanding of our objectives."

Kikkan had to guess at the meaning of some of Quillion's words, but the former slave had come to know the northerner well enough over the last few months to be confident of his gist.

"My purpose is to eliminate slavery," he said.

Quillion nodded. "A noble cause. But I think you need to adopt a better strategy than marching up and bludgeoning people to death."

Cole finished Kikkan's bandage and moved over to sit on his bed. Kikkan shifted his weight and gazed up at the rusted metallic rafters. "You always seek to complicate things when the answers are simple."

Quillion laughed. "That's where you're wrong—nothing is simple."

"Slavery is evil," Kikkan retorted, "slavers must be killed. Simple."

"True," Quillion replied. Kikkan arched an eyebrow as Quillion continued. "But what if you kill two or three slavers and then we're hunted down and hanged?"

"I will have done some good," Kikkan replied after a moment.

"Yes, but you might have done *more* good. If you fail in your quest because you lacked the discipline to proceed with foresight, then you are as guilty of contributing to oppression as the slave owners."

Kikkan's face tightened and he began to lift himself from the bed. Before he could do himself any damage, Cole sprang to his feet. "Easy, Kikkan; you know how he is, he's just try-ing to get your attention."

"Trying to get a rise out of me is more like it," Kikkan snapped. He settled back into repose but he fixed a hard stare on Quillion.

Quillion took a swig from his flask.

"What's the matter? Can't you take the truth?"

Kikkan scowled again and Cole turned on Quillion with a hard look of his own. "Show a little diplomacy, why don't you?"

"There's no time for diplomacy!" Quillion shouted. "Isn't that right, Kikkan? Isn't every moment that a single person lives under the bondage of slavery an abomination? Isn't it our goal to eliminate that? Should I really waste time we could spend pursuing that objective trying to figure out how to communicate with you without hurting your *feelings*?"

Kikkan's face tightened again, a menacing smile playing about his lips. "What are you worried about? That there will be consequences over that last little incident?"

Quillion shook his head and leaned back in his bed to gaze up at the ceiling. "There are always consequences."

His voice trailed off and the stout mercenary suddenly began to project a profound sadness that caught both Kikkan and Cole's attention. Quillion's manner became submissive, and his two companions caught a glimpse of the vulnerable, preoccupied man that existed beneath the cocky exterior.

"Consequences inflicted by other men are of little con-cern to me," Quillion continued, the iron back in his voice. "Nobody's going to come after us. Even if they tried, they'd be too incompetent to ever hand down proper justice. That's the whole *problem*! Nobody cares enough to see that justice is served!"

Cole nodded, and Kikkan found himself sharing the sentiment.

"It doesn't matter what people do anyway," Quillion said. "We can't escape our actions. We'll feel that man's blood on our hands until our dying day. At least, I will. I feel the blood of every man I've killed, even the ones I've killed with cause. Even when I've celebrated the death, or the victory, the snuffing of life takes its toll—it dampens your enjoyment of beauty from that point forward. Perhaps conscience is my weakness. The world is populated with those born bereft of remorse who are thus able to achieve high stations and force good people to toil beneath them."

Quillion sat up and started fishing through his pack. After a brief search, he drew forth the worn copy of 'The Demon Haunted World' that Adam Lockhart had given him.

"Have you been able to make any sense of that?" Cole asked.

Quillion snorted and shook his head.

"I've studied it extensively. There are phrases that linger, but I lack the vocabulary to catch their complete meaning. The book is a torment. It takes you to the precipice of greater understanding, then drops you flat without warning and with nothing to show for the effort." Quillion dragged his thumb along the book's edge, causing the pages to hum.

"Lockhart left notes in the margins," he said, opening the book to show extensive writing framing the printed text in blue and black ink. "Some of the scribbles make sense, although there are phrases that seem more of a descent into madness." Quillion paused at a passage. He cleared his throat to read, "'*If you eliminate cognitive dissonance, you greatly reduce the compulsion to obey authority. False power structures strive to sabotage personal autonomy for the sake of control.*'" Quillion looked up from the page in annoyance. "'Cognitive dissonance,' what do you think that means?"

Quillion thumbed the edge one more time, then became frustrated. He cocked his arm, ready to throw the offending object away, and froze for a moment, his body tense. But, instead of hurling the book, Quillion relaxed and slipped the worn volume back into his pack.

"Those slaves at the last farm seemed to resent their freedom, Kikkan," he said. "Have you considered the ramifications? They said they had been treated well."

"He probably had them drugged," Kikkan said. "They needed time to contemplate their new reality."

"Is it not possible for a slave to have a gentle master?" Quillion asked.

Kikkan scoffed. "How is a person who has never known freedom in a position to know what 'gentleness' is?"

"It seemed they resented our intrusion," Quillion persisted.

"Even abusive relationships have moments of shared happiness. That's part of the method of the master," Kikkan said. "To inflict horror in every waking moment of the day would require more effort than would be saved by possessing the laborer—making the institution of ownership impractical. To the outside observer, abuse, even terrible abuse, can masquerade as normalcy for the greater share of the time. The abuse is in the knowledge that judgment—that punishment—is inevitable. A slave might be fooled into feeling gratitude when the master provides a meal or ceases a beating, but do not be confused. The slave owes no loyalty to a person who limits one form of sub-human treatment while maintaining another."

Quillion let the words echo in the large, abandoned structure. He hung Kikkan's thought in his mind to reflect on and gave Kikkan a look of profound respect.

"I think we have made some progress."

For a moment, the hint of a smile appeared on Kikkan's face. Then the former slave leaned back on his bed, wincing as the shift in weight caused a jolt of pain to travel up his leg.

"This world must fall. It is designed so that the incompetent can dominate the weak," he stated.

"I agree," Quillion replied, "but I would add one thing. The world must fall, and *we* must emerge unscathed."

Cole laughed, but Kikkan had an objection.

"I would gladly give my life to end slavery."

"That's easy to say now," Quillion said, "but you might change your position when you have a knife at your neck."

A fire sprang to life again in Kikkan's eyes, but Quillion lifted his hands.

"Let's agree that we all wish to stay alive as long as possible. I propose we do so by picking our battles and making sure our strikes maximize damage and minimize risk."

"Meaning?" Kikkan said.

"Meaning that there will be times when we let villains go free in order to pursue those of greater consequence. We cannot be reactionary; we have to leave some space for strategy."

Kikkan shook his head. "I'm not sure I am comfortable with the notion of allowing perceived evil to endure."

"We will mark our targets, observe them and trick them into revealing others of their kind. We will not begin our extermination until the whole network is known. When we strike, it will be with the confidence of knowing none will escape. This is the best way."

The words appeased Kikkan.

"Agreed, the proposal is simple enough."

Quillion's eyes widened. "Perhaps it seems simple now in this moment of repose, but I have no doubt things will only become more complicated the closer we get to Edentown."

Chapter 5: Pursuit

Go home, Simyon.

The command resonated beneath his throbbing temples. The warning rang true, but he would not heed reason.

Don't be a fool!

The self-chastisement did not faze him. City streets rolled beneath his pounding feet as he strained to keep Valeria's carriage in sight.

The cost is too high, she's beyond you now!

"No," Simyon said aloud, tired of the internal conflict. "The price is well paid. Or shall I stop here to carve my beating heart from my breast and end this torment?"

The dissenting voice fell dead.

A pair of street vendors looked up at Simyon in confusion at the random outburst, but the thief paid them no heed. Those that toiled in desperation could be dismissed. Did they truly believe nobility could be born from suffering?

Simyon scoffed.

These cowards were so broken, they submitted to open theft. He could palm what he wished and march on, while they pouted in silence. Too bad they had nothing worth taking. The vendors chose long ago to bury their rage rather than allow heat to forge iron in their spines.

Simyon wouldn't make the same mistake.

Seneschal!

"Enough!" Simyon howled, now there were none to hear. The streets and alleys sped by as he flew in mad pursuit. The more he strained, the more the carriage seemed to pull away. "He's not a Seneschal; he's just a pampered dandy playing dress-up to impress a girl."

Are you sure?

Simyon slowed to a halt and glanced around. The derelict buildings were sparser now, and the upper floors would afford him a view. He abandoned the street, looking for toeholds in the wall.

You're going to draw attention! A dandy dressed like you would not act this way. They'll send the red cloaks!

Simyon set his jaw and climbed. The voice was correct; nearby street people stopped in their idle meandering to stare at him.

"Official business," Simyon howled. He clutched at a loose piece of cement and sent it hurtling into the crowd. Sheep scattered. The sight brought a smile to Simyon's face.

The young thief's fingers tore as he plunged them deep into ragged holds, but the pain was nothing compared to his agitation. He flew up the wall, swinging into an abandoned alcove in a matter of minutes. Squinting, he quickly discerned the carriage in the crowd before glancing around in search of a route to the next level. His eyes fell upon a stairway and he sprinted toward it, leaping over steps three at a time and spiraling ever upward. He gulped down deep breaths and came up coughing after drawing in a lungful of dust.

This isn't you. She's awakened something. Think of all you risk! Why do you kneel to her control?

But the words were dimmer now, fading back into oblivion.

Simyon stumbled over to the ledge, kicking aside debris of metal and glass.

Scouring the landscape revealed the carriage again. Simyon guessed where Valeria and her companion were heading. The walls rose up in the distance, the last barrier before the shore. Though Simyon had lived in Edentown all his life, he had never passed through that distant gate.

Few in San Borja had, but the rumors leaked through. The walls marked the boundaries of the richest quadrant of the city.

San Aryan.

Simyon watched as the carriage approached the wall. There weren't any guards visible at the gate. Entry was allowed by a mechanism that could not be forced and which would only open to those who had the right of passage.

A tightness developed in the young thief's breast, but he knew he couldn't reasonably hope that passage would be denied. True to his fears, a white light appeared in the center of the gate, growing steadily wider as the doors opened until the carriage could pass through.

"Valeria," Simyon whispered. As he watched the passage close, a crippling weight descended. He hadn't seen her for years, yet the loss of her crushed him.

The strength seeped from his limbs. The muscles in his legs burned from his desperate chase. His fingers seared with the mistreatment of the climb. He panted to recuperate air.

The seconds ticked by and darkness encroached.

She is lost to you . . . again.

Darkness.

The hollow city awaited below, an empty cardboard approximation of life: dry, tasteless, without emotion.

Good enough for one such as he.

"No!"

The vocalized declaration brought resolve, and with the resolve Simyon felt his heart beat again. Strength flowed through him, once more numbing his fingers and his muscles to their discomfort.

"It does not end here."

You can't go into San Aryan. You'll die in the attempt just like all the others.

"I've broken into the most heavily guarded houses of San Borja. I've taken all the precious items that can be found in this derelict graveyard. The city bores me. I will pass beyond or be undone. Either way, my misery will end."

How?

Simyon smiled, for he had considered breaking San Aryan before. No thief who ever prowled the streets of Edentown had not contemplated cracking the grandest jewel of them all.

How are you going to find her when you get there? What about guards? What about weapons? You'll be killed! What if she doesn't want to come back with you . . . ?

"Shut up!" Simyon howled, clutching his head between his hands. "Shut up! Shut up! Shut up!"

He stood trembling for a long moment on the ledge.

Why don't you jump? Just jump; it will be cleaner.

Simyon's eyes widened and he issued a soft chuckle. The chuckle became a laugh which magnified until the thief was howling. He made such a scandal that again, people in the streets below stopped and stared.

"Scurry, rats!" Simyon screamed, reaching down for a stone which he hurled below. The stone landed with a crack, grating across the worn thoroughfare with a terrible echo. "Scurry to your holes!"

With a final laugh, Simyon spun on his heel and trotted back into the dark shadows of the building.

It didn't take him long to find what he sought, buildings of this size always had a chute next to the stairwell that ran through the belly of the stone into the darkness below.

Cables dangled down into the black pit at the center of the chute. Simyon's passion had dissipated enough that he spared the time to withdraw a pair of leather gloves from his pocket and slip them onto his hands. The cable would be rust-covered and full of slivers; this, he knew from experience. He reached out to grasp the dangling, braided metal lines. A hard tug demonstrated that they weren't rusted to the point of collapse. Satisfied, Simyon swung out over the dark and began his descent.

If he went deep enough, there would be little resistance. The underworld was populated with demons, but there were no red cloaks or Seneschals.

Simyon could get through.

Not even the residents of San Aryan could control the heavens above them or the haunted depths below.

They would have you believe they can.

"They are liars," Simyon said. He lowered himself, knowing full well that the rest of his life would be defined by that assumption.

Chapter 6: The Creature in the Cage

A few days' rest mended Kikkan considerably, and the three companions resumed their journey through the concrete wilderness. Kikkan limped but would soon improve, though the wound limited the distance they could cover in a day.

With every step, the shadows seemed to grow longer and the dust and filth grew deeper. High up on the buildings, where windows remained, their panes were so coated with grime that they appeared carved from stone. The wind that thundered down through the unnatural canyon walls carried a toxic scent, each gust causing the three companions a round of labored coughing.

Looking upon the ruins, Quillion could not escape a sense of fundamental fury. Though only shameful, broken skeletons remained, he could imagine the beauty they once possessed. This intangible, glowing image of former glory left him trembling with rage. What folly had brought the world to ruin?

Quillion wondered whether they were misguided in seeking out Edentown. The rot seemed to worsen along the way. Part of him longed to return to the wilds: Acheron, Nirdeen, and Oshia were at least known dangers that the three of them had learned to navigate with relative comfort.

Yet Quillion did not entertain the idea of retreat for long.

Edentown contained the last fragment of the heritage Quillion sought. Adam Lockhart had said they would find a teacher there, but beyond his cryptic description of someone with a star-shaped birthmark, Quillion knew nothing of the person they sought. Would he be a man like Quillion; one who had stolen his scholarship at the behest of some inherent fundamental longing? Or was he a fallen guardian of the old world; a senile lunatic such as Adam Lockhart? Did he even exist, or were they marching into folly?

The mystery disgusted Quillion. Yet even with his repulsion, the mercenary knew he could not live in the shadow of Edentown without making an effort to explore.

Of all the slavers in all the districts, his curiosity was the fiercest – at least, that he had encountered so far.

*

The companions began to notice a pattern in their new surroundings. Long stretches were overrun and abandoned, followed by zones developed into modern settlements.

In these zones lived people. Shuffling, pathetic people, drifting through the promise of a life as decayed as the buildings rising up from the charred earth. The sight of these locals evoked a profound sadness within Quillion. He had hoped to find evidence of a better life here, but if something better did exist it was well hidden.

People in the first few settlements they passed ignored the three mercenaries. Fleeting shadows closed windows and locked doors in a flurried shuffle of movement and noise, but no one hailed or molested the companions. The ease of their passage was disconcerting. Quillion sensed danger lurking, but he did not know what form the threat would take.

As the days stretched on and their journey continued, the settlements increased in size, the population emboldened by their numbers. Children with scuffed knees and ragged apparel played in the dirt. They could often be seen in large packs, chasing a ball back and forth down square fields marked with stones at the corners. Fights broke out frequently, and many of the children sported swollen eyes and blood stains on their shirts.

Cole had paused to watch one such match when a child disengaged himself from the contest. He ran over to the lean swordsman and waved.

"Hello," the boy said.

"Hello," Cole replied.

The child stood and regarded the three.

"You aren't from here, are you?"

Quillion tensed and glanced around in all directions in case the boy was some sort of distraction. The mercenary saw nothing in the nearby structures, but was all too aware that he lacked the experience to know where an attack would come from in this cursed place.

"No, we're not," Cole replied. "How could you tell?"

The child shrugged. The other players yelled at him to return to their game, but the boy shushed them with a dismissive wave.

"It's obvious."

Cole reflected on the statement. "Aren't you scared of us?"

"Naw," the boy laughed, "you're too dumb."

"How so?"

"Well, you've got an escaped slave with you for starters."

Kikkan swiveled on the boy with clenched fists.

A flash of panic crossed the lad's face, but he managed to keep up a smile even as he took a cautious backward step.

"You see? You gave yourself away. You'll have to be smarter if you get questioned by the grifters."

The admonishment settled Kikkan down, but his eyes remained narrow as he appraised the boy.

"Grifters?" Cole asked.

"City guard, red cloaks. You're getting close enough to Edentown that you'll start to see patrols soon. They say their duty is to protect us from the underworld demons, but really the grifters are just thugs who like beating, looting and rape. Scurry when you hear 'em come."

"Demons?" Cole asked.

"You don't know what demons are?" the boy said. "You don't know anything, do you?"

"Son," Quillion said, "why are you talking to us?"

The boy smiled and tilted his head.

"I'm looking for *Bliss* and I think you have some."

Quillion tensed. The boy laughed again.

"You *do* have some! You guys give *everything* away."

"Why do you think we would be carrying that?"

"Please," the boy snapped, "don't try to pretend you don't. I can smell it."

"*Bliss* turns people into sniveling dogs, you should know that," Kikkan said, tossing a dark look at Quillion.

"So you do know about demons after all!" the boy replied. He continued before the companions could respond. "Sure, it's dangerous if you take the whole pill. I only want a jolt; grind the capsule into powder and snort it. It's safe like that."

"Get out of here," Quillion snapped. He began walking and Cole and Kikkan followed.

The boy's face went dark and he kept pace with the trio for a few steps before abruptly stopping in the road behind them. Quillion kept his eye on the boy. When there was some distance between them, the boy called out, "Could be you're going to regret holding out on me. Could be there's a pack of grifters around that will provide a nice reward for information about you."

With that, the child spun on his foot and ran off in the opposite direction. Again, Quillion snapped his gaze around a wide perimeter: still he saw nothing. A pit began to grow in his stomach.

"What hell have we wandered into?" he whispered.

The silent grave surrounding them offered no answer.

*

A few hours later, the three came to a small market. The market had formed at a natural intersection of roads. There was a clear plaza in the center, surrounded by a variety of colorful tents. Men and women called out from beneath red and gold awnings and gestured toward the wares on display before them.

Upon entering the market, Quillion became acutely aware of Kikkan. The former slave was as skittish as a stallion unwilling to be led. Kikkan's anxiety made Quillion anxious as well. The large man was too big to hide in plain sight, and if he kept blowing and snorting like an animal, he was bound to draw attention.

The encounter with the young boy weighed on Quillion. The northerner considered himself adept at deception, but that meeting had led him to wonder whether his cache of ruses was sophisticated enough for Edentown.

"Look," Cole said beneath his breath, to prevent Kikkan from hearing. Cole flicked his eyes to the southern side of the market, then turned his head to regard a slender young woman who smiled at him in clear invitation.

Quillion turned to regard the woman, but in his peripheral vision he saw what concerned Cole. A group of seven men in scarlet cloaks were making a leisurely circuit of the market's perimeter. Their movements were undisciplined and brutish, but the sheer size of each man stupefied Quillion. Every one of them was nearly as tall as Kikkan. Unlike the lean former slave, however, these men swelled with unnatural muscle.

"Grifters?" Quillion hissed.

"They have to be," Cole replied.

The smaller swordsman stepped closer to the young woman, who purred with delight at his approach.

"Hello, stranger," she smiled.

Cole nodded in greeting.

"I'm new in town, what's the best way to stay out of trouble?"

"Ah," the woman said, reaching over to place her hand on top of Cole's, "wouldn't you like a little trouble?"

"It all depends," Cole replied, a touch of a smile playing across his lips. "But I'd rather it lasted a few hours. If I find myself clasped in irons within a heartbeat of getting started, I think I'll explode."

The girl purred again.

Quillion looked away; the interrogation didn't seem to be getting anywhere. He scoured the market for signs of further threats, and saw something that made his mouth go dry.

Hunched in a corner, on the far edge of the market, sat a motionless figure in a cage. Even from his considerable distance, Quillion could see the man was covered in blood. Flies buzzed around his staring eyes, and Quillion thought he must be looking at a corpse. Then a passerby casually poked the prisoner with a stick. The response was a lethargic and pitiful swipe. There was something terrifying in that meager proof of life. The creature in the cage already resided on the other side.

A slave.

Quillion turned to Kikkan, whose body was virtually trembling with fury. He had seen the captive.

"Leave it, Kikkan!" Quillion hissed.

Kikkan made no sign he heard. Every muscle in his body was tense.

A gust of wind kicked up against Quillion's back. The air passing through the marketplace ruffled the edges of the tents, and when it reached the slave a twinkle of life suddenly appeared in his eyes.

The *Bliss.* Addicts could smell it . . .

Quillion reached over to tap Cole on the shoulder. The woman had managed to wrap herself about him with impressive dexterity, and the lean swordsman found himself staring into the crease of an ample bosom.

"Cole," Quillion hissed, "we have to go."

"We have to free that one," Kikkan snapped.

"No." Quillion turned to face Kikkan. A flash of insight struck the northerner, enabling him see past the chaos to the terrible truth hidden beneath. "Don't you see, you fool? That tortured creature is an alarm."

As if on cue, another, stronger wind stirred up, and this time there was no mistaking the effect when the wall of air hit the caged man. In a silent, deliberate motion, the slave stood, and Quillion gasped at the horror of the sight. The man, if he could still be called a man, was as thin as a skeleton. His hair was attached to his head in scattered, greasy clumps between largely bald patches. Flaps of skin peeled away from various sections of his body. But his eyes blazed with the clarity of desperation.

Quillion had seen that look before.

He had seen it in the company of Captain Tark and Cassius the Seneschal when they were attacked at night on the plantations of Oshia. It was the dark twinkle manifested by the zombies when the last of their humanity was consumed.

"Run," Quillion said.

As he gave the order, the creature in the cage found his voice. It was hard to imagine that such a broken husk could generate so powerful a sound, but the bellows that remained beneath the man's fractured chest served to amplify a final, sub-human wail. The creature screamed, and everything else in the market with a pulse stopped, turned, and stared in open-mouthed terror.

Quillion grabbed Cole and shook him loose of the young woman before turning to escape. Yet the second he spun around, he found himself face to face with the seven brutish men in scarlet cloaks that he had marked as dangerous the moment he stumbled into the plaza.

"Hello," the first one said with a wide grin, "what have we here?"

Chapter 7: San Aryan

Valeria gazed out the window of the moving carriage. People milled about in the street outside. The vehicle's passage was largely ignored by the impoverished peddlers. Valeria watched, but the ragged masses knew better than to risk eye contact.

She reflected on Simyon. Sitting with him had been a mistake. The thief had no prospects, no future. Certainly, Simyon could not contend with the Seneschal who now kept her company. Yet some sorcery had compelled her to pause. She had long known she lacked the power to save Simyon from his fate. The young thief beckoned from his perch at the edge of the void. The fall was inevitable; she could only prevent him from taking her down as well.

"Are you troubled, Valeria?" her companion asked. His voice was deep and rich. Not unkind, but authoritative and confident.

Valeria looked at the Seneschal and allowed her lips to fall into a disinterested line. He was strong and handsome, but she could defeat that with feigned boredom. Boredom always played well. That and uttering her target's name. Sometimes, simply speaking the word was enough to submit a mark to her control.

"No, Janus," she said, returning her gaze to the window and observing his reaction out of the corner of her eye. Janus only smirked.

Valeria let her right hand fall to her breast. Janus stiffened at the casual gesture. Valeria was pleased with any trick that functioned on him. Janus was a mystery: a man of great social and political power. The challenge with this one dwarfed the conquest of lecherous merchants.

Valeria played with the soft fabric of her garment, feigning ignorance of the effect. Her finger alternated between stroking her skin and sampling the slippery silk of her dress. Did Janus imagine that same finger upon his own body? Or did his fantasy tend toward aggression?

Could she defend herself from this one? She had her own vial of street deterrent, but she preferred finesse.

The scenery through the carriage window remained largely unchanged, and Valeria's attention focused on Janus. In the heat of passion, the man's true character would be revealed.

Monsters were not common. Most of her marks were sincere in their simple longing, yet those who drew nourishment from torment did exist. Valeria had seen the deflated remains of others in her trade get flushed through the waterways of the underworld. Forgotten husks of something that had once been human, devoured by a beast roaming the surface. She had always known she would meet one eventually. Yet she had no energy to spare feeding fear.

She slipped one leg over the other, careful to reveal a tantalizing flash of skin. She sensed Janus inhale, savoring her presence. He devoured the air.

She was protected.

Her dress was her armor. As long as he regarded her as a desirable thing, she would come to no harm.

The dress supported her, lifted her, made her strong.

But should she be defiled . . .

A maiden could be made a wretch in an instant. The city was full of vanquished beauty: torn vestments, scuffed knees, missing teeth and hair. The downward spiral happened quickly – blood trickling from the mouth or nose.

If she embodied an unblemished vessel, the spell would function. However, inelegant moments, a stumble on the cobbles perhaps, allowed cracks to form and compromise the illusion.

She stared out the window.

Boredom and annoyance.

Keep the pressure on him.

Outside, the streets began to take on a different color. Valeria was so occupied with her own thoughts that she didn't notice the change at first, but when she did a rush of fear shot through her.

"Janus," she said, looking his way, "where are we going?"

There was a twinkle in his eye as he replied.

"San Aryan."

Valeria broke her gaze, fearful that her surprise had already been revealed. Why was he taking her there? It was forbidden. Was this the source of the thrill he sought? What would the consequences be for her?

The tension in the carriage shifted, Valeria sensing Janus now had the upper hand. Still, his body language was not menacing, just smug. She didn't panic.

The carriage came to a halt at the gate, and suddenly Janus became annoyed. With trepidation, Valeria felt his attention drift from her. An afterthought had no power.

"This gate is usually unmanned," he growled.

A crease appeared in the wall and a smartly uniformed guard stood off to the side. Janus watched him with outward calm, but Valeria could tell he was irritated.

"Sir," the gateman said, "Orion has requested your presence at his estate immediately."

Janus nodded his acquiescence.

The coach started again, moving at a leisurely tromp. Janus was quiet, almost as if he had forgotten Valeria's presence entirely. After a time, he glanced over at her and tried to force a casual smile.

"I do apologize," he said, "but I am obligated to attend."

"Of course," Valeria replied. In light of his agitation, she knew to drop the pressure. "I don't mind."

Janus sighed. "You'll have to come with me. There's no time to take you back, and I can't leave you out in the carriage."

The Seneschal spoke to himself as much as to her. The young woman had never seen him quite so preoccupied.

"It will be better if you speak as little as possible."

Valeria blanched. The statement was rather rude and she knew that allowing such words to go unchallenged would damage her crafted image. She took a deep breath and folded her hands on her lap.

Janus noticed the inhalation.

"I'm sorry," he said, "I didn't put that well. My superior is a unique man. I mean you no disrespect, but we have little time to prepare for this meeting so I'm afraid I must be blunt."

Valeria glanced at Janus. He kept his eyes on her and the two of them shared the gaze for a long while. After a moment, she felt the damage begin to mend. When they had again achieved an approximate level of parity, she cracked her facade.

"Apology accepted," she said, and then turned to regard the window, breaking eye contact.

Janus smiled, though he remained preoccupied.

The carriage rolled along, affording Valeria her first glimpse of San Aryan. Long had she wondered what lay hidden behind those vaunted gates, and now, having passed through, her senses drank in the strange new surroundings. Their passage through the wall seemed to have changed the whole world.

The streets were flat and well maintained. In San Borja, and in other districts, even the best roads were not the quality of this entry passage into San Aryan. Walls lined the street and she could not see into the estates they encompassed. Some of the walls were posted with images, unsullied by the thick layers of grime and decay that were commonplace in San Borja.

The overriding impression was that San Aryan was new.

Valeria glanced over at Janus to see if he had noticed the wonderment on her features, but he was still focused on the road, grinding his jaw.

The carriage continued for a series of turns before finally stopping in front of an ornate, wood-paneled gate. They waited. Nobody came to greet them or demand their identities, but after a moment the gate opened, seemingly of its own accord. The motion startled Valeria, and she wondered what wizardry was responsible.

"Remember," Janus said, "speak as little as possible. Hopefully, this meeting will end quickly and we can resume our excursion."

Valeria said nothing.

The carriage rolled in and this time Valeria couldn't hide her gasp of surprise at the sight before her.

She had found the streets delightful in their cleanliness and newness compared to her daily life in San Borja. However, the common byways of San Aryan were nothing compared to what lay behind the exterior walls.

Before her was a field of green unlike anything she had ever witnessed. Grass in San Borja existed in small patches that were usually stained with the dust and grit of the city. Here, however, the color was pure and unblemished and shone with a tone that appeared to transcend the bleak, desperate coloration of the world. The road too switched from uniform black to a patchwork of colored brick that meandered to an estate at the top of a small rise. The estate itself was breathtaking. Valeria had never seen such a soaring construction. Red walls and white trimmed windows peeked out from behind a glorious garden of trees, climbing vines, and bushes. Four white pillars marked a greeting area in the front, and beside one of those stood a white-haired man dressed in matching cream-colored shirt and pants.

"It's beautiful," Valeria said.

"Yes, Orion has one of the grandest estates in San Aryan. He's been here the longest."

The two of them fell to silence as the carriage approached the welcome area. As they neared, Valeria kept her eye on Orion and his features came more and more into focus.

He was a handsome man with a large and inviting smile, but something about him made her instantly nervous. Perhaps it was the house, or the estate, or the newness and strangeness of her surroundings. Valeria had met powerful people before; she had even learned to distinguish those who tried to present themselves as more than they were. They all, even Janus, paled in comparison to this one. Furthermore, she couldn't help but suspect that even the apparent opulence manifested only a fragment of Orion's true influence.

How dangerous must a man be to so casually own and occupy such a property as this?

The carriage pulled to a halt and Orion grasped the handle.

"Janus, thank you for coming so soon," he said. "I trust I haven't interrupted your diversions for the day?"

"Not at all," Janus replied.

Orion smiled and nodded before turning to Valeria.

"My," he said, "what a beautiful creature you are. Welcome to my home."

He reached out his hand and Valeria could see no escape from clasping her fingers around his. She expected a simple shake, but once he had hold, Orion seemed reluctant to release her. The feel of his skin was intrusive. Valeria felt herself recoil.

"Janus has always had an eye for well-formed objects," Orion continued. He placed his arm around Valeria's shoulder. Valeria knew any objection she might have was irrelevant. She felt suddenly like a morsel on a fork.

Her mind raced, but she could think of no extraction. Orion applied gentle pressure to her back, and she realized he was attempting to guide her toward the house. She acceded, fearful of the consequence of resistance.

As they walked, Orion's hand on her back began to move from side to side. He kneaded her muscles with his gritty fingertips.

Janus came around to stand in front of the awkward pair.

"Delightful, delightful," Orion said. "How old are you, my darling?"

The question was meaningless. Valeria replied with a blank stare.

"Oh yes, you wouldn't know what that means," Orion said. "How charming!" He leaned back to give Valeria an appraising look. "Firm body, perky breasts, yet no baby fat. I'd guess you are between twenty and twenty-five." Orion reached for one of Valeria's arms and then began running his fingers across her flesh. "No blemishes or abrasions on the skin, now that's truly remarkable."

Valeria knew something was wrong. Orion was taking too many liberties, surely more than he would with a woman of San Aryan. But she could not object. She had observed high born women before and knew they waited for their escort to intervene on their behalf. Janus had to react.

Why wasn't he doing anything?

Orion stood for a moment longer; his fingers had crept up to her shoulder.

"You're tense," he said, with the same deceptive smile. "Why are you so tense?"

Valeria didn't answer.

Orion looked over at Janus. "I didn't know you had such appetites, my friend. There is a protocol violation in bringing her here, but I'll allow it. You see, I too have found enjoyment in the willingness of San Borja girls to perform the acts our ladies of San Aryan find detestable. It's good to have an outlet for impulses deemed socially unacceptable, don't you agree?"

Valeria went cold.

The illusion was broken.

She had been exposed.

Chapter 8: Mercy Killing

"Is there a problem?" Quillion addressed the thick warrior. The terrible, soul piercing screech of the slave continued to echo throughout the market.

The red cloak smiled. His lips, nose and cheeks were swollen as if engorged. He lifted up a stubby finger and pointed.

"Our hound over there doesn't like something."

"That's his problem," Quillion said.

"No," the red cloak replied, "it's *my* problem. I'm the one that has to shut him up." The burly man snapped his fingers and one of his men scurried off in the direction of the slave. Quillion never took his eyes off the captain, but he sensed Kikkan tightening up beside him.

There was a loud crack in the distance, followed by silence.

"His reward was death, then?" Kikkan asked through clenched teeth.

The captain turned to regard Kikkan. Quillion took advantage of the distraction and surreptitiously slipped his hand into the satchel slung at his hip.

"His reward is a refreshing nap," the captain said. "Now, I'd like some answers from the three of you."

"Answers to what?" Quillion asked. The dispatched soldier returned from his task and took his former position.

"It's illegal to carry weapons in town," the captain said.

"We're not from here," Quillion replied.

"I'd guessed that. Do you have any *Bliss* on you?"

"Yes," Quillion replied.

"It's illegal to bring *Bliss* into the city."

"How do you control your slaves?"

The captain scowled.

"Don't play dumb. You know darn well people are snorting it and we've had plenty of northern mercenaries smuggling the stuff in for profit. Now, I'd like the three of you to drop your weapons and come along with us."

"Where are we going?"

"Questioning."

Quillion nodded. A thunderclap erupted from his satchel. The captain reacted as if he had been pushed in the chest; his arms flailed out as he fell back. Confusion ensued. Several red cloaks reached for their leader, while the others began to draw weapons.

Quillion withdrew a smoking handgun from his satchel and pointed it at the nearest soldier. The weapon cracked and the man spun to the ground. Quillion sought another target, then two more. He put all of his five shots into the bodies of the soldiers, but in the chaos of battle he couldn't discern whether the wounds were fatal.

In the meantime, Cole had drawn his sword and Kikkan brandished his pipe. The two stepped forward. There were still two soldiers untouched by Quillion's shooting, and they pushed aside their wounded fellows to meet the companions with edged steel.

Something about their battle stance seemed unnatural. The soldiers were so thick with muscle that their movements were slow and deliberate. Quillion slipped the gun back into his satchel and drew his own sword.

Kikkan connected first. He stepped forward and swung his pipe in a horizontal swipe. The metal made a hollow ring as it crushed the face of a soldier still moving despite Quillion's bullet. The man went down in a heap and Kikkan stepped over the body to engage the next foe.

Cole stepped into the space created behind his advancing companion and drove two deft stabs into the soldiers on the ground to ensure they would not rise to attack. Quillion's first shot had left little life in the captain, and Cole's blade took the rest. Flank secured, Cole maneuvered to stay in a position to defend Kikkan's blind side.

From the back, Quillion could see that the two men who had escaped the bullets would be a problem. They pushed at the backs of their wounded companions with terrible force, and Quillion was tempted to to try to reload his gun. He cursed himself for carrying the extra bullets in his pack rather than his satchel, and decided he was better off with a functional sword in his hand than to be caught fiddling around with the tiny cartridges.

Kikkan continued driving forward, striking the men Quillion had wounded and sending them to oblivion. Some were easy targets, flopping around on the stone and slipping in the black blood rapidly pooling at their feet. Others managed to lift their arms in defense, which enabled Kikkan to strike twice: once to shatter the bones that thwarted him, and once more to rupture the skull.

By the time Kikkan came face to face with the two unwounded red cloaks, the other five were dead.

Kikkan panted with the effort. Sweat glistened on his exposed arms, and a hateful fire burned in his eyes. He had been repressing his need to lash out, but the incident with the slave at the edge of the market was more than he could bear. When Quillion started shooting, Kikkan's spirit soared for the opportunity to correct a wrong even if prudence might have dictated a less overt tactic.

The first of the two soldiers came at Kikkan with a crude overhead stroke that the former slave deflected with ease. Kikkan felt the power of his opponent resonate down the pipe, but the red cloak had not set his feet before the attack, minimizing its effectiveness. Kikkan carried his own momentum forward and shoulder-slammed his assailant in the chest. The soldier staggered backward to the ground, but before Kikkan could finish the fight he found himself occupied by several wild sword swings from the man's companion.

By then, Cole had stepped up to provide support, and as Kikkan parried an overhead blow, Cole ran his sword deep into a weak point in the soldier's armor just below the armpit. The sword got hung up on its lethal path, and Cole struggled to get his weight behind the thrust. In a flash of inspiration, he reached forward to grasp the soldier's back plate, which he used as leverage to ram his blade through.

The remaining soldier struggled to regain his feet, but Quillion pounced on him and managed to get his blade against the man's neck.

The soldier paused and stared at the stout northerner, rage dancing in his eyes.

"It's a death sentence," he growled. "Attacking the city guard is a death—"

Quillion gave his sword a sharp jerk, ending the red cloak's life in a spout of blood.

"Why did you do that?" Cole asked.

"We've already earned a death sentence," Quillion quipped, "sparing one soldier wouldn't change that."

"But we could have questioned him!" Cole snapped.

"Too bulky to carry; besides, there is a better option." Quillion nodded into the crowd. Kikkan and Cole turned, both instantly recognizing what Quillion had seen. It was the boy they had met in the street. Seeing that he had been recognized, the boy turned to flee.

"Kikkan!" Quillion shouted.

The former slave did not need to be told twice. He sprang forward as if stung, and the crowd parted before him, creating a perfect alleyway to his objective. In less than a dozen strides, Kikkan had covered the distance and he swallowed up the boy in his arms.

"No!" the boy screamed. But Kikkan's embrace was not tortuous.

"Shhh," he said, "we will not harm you."

"So you say!" the boy yelled, still struggling against Kikkan's grasp.

Kikkan spun the lad to face him and fixed him with a piercing stare that left no doubt as to his sincerity.

"I give you my word as a free man that I will not allow any harm to come to you. We need only information. Now, stop struggling."

The words took the wind out of the boy and he went limp. Kikkan spun on his heel to return to Quillion, who had just finished a circuit of slitting all the prone soldiers' throats.

"I wish we had time to fish the bullets out," he said. Then he looked around at the remaining crowd in the market. Many of the people had fled the scene the moment the shooting started. From his vantage point, Quillion could see that several tents had been toppled, and trinkets, recently for sale, had spilled to the ground. Already, children were sneaking forward to claim prizes that had been scattered by accident in the mud. Few seemed to exhibit any reaction of surprise or horror regarding the recent slaughter.

"Is there nothing but savagery everywhere?" Quillion wondered aloud.

"This quiet isn't going to last," Cole hissed.

Quillion came back to the moment. People were looking at him. He glanced from face to face, seeing the same silent emptiness behind every the darkened eye. A thought occurred to him, and he reached into a different pouch on his belt and withdrew a handful of *Bliss*.

The gathering reacted as if they were a single living thing. They twitched, like dogs perking up at the smell of food, and paused in expectation.

Quillion cocked his arm and threw the pills as far from him as he could manage. The act caused an eruption of motion and the witnesses turned into a mob scurrying over one another in the grime for the tiny capsules that would bring them a sliver of peace for a few short hours.

"Let's go," Quillion said.

The companions moved in the opposite direction to the frenzy and their heading brought them past the cage with the broken slave. As Quillion approached, the smell of *Bliss* caused the pitiful creature's eyes to snap open. He began to hyperventilate, and lifted an arm to beg.

Quillion glanced at Kikkan.

The tall warrior looked at the half animated corpse with pity.

"Give him some," he said, "he's too far along for redemption. Let a fog take the edges off his suffering."

Quillion nodded and withdrew another handful of powdery pills, which he tossed into the cage.

The slave came to life and his bony arm snapped around too fast for the eye to see as he gathered up the capsules of *Bliss* and brought them to his mouth. Only after all the pills were consumed did he relax against the bars in a posture that seemed agonizing to Quillion.

His panting slowed, going from frenetic palpitation to a long and deliberate sigh.

The sigh lengthened.

Then stopped.

Kikkan watched the slave's final moments with scorn, and when he was sure the caged man was dead, he turned to Quillion in rage.

"This is no victory," he snapped.

Quillion nodded.

"Sometimes you can do no more than grant a painless death."

Kikkan's jaw tightened in fury. He was about to retort, but Quillion cut him off. "Save it, we need to find shelter."

Chapter 9: Mnemonics

Simyon slid down the cables, holding his own weight with ease. His muscles tensed, and the thief was grateful for the outlet to exhaust himself. Some inner part recognized he would only be able to climb for an hour or two before his strength gave out, but at that moment, he felt angry enough to rage against infinity.

He slid down, breaking his speed by pinching his feet against the cable or clutching the splintered metal tightly in his fist. He avoided pressing his body against the rust for fear of staining his fine clothing, but the cloud of dust dislodged by his passage clung to him. He lamented not taking the time to change, but he expected his disguise would be necessary if he wanted to walk unchallenged in the streets of San Aryan.

Down he went to the bottom floor of the building, where a cube of wreckage as tall as a man sat nestled in the darkness. Simyon dropped down through a trap door, and pried open a crack in the wall. Most of the buildings in San Borja contained a room like this, and Simyon had learned the tricks to manipulate them. He opened one door, then another, and emerged out into an abandoned hall.

A floor of broken tiles reflected the meager light that had managed to find its way into the infernal depths.

Simyon stopped and waited for his eyes to adjust.

He had learned the secret of the underworld long ago: light existed in the depths. The light was another in an endless series of mysteries from the past. The illumination was faint but functional, and once the eyes adjusted, it became possible to move around.

As the vague blur that surrounded him slowly took form, Simyon scoured his surroundings for signs of passage.

In a city, nothing was ever completely abandoned. For the half a hundred years Edentown had sat in ruin, few rooms or doors had been left unexplored. Human beings were closer to rats than they would ever wish to believe. When they passed they left traces, and a man of perception could always follow the movement.

Simyon looked, and after a moment found what he strained to see. A veritable river way of scuff marks stretched off into the depths. Not footprints; the darkness dwellers were too clever to leave those behind; but stirred dust looked different to dust that had lain dormant for decades. Simyon made his way along the demon flow.

He passed through another doorway, down a flight of stairs, and came eventually to a hole in the ground accessed by a rusty ladder. This he climbed to arrive at a circular tunnel with a trickle of water running through the bottom.

Here he stopped and gazed at the walls, preparing to ply a trick which he had once been promised would make him powerful.

He scoffed, too loud for the darkness, and the noise echoed. Simyon flinched.

Powerful.

The empty promises of an old fool. What time he had wasted! Yet even in his contempt, Simyon had to concede the most worthless of traits could flash moments of utility.

Grease and organic matter smeared the wall. Some suggested the mold provided the meager luminescence that made the underworld passable. Simyon didn't know, but the dim glow served a valuable purpose, and the young thief had more pressing problems than to question random chance that played out in his favor.

He studied the wall and found what he sought. A splash of white hidden behind the ladder.

He reached forward and wiped the panel clean.

There were three black symbols on a white field. The middle one was self-evident: an arrow with points on either end, indicating the direction of the tunnel. The other two symbols would have been meaningless to most, but Simyon knew them. They were letters. The letters W and E to be exact. Here in the context of the underworld, however, their meaning was unclear.

The letter E, master, is special because it's a vowel.

The memory caused Simyon to furrow his brow in irritation. He pushed the past away and returned his focus to the challenge before him.

The discovery perturbed Simyon. He had been hoping for an indication of the whereabouts of San Aryan. Letters served no purpose.

There's more meaning to them than that.

Simyon closed his eyes. His mind ached. The weight of his memories crushed down upon him. There was a diamond hidden beneath the recollections. Some kernel he had not contemplated in decades. The labor of moving aside the irrelevant thoughts taxed him. His former master's face floated into his thoughts once more.

What is the significance of W and E?

The master had taught him tricks to aid his memory in times like these. "Mnemonics," they were called. The human mind was unruly, and it took an artist to extract the full potential of one's own ability to think. Simyon leaned back and tried to remember.

Association . . .

Where had he seen W and E before?

He discarded several flashing images. The first wave of memory was little more than a series of words that contained the two characters: we, wet, were. Meaningless static to distract his thinking. That was to be expected.

You must be patient with the mind, it likes to play games.

More images came as different kinds of memories were stimulated by the persistence of Simyon's thought.

The cover of a book flashed. 'We' by . . . whom? Simyon's focus hardened and the name came to him: Yevgeny Zamyatin. The image of the name upon a cover gave Simyon pause. He remembered the feel of the relic, the septic smell of the pages. The book had suffered abuse before coming to Simyon. He remembered reading the words with the master . . .

Stop.

That line of thinking was making him lose focus. Not the book, but the images should command his attention.

Where else had he seen . . . ?

A map!

The realization came with a flash of certainty. Simyon remembered the tiny icon at the bottom of printed maps with the N, S, W, and E labels.

"Compass directions," he said aloud, excited with the progress. His success seemed to alleviate the general ache that had settled into his mind to dissuade him. With progress came encouragement. Street dwellers of Edentown such as Simyon used landmarks as guidance rather than compass points. Travelers from the provinces dropped the words on occasion, but Simyon himself had never had a reason to learn them. Sunset and Sunrise were the most frequent direction indicators. Yet, deep in the recesses of his mind, Simyon sensed that he had studied the ancient labeling.

With a new stimulus to guide his search, he went through another series of mnemonics.

"North, south, west, and east," he whispered in a singsong voice. Was there a rhyme that he had learned that might give him a clue? He said the phrase a couple times. The repetition of the s called up the word "moss."

"Mossssss," Simyon said, hissing the final s.

"A rolling stone gathers no moss."

Worthless.

"Moss grows on the north side of trees."

That was something.

Why the north side? Because of shade. He had seen examples on the walls and floors of the derelict buildings all around. That meant the sun passed through the southern half of the sky so a tree or a building blocked the light. Simyon still wasn't oriented, but he sensed progress.

As if encouraged by his attitude shift, the floodgates opened. The long forgotten ideas came too fast for Simyon to process. He was delighted by the deluge of information. The words made him curious. He had simple knowledge of most, but he hadn't taken the time to examine them in adult contemplation. The thoughts had been programmed into him by the master and now, as an adult, Simyon caught the fleeting perception of greater significance.

Again, he had to stop himself and remain on task. He closed his eyes. He knew he was close to a revelation. When the knowledge finally came, understanding was instant and absolute.

The sun! The sun rises in the east and sets in the west. The archaic term for Sunrise is East.

The realization sobered Simyon and dredged up a new set of musings. When he and Valeria had run the city together, they had often climbed to the top of structures to witness the morning colors as the sun rose from the sea.

"Look at how it lights up San Aryan," Valeria would say. She had been dazzled by the prospect of that cursed district even then.

Simyon's hand closed into a fist and he lifted it to tap the E on the sign before him.

"San Aryan is east," he snapped.

He lifted himself and continued in the indicated direction. Thoughts of Valeria dampened the delight he had felt wandering through the world of memory, and the near darkness of rage overcame him.

Chapter 10: Separation

Quillion, Kikkan, and Cole took flight down the winding streets, taking random turns to confuse any potential pursuers. Kikkan carried the boy slung beneath an arm. When the companions' muscles began to burn, they looked for shelter, finally ducking into a building. The structure happened to be one of the larger ruins with columns stretching skyward in a seemingly infinite reach.

The first floor was a wide open space only broken by lines of oval pillars. Quillion assessed the layout before directing the group toward a door hidden in the shadows. The door opened to a flight of stairs dank with mildew and a musty smell.

Up and up they went, winding around in circles until Quillion eventually called for a halt and pushed through another door. This one opened into a narrow hallway. Selecting a door at random, the small group entered a room with grimy floor-to-ceiling windows.

"This will suffice," Quillion panted. He pointed at the windows. "These will allow us to watch the street in case anyone is coming after us."

For a moment, the three men stood panting, allowing the fear of battle and flight to purge itself from their hearts.

Kikkan stood glowering, and when he finally found enough breath to speak, his words held an edge. "Maybe you'd like to explain yourself?"

Quillion looked up in surprise.

"Why are you angry?"

Kikkan let out a loud bark of laughter. He was still holding the boy from the market in his arms, and the lad jumped at the sound.

"What happened to avoiding conflict? Why should I stand motionless, while you're free to slaughter anyone you please?"

Quillion ignored Kikkan. The stout warrior scanned the room and walked toward a dusty chair. As he approached the object, he paused to retrieve a flexible cable from the floor. He scooped up the chair and set it upright at Kikkan's feet.

The former slave could barely mask his fury.

"Well?"

"I don't control everything, Kikkan. I had to make a judgment call. Those red cloaks would have taken us prisoner and stripped us of our weapons and leverage. We don't know enough about this place to allow that to happen." Quillion pointed at the boy and held up the cable. Kikkan just looked at him. The boy said nothing.

"Do you have family? Parents?" Quillion asked, addressing the boy.

The boy shook his head.

"Dead?"

The boy nodded.

Quillion growled, "This world is nothing but a flesh farm. Human beings should not be a product to be discarded." He caught himself mid-thought and looked up at Kikkan. "Do you agree?"

Kikkan eyed him warily.

Quillion looked at the boy again.

"I'm not in the business of slaughtering children. We won't hurt you, but our current situation is delicate. I'm afraid we're going to have to tie you up for the moment."

Quillion gestured for Kikkan to put the boy in the chair. The tall man hesitated, staring at Quillion before finally acceding.

"You have my word you will not be harmed," Kikkan said, as much in warning to Quillion as comfort for the boy.

The boy nodded, and submitted to being tied without a struggle.

When the lad was suitably restrained, Kikkan fixed his angry stare upon Quillion. The stout northerner lifted his hands, palms outward in supplication.

"Where would we be now if I had not decided to take control? Disarmed and in custody at the mercy of those thugs!"

Kikkan looked skeptical, but Quillion surprised him by turning to the boy.

"What do you think? You were the one who named them looters and rapists. Was I wrong to cut them down?"

The boy didn't meet Quillion's gaze, but he responded in a whisper. "No you were not."

The boy's voice calmed everyone, even Cole, who had been pacing around the perimeter of the room. He came to a halt.

"Did you alert the red cloaks to our presence?" Quillion asked.

"Yes," the boy replied.

"Why?"

The lad shrugged. "They grabbed me. I had to give them something."

The three travelers stood in silence until Cole spoke. "What is your name, lad?"

The boy looked up. "They call me Weasel."

Quillion snorted. "That's not a very nice name. Do you want to pick a new one?"

Weasel shrugged again. "I'm used to it."

"Very well then, Weasel." Quillion pulled up another chair and sat down. "I don't entirely trust you, but you're the only source of information we have. You're going to have to help us figure out what to do."

Weasel fell silent.

"First," Quillion continued, "why are those red cloaks, or grifters as you called them, so darn big?"

Weasel took a deep breath. "They say they put something in their food. Whenever new recruits join up, they start to put on muscle. It usually takes them several months to get to that size."

"*Bliss* for soldiers?" Cole offered, looking at Quillion.

"No," Weasel replied, surprising Quillion with his boldness. "*Bliss* makes folk docile; they don't become monsters until the supply is revoked. Whatever the grifters take makes them aggressive. The change is complete. After a few months spent with the grifters, you're a different person; even your own mother wouldn't recognize you." Weasel's voice dropped. "I heard it makes their balls shrivel up."

Quillion fixed him with a gaze. "They become sterile?"

The boy shrugged.

Quillion ran his hand through his hair. He stood and paced, walking to the window so he could stare down into the street. Below, the city was silent.

"Months, you say?" he asked, turning on the boy.

Weasel nodded.

"Months . . . months . . . months . . . ." Quillion whispered.

Cole had spent enough time with Quillion to be able to guess what he was thinking.

"You mean to join them?"

Quillion locked eyes with Cole and gave a slow, resigned nod. "It will be the best way, the quickest way, to familiarize ourselves with the politics of Edentown."

"What about the bodies in the market?" Cole continued. "Don't you think they'll have an investigation? It would be a hell of a thing if they found out about us when we were already in their custody."

Quillion turned back to the window. He stared below to confirm that the pursuit he had feared was only a figment of his imagination. "They'll make a show of investigating, then find a scapegoat to take the blame. Groups like these always have targets picked for the necessity of public slaughter. Punishment is part of a larger agenda. They see no need to ferret out any truth beyond what they already believe. We'll use that."

Kikkan scoffed.

"It would seem the red cloaks are nothing more than another form of slavery. Are you seriously considering submitting to that?"

Quillion glanced at the boy before turning to Kikkan.

"We need to get into the city and we need cover so as to go unmolested. Also, I want to see how this organization works. In a couple weeks, I think we can learn everything we need and we'll slip away. At that point, we will be better equipped to plan our next move."

"What if your brain gets rotted by whatever they feed you before then?" Kikkan replied.

Quillion turned to Weasel.

"It is in the food, you say?"

Weasel shrugged. "Nobody knows for sure. Maybe they give them pills like *Bliss*; maybe it's in the water."

"But it takes two months for the effects to show?"

The lad nodded.

Quillion folded his arms and furrowed his brow. He continued to pace.

"This is madness," Kikkan said. "I will not submit to this plan."

"No, I didn't think you would." Quillion eyed him. "Also, it would be foolish for us to commit fully to this course."

"What do you mean?" Kikkan replied.

"I want you on the outside," Quillion said. He turned to Weasel. "Tell me about Edentown. Is there a city within the city?"

The boy's eyes twinkled. "I'm starting to think you're not as dumb as most of the travelers the wind blows in. Where are you from?"

Quillion's face hardened. "I'm from many places, now answer the question!"

"Yes," the boy said.

Cole looked back and forth between the boy and Quillion. "City within a city? What does that mean?"

"The place where thieves go to hide," Quillion said.

"The underworld," the boy replied.

"Free people?" Kikkan asked.

Weasel shrugged. "Perhaps there is that potential."

"Then we should go there," Cole offered. "Why waste our time taking a risk with the red cloaks?"

"Because we have to discover who the enemy is," Quillion answered. "The red cloaks are just puppets, I need to find out who is pulling the strings. We can't form a rebellion until we find out who we're fighting."

"But once we join the red cloaks, how will the resistance ever trust us?" Cole asked.

Quillion pointed at Kikkan.

"He'll speak for us when the time comes."

Kikkan tilted his head, genuinely surprised.

"Why will they trust me?" he asked.

"Because you will bring them this." Quillion offered him the tattered copy of 'The Demon Haunted World' that he had received from Adam Lockhart.

Kikkan took the proffered book.

"The boy will have to stay with you," Quillion continued, turning to address the lad. "I'm sorry, but you know enough to blow this whole thing up."

The boy didn't seem too concerned. "Running from the grifters is what I do anyway."

Quillion held his gaze. "Unless you have a kernel of information to sell them, that is."

Weasel shot him a suspicious look.

"It doesn't matter," Quillion said, "we all do what we can to survive. As long as you understand that Kikkan will be protecting you now. Do you trust that he is capable?"

Weasel looked at the large warrior, remembering how he had cut down two of the red cloaks back at the market. "Yes."

"Good." Quillion lifted the pouch of *Bliss* and offered it to Kikkan. "You better take this, too."

"That, I do not want," Kikkan said.

Quillion didn't retract the item. "Take it, you know it has value here and you know I cannot go to the red cloaks with it."

Kikkan delayed for a moment, then reluctantly reached out to grab the proffered item. He said nothing but tucked the bag into his belt.

"Seal it better," Weasel said.

Quillion looked at the boy.

"The bag of *Bliss*; you need to seal it better or you'll draw the hordes up. The winds have favored you thus far or we'd be overrun already. You were right to wrap it in plastic, but you need more layers. There," he nodded at the piles of refuse that littered the ground, "plastic can contain the smell, the thicker the better. Though at depths, the hunger of the demons is strong."

Quillion stooped to retrieve the indicated piece of plastic and passed it to Kikkan, who wrapped the package while locking eyes with Quillion.

Quillion turned back to Weasel. "How are you and Kikkan going to enter the under city?"

"We'll go in through the sewers."

The term was unfamiliar to Quillion, but Weasel noticed his confusion and elaborated.

"A network of tunnels below ground."

Quillion nodded. He slipped his sword from his belt and handed the weapon to Kikkan. Kikkan took the blade with surprise.

"You heard the red cloaks," Quillion explained, "it's illegal to walk around the city with a weapon."

"You'd disarm yourself?" Kikkan said.

"I'm disarming both of us." Quillion glanced meaningfully at Cole.

The smaller swordsman shook his head, but he stood to loosen his own blade from his belt and handed it to Kikkan.

"I hope you know what you're doing," he grumbled.

Seeing Kikkan holding the swords gave Quillion pause.

"Maybe you should consider wielding one of those in our absence."

Kikkan shook his head.

"My pipe is battle-tested."

"Suit yourself." Quillion turned to Weasel. "Where do the red cloaks gather?"

"Fort Brinewater," Weasel said. "Captain Jesse is their leader, and she is without mercy."

Chapter 11: The Diligent Captain

The clouds hung low over the outskirts of Edentown, and the evening light made the city glow red. Captain Jesse stood in the courtyard before her assembled officers. Her features were bland, unremarkable except for a constant expression of irritation. She was a short, squat woman and when she moved, her body contorted in manic twitches and jerks. Her eyes darted about in search of transgressions worthy of punishment; never failing to find something or someone out of place.

"Where's Commander Marcos?" she barked. Her question was met with silence as none wished to draw her attention.

No sooner had the words passed her lips than the immense gates of Fort Brinewater opened. A man on a lathered horse arrived. His graying hair indicated age, but he slipped from his mount with the dexterity of an accomplished soldier. He passed the reins to an attendant and marched to take his place in the assembly.

At the man's arrival, Captain Jesse stared down at her feet. When she spoke, her voice was thick with disappointment. "You are to be in assembly at sunset, Commander Marcos."

Commander Marcos glanced over at the horizon to see the last light of the setting sun slip from view. He had arrived at the appointed hour, but he knew better than to correct his superior.

"Report," Captain Jesse ordered, keeping her eyes averted from the horizon.

The first officer gave a brief report, stating all of his responsibilities were in order. Jesse nodded, not listening, and moved through the line of assembled men. The question was repeated, and the captain stood passively while the reports were given. She was in no hurry as she made her way to stand before Commander Marcos.

"Tardy," she said, finally lifting her eyes to look at him. "That is a demerit. How many demerits has this man accrued?"

The Inquisitor, Captain Jesse's primary adviser, stepped forward. The Inquisitor was an imposing man, taller than the captain, but ethereal, like a shadow.

"Three, Captain," the Inquisitor said.

Commander Marcos scowled.

"Three," Jesse repeated, returning her gaze to the commander. "A punishment is warranted then. What is your report, Commander? Are all your patrols accounted for?"

"All but one. Sergeant Erik's group has not checked in yet."

Captain Jesse's eyes widened, but Commander Marcos thought he detected a tinge of delight as well.

"You're in breach of protocol," Jesse said. "The code clearly states that all day patrols must return before sundown. Why have your charges failed to appear?"

Commander Marcos stood at attention and tried to calm himself. Before being pressured to take this post, he had been enjoying a quiet retirement. His current assignment was to assist a privileged youth from San Aryan take control of her first command. Marcos had accepted the position as a personal favor to Jesse's father, but from the beginning, the captain had resented his presence. "Captain, I have just finished my initial investigation of the matter. I can only assume that foul play . . ."

"Assume? You dare to waste my time with assumptions?"

Marcos stiffened. He lifted his chin higher. "Captain, I wished to return from my initial inquiry in time to present myself at assembly."

"And you arrived late," Captain Jesse reminded him.

"Captain, I was not late," Marcos said, "I was in formation at attention with the last light of the setting sun as the code requires."

Jesse did not reply, but she stepped back from the formation and nodded to a burly man watching the proceedings. Sergeant Keene nodded back at her. Keene was a towering brute with short cropped hair and beard; a perpetual smirk on his face. Commander Marcos had disapproved of Sergeant Keene from his arrival.

"Men," Captain Jesse said, "it seems I have an opportunity to reiterate the philosophy of my command. Work hard, complete your duties, and you will be rewarded. There are no excuses and no shortcuts. Nobody is handed anything based on reputation or prior achievement."

Marcos felt eyes upon him. He was the most experienced and decorated officer stationed at Fort Brinewater, but over the months, Captain Jesse had never missed an opportunity to disparage his reputation. Marcos had grown used to hearing his name mentioned in whispers followed by guttural laughter. Such slovenly command was Jesse's way, but Marcos had no intention of succumbing to her level. He stood at stoic attention, eyes forward.

"It seems I have been too tolerant," Jesse continued. "Sergeant Keene!" The last was an order and Sergeant Keene hopped forward to stand in front of Commander Marcos. Marcos watched the man approach, but couldn't perceive much beyond the ever present half-grin. When Keene's nose nearly touched that of the besieged commander, the sergeant stopped to await further orders.

Marcos had to keep himself from recoiling at the smell. There was something bestial about the hulking Sergeant Keene.

"Take him," Jesse snapped.

She wouldn't dare.

At Jesse's command, Sergeant Keene grasped Marcos's arms and wrestled the older commander into a submission hold.

Commander Marcos did not resist the mistreatment as Keene marched him forward, but the brutish sergeant didn't allow the commander any opportunity to save face. The sergeant wrenched the older man's arm so Marcos twisted and recoiled like a puppet on a string. The soldiers assembled in the courtyard shared a laugh at the commander's expense.

This is insanity. Preserving the sanctity of chain of command is paramount.

"Commander Marcos," Jesse snapped, "you have been found derelict in your duty and have earned a third demerit. Your punishment will be five strokes of the lash, administered immediately,"

Marcos blanched. At his advanced age, five strokes could prove fatal. What game was Captain Jesse playing? He was fully aware she harbored resentment, but had never considered his life might be in danger.

"Captain, I request an appeal."

"Denied."

Sergeant Keene maneuvered Marcos over to the flogging post. Though Commander Marcos didn't resist, the brutish sergeant smashed Marcos's face against the polished wooden surface. Marcos felt a cut open above his left eye. Desperation descended.

"Captain," Marcos said, "the patrol was missing and I went to find them as protocol required. What more could I have done?"

"You should have found them. I have no place for incompetence under my command," Jesse replied.

Marcos felt the wind leave his chest. "What could I have done?" he cried again, panic in his voice.

Jesse made a dismissive gesture. Her Inquisitor offered her the handle of a whip. "You see, gentlemen," she said, turning to those assembled, "he asks for advice on how to fulfill his commission. I do not have the time to train incompetents in how to perform their duties. This is what happens when an unqualified person assumes a position beyond his level of ability. There are no shortcuts! You must earn your place by going through the proper channels. Only through diligent labor can you improve your station."

"That was not the case with you," Commander Marcos shouted, anger replacing his desperation. The words seemed to paralyze Captain Jesse. Marcos seized the opportunity. "Your father got you placed here. Do you deny it? You have not earned this post, otherwise you would know better than to subject a man of my reputation to this punishment. Do you think there will be no consequences?"

Captain Jesse stood still as the words echoed over the courtyard.

"Release me, insolent child," Marcos demanded, "and let us seek out that lost patrol as any competent captain would have long since ordered!"

There was a pause. Captain Jesse threw the lash to the ground.

"Captain?" said the Inquisitor.

Captain Jesse said nothing.

"Release me," Commander Marcos shrieked, jerking against his restraints.

Captain Jesse looked up. Again she made eye contact with Sergeant Keene; again the brutish man returned her look with a malicious smirk.

"Get a pole," Jesse said.

Sergeant Keene saluted and sprinted off, tapping several men on the shoulder to accompany him. At the order, Commander Marcos went limp, his building bravado suddenly replaced with abject terror.

Captain Jesse walked over to stand before the stuttering commander and fixed him with a firm look. "If anyone cared what happened to you, you would have never been assigned here."

Before Marcos could reply, Keene and several others returned carrying a pole that looked to have been cut from the core of a mature tree. The men threw the heavy object to the ground, and Keene wrestled Marcos off the flogging stake to prostrate him across the pole. Now Marcos resisted with new strength born of the terror of his imminent death, but even in the face of that horror, he could not overpower Sergeant Keene. The younger man struck Marcos in the face, rendering the beleaguered commander half unconscious, before placing a knee upon the elder man's chest and positioning his arms above his head, crossed at the wrists.

"There are no shortcuts," Captain Jesse reiterated. "Work hard and you'll be rewarded. Incompetence and insubordination will be paid with death. Let the witnesses spread the word on what transpires here." Captain Jesse nodded the final order.

Keene smiled; he had procured tools along with the pole. In one hand he held an iron stake against the commander's crossed forearms, in his other he clasped a heavy mallet. At Jesse's nod, Keene slammed the mallet against the head of the spike. The spike drove through Marcos's arms and bit deeply into the wood beneath.

Despite the commander's semi-coherent state, the blow elicited an anguished scream. Keene continued to hammer until the stake was fully buried in the commander's forearms. When the sergeant finished, several men came together to lift the pole into one of three well-holes spaced along the courtyard's northern wall. Displaced water shot out as the pole settled into place, with Commander Marcos dangling in the air.

"When he starts to stink," Jesse said, "take him down." She paused to watch Commander Marcos twitch.

Sergeant Keene approached to stand beside the Captain.

"Go find Erik's patrol," Jesse said. "With any luck, they'll turn up drunk before morning."

Still wearing his perpetual smile, Keene turned and headed off to fulfill his orders.

"Forgive me, Captain," murmured the Inquisitor, "but what do we report if Sergeant Keene does find the patrol?"

"Commander Marcos's death has been a long time coming," Jesse replied. "I knew he was going to be a problem the first time I laid eyes on him."

"Yes, but he was well known. What might the Seneschals say?"

"My duty is to enforce the code," Jesse replied. "I don't make decisions; I am a conduit. The procedures were set by wiser souls long ago."

The Inquisitor nodded. "And if the patrol is not found?"

"Keene will send a report to San Aryan. My superiors can deal with any abnormalities. As far as I'm concerned, the trespass has been paid."

Chapter 12: Forced Entry

Simyon walked in the near-dark with the practiced care one who had spent a lifetime in shadow. Every so often, he came upon a ladder bolted into the wall; most had grime-covered directional plaques set beneath. Some plaques were nothing more than compass directions and arrows, while others displayed intricate maps with unfamiliar names and places.

With every step, Simyon's agitation grew. The thought of Valeria alone with that Seneschal made the young thief's skin crawl.

"Fool!" he whispered. He was tempted to scream, but even in his agitation he knew that could not be risked. He occupied the fringes of where the demons lurked, and Simyon had no desire to battle a horde of *Bliss*-craving skeletal monsters. Instead, he clenched his fists until the knuckles turned white.

Did Valeria really think she could make the Seneschal love her? Her ambition bordered on hubris! True, her physical attributes were enough to throw a gutter-rat like Simyon into a frenzy, but to a Seneschal . . .

Simyon's foot hit a slick rock and he stumbled knee deep into a foul-smelling pool. His flailing hand traced out a line of slime on the wall. Simyon crinkled his nose as he regained his balance, shaking his fingers to dislodge the muck.

Dull luminescence was visible on the edges of where his hand had passed. Curiosity compelled him to scoop up a glob of slime. He squeezed it together between his palms. He lifted the mass close to his face and opened his fingers to peer inside.

At first there was nothing. But a moment later, he thought he detected heat emanating from the wad.

Simyon closed his hands over the mass once more, squeezing so hard that liquid dribbled from the gaps between his fingers. As he applied pressure, he sensed the heat increasing. This time when he opened his fingers, he was startled by the emanation of a pale blue light. The light in the grime was both subtle and beautiful, and Simyon gazed in wonder.

With the benefit of the light, Simyon reached to clear off a section of the wall. A couple quick swipes revealed the beginning of an image, but Simyon stopped himself from clearing more. He had already stained his disguise, perhaps irretrievably. The young thief pulled his hand back from the wall and lifted the light.

The image seemed to be a representation of people. Strange people dressed in clothing unlike anything Simyon had ever seen were shown standing in a park. A woman stood in the foreground beside a monkey on a chain.

"Another relic of the ancient world," Simyon whispered. Profound sadness threatened to overtake him, a weakness he could not entertain in this place of vulnerability.

Simyon drew away from the mystery. His quest lay ahead; the past could not assist him now.

*

Some time later, a subtle increase in the ambient light roused Simyon from his dark reverie. There was no obvious source to account for the change, and but for the recognition that his stumbles had become less frequent, the young thief might not have noticed. He continued on his way, keenly aware of the growing light, until he was finally able to make out a white point in the distance.

Simyon proceeded toward his objective, and as the point grew in size, he realized he was looking at a door. The illumination that revealed the door was white and encased in a metal cage. There was no flame that Simyon could detect; instead, the source seemed to be some manner of enchantment trapped within a thick piece of glass.

Simyon reached up to touch the glass, but quickly pulled back his hand from the hot surface. He turned his attention to the oval-shaped, metal door. Simyon pushed experimentally, but the surface was unyielding. There was a lever in the center, but this too was solid and could not be forced.

The thief nodded.

The obstacle was formidable, but Simyon had broken too many houses to be perturbed by the presence of a stubborn door.

He stepped back and examined the wall, tracing out a circular, ever widening perimeter from the portal's center. There appeared to be no weaknesses. The frame—also metal—showed no sign of rot or improper installment. Even the stone that housed the portal was of a different variety to that of the tunnel. These stones were white, and had the shine of newness. They had not been abandoned to decay and slime for decades, like those along the path.

There is a way in, there always is.

The rough wall was still slick with moisture, but without the slime of living moss.

"Hmmm," Simyon mused. He had hoped to find loose bricks in crumbling mortar. He didn't have the time to chisel through stone.

He kept scanning. By now, he had begun to suspect that this was the border of San Aryan. As the obstacle continued to thwart him, Simyon's agitation magnified.

He groped in the strange light for the secret of the door. The young thief was unsure what he was looking for, but he diligently patted at the walls. His quest drew him away from the door to a section of wall bathed in shadow. There, he felt his palms connect with a metallic cover rather than the expected rough patch of molded stone.

Simyon patted around the edges of the metal plate and came upon a ring. He gave this a tug, pulling away a thin cover to reveal a keypad outlined in glowing red.

A surge of memories from his youth returned in a rush.

"What are these symbols?" a voice echoed in his mind. It was the stern voice of his teacher, and Simyon couldn't help but answer.

"Numbers: one, two, three, four . . ."

A keypad! But what was the code?

Simyon returned to the door, once again questing for answers. Whether he had learned the discipline from the teacher of his youth, or from his years of labor on the streets, Simyon was methodical. He returned to the beginning of the problem and began his examination again, this time specifically looking for numbers.

Every time his eyes passed the light, something nagged at him. By the third time, he stopped and regarded the mysterious illumination once more.

Why a light?

The light was positioned directly over the door. The keypad was outside of its illumination, but the keypad had its own light source.

What was the overhead light there to reveal?

Simyon took a step back.

The light's housing directed the beam straight down.

Simyon kneeled and pawed at the dust that had collected at the base of the portal. The spot was oddly dry and the dust that had gathered there was of a fine, soft powder. With a couple quick swipes of his hand, Simyon discovered letters carved into the stone. Letters, not numbers, but the message was clear. "Ninety-two, twelve."

Simyon rocked back.

The code was desperately simple. The keypad contained numbers and the code was written out in letters – completely disguised, yet instantly visible to those with the requisite knowledge.

Simyon stood and walked back to the keypad.

He entered: 9-2-1-2. Then he stood back to watch.

For a moment, there was nothing.

Then the portal came alive. Working of its own accord, the lever in the center of the door swung over to the right. There were two popping sounds, then the door itself swung inward.

Simyon swallowed hard. He was tempted to observe for a moment before proceeding, but he feared the door would shut again. "Valeria," he said to himself, and jumped through the portal into darkness.

He took a hesitant step, then another. The room beyond the door was black and silent. His third step provoked a grating noise of metal upon metal. Behind him, the entryway slammed shut, leaving Simyon in total darkness. His heart raced, but before he could react, he felt a prick on his arm like the sting of an insect. The sting was followed by a jolt of agony that stiffened every muscle in his body.

Simyon toppled over, caught in the throes of uncontrollable spasms. His chest tightened, and the young thief found himself unable to draw breath. Powerless to resist the force that had felled him, Simyon's twitching and pained vocalizations continued even after he lost consciousness.

Chapter 13: Preparations

"Of all your plans, this is the worst," Cole said as he and Quillion made their way through the stone streets of outer Edentown.

"Why?" Quillion replied, keeping his voice low to avoid an echo. He was paying greater than usual attention to his surroundings, glancing about as if searching for something.

"What were you thinking, leaving Kikkan with that red cloak informant? How's he going to keep that kid under wraps, inclined as he is to liberate every oppressed soul he comes into contact with?"

"What do you think will happen?" Quillion asked.

Cole responded instantly. "I think the kid will give him the slip, the red cloaks will come running, and Kikkan will hang before the night's over."

Quillion nodded at the grim scenario.

"I suppose that's possible."

"Possible?" Cole barked, his voice dripping with disgust. "So you *did* think of it!"

"The scenario you mention crossed my mind."

The two mercenaries fell into silence as they continued marching. Weasel had said Fort Brinewater was a mere five or six miles distant. As they were unarmed, Quillion was confident the red cloaks would take them into custody without violence, although even that end was uncertain.

"I think we all have a few harsh lessons ahead," he mumbled.

Realization dawned on Cole and he flashed Quillion a judgmental look.

"You did it on purpose! You've set Kikkan up for a choice he cannot make."

Quillion snorted. He continued to survey their surroundings with extra care.

"I won't take the blame for that. It was not I who constructed a world that makes you choose between honor and survival. Kikkan needs to develop a more flexible sense of morality. If he does so, and survives, he will be of further use to us. If not, it's better we don't get caught in the fallout."

Cole didn't respond, but he set his jaw.

The dark stretched out above them and there was nary a light in a window for as far as they could see. Weasel had said they were entering the last stretch of uninhabited buildings before the main city. Quillion was relieved to observe the boy seemed to have told them the truth.

"Just so you know," he said, after giving Cole enough time to cool his head, "I do believe Kikkan will perform his task. Even if he doesn't know it, survival is his principal motivator, just as it is for us."

"Marching up unarmed to hand ourselves over to the enemy is a tactic for survival?" Cole snapped.

Quillion shrugged.

"Adam Lockhart's book suggested that one must always judge things in terms of their context."

"I thought that book didn't make sense to you?"

"It didn't," Quillion admitted, "not at first. But some passages have lingered with me. Maybe grander schemes do not reveal their full importance all at once. Comprehension comes in fragments, like searching with a candle in the blackness of a starless night. Slowly, with persistence, a larger image is revealed."

"What pieces have you collected so far?"

Quillion fixed Cole with a firm expression.

"Not to abandon my perceptions and my conclusions due to the pressure of a more powerful entity."

"Uh-huh," Cole said, losing interest.

Quillion stopped and gave Cole an intense look. "I mean, we will not submit to the dominance of lesser men."

"I thought that was how we operated already," Cole replied.

"To an extent." Quillion's voice softened. "But I find there are more ways to dominate a person than I ever imagined. If we aren't vigilant, we can slip into bondage without even noticing."

"I'd think I'd notice if my hands were tied."

"Certainly," Quillion replied. "But you might not notice if they tied your mind. Now, look there."

Quillion pointed and Cole followed his direction. Before them stood a large building; at the very top was a dingy red sign depicting a man with a white beard drinking a black liquid from a glass bottle.

"What of it?" Cole asked.

"Do you think you could find that building again?"

"Yes, that sign is a landmark, it can be seen from a great distance."

"Good." Quillion trotted forward to the building and ran his hand against the wall, circling the perimeter in a secret quest. Cole followed, slightly confused.

In a short while, Quillion came to a metallic green door. He tried the handle. At first, it appeared to be rusted shut, but Quillion worked at it and the resistance eventually gave with a snap. The stout northerner pulled the door open and stepped inside.

The room was dark. Scattered about the floor were various scraps of metal and items of long forgotten purpose. Along one wall was a row of metal boxes reaching all the way to the roof.

"That will work," Quillion said.

Cole began to suspect what his friend was up to.

Quillion opened boxes at random, but as he did so, he saw something he liked better. At the far end of the room, protruding out from the wall, were a series of capped pipes. The pipes were as wide as the breadth of Quillion's hand. Handles protruded from either side of the caps.

Quillion grasped the handles of one cap and began applying pressure. The cap, like the door, resisted his effort. Quillion strained, his muscles shaking with exertion. After a while he stopped, rested for a moment, and tried again.

"It's rusted shut," Cole said.

"It's loosening," Quillion replied.

It took two more efforts, but the cap finally broke free and Quillion spun it loose. The cap popped off the pipe, swinging on a lightweight chain that kept it from falling to the floor.

Quillion kneeled and peered into the pipe. He reached his hand in and found it dry.

"Good," he said.

He reached into his satchel and pulled out the gun. He wrapped it in a piece of leather and inserted it into the pipe. Then he dug through his belongings for the boxes of bullets before also inserting them into the hiding place. When he was finished, he looked at Cole.

"Do you have anything you wish to keep safe?"

Cole considered for a minute before shaking his head. Quillion nodded and replaced the cap. When he was finished, he stood.

"You're confident you can find this place again?" he repeated.

"Yes."

"Good." Quillion made his way outside. He squinted and pointed to the distance. "There are lights ahead."

*

"Your friend is a lunatic," Weasel said.

"He's not my friend; we've just been traveling together for a time."

The man and the boy were making their way down a flight of stairs. To Kikkan's surprise, Weasel had guided him below the surface level of the building where they had been staying. The stairway wound down flight after flight into darkness. Kikkan lifted a torch over his head, but he knew it wasn't going to last long and the thought concerned him.

"I don't want to be trapped in difficult terrain with no way to see," the former slave said.

"Don't worry," Weasel replied, "there is light below. It's not that bright, but it's enough so that we can get around."

Kikkan scowled. What choice did he have but to believe?

"He's going to get killed, you know, and the smaller one too," Weasel continued. "The red cloaks aren't all that accommodating."

"Then that will be his fate."

"He likes to provoke doesn't he, this Quillion?" Weasel laughed. "It would almost be worth watching the reaction he gets from Captain Jesse."

"Who?"

"She's their leader, the grifters, I mean, the red cloaks; at least in this district. Very little sense of humor."

Kikkan nodded. "Provocation is how he gets the measure of people. He likes to push to see where the limits are."

"That's a dangerous game," Weasel replied. "There are those who will not wish to continue in his fellowship once they've been tricked into revealing more than they intended."

"I've seen him interact with people," Kikkan said. "He tries to get the information he needs before the breaking point is reached."

"That's what he thinks," Weasel stated. "Provincial tactics don't work in Edentown."

Kikkan fell into thought as the two continued their descent.

The further they went into the heart of the building, the more refuse and debris cluttered the stairwell. It became difficult for Kikkan to maintain his balance, and more often than not he found himself bracing the floor or wall with his arm as he progressed. Rocks and loose tiles shifted beneath him, causing the torch he carried to swing, casting long shadows against the walls.

Finally, the stairs opened up into a hallway. Kikkan lifted his torch high and stared forward and back.

The hallway had curved walls, there was a footpath on either side, and a recessed trench running down the middle. Kikkan held his torch over the trench and the light reflected back off two parallel metal rails.

"We're deep enough now," Weasel said, "you can put out the light."

Kikkan gave Weasel a hard look and, not for the first time, wondered if the boy had some trick in mind.

"Come on," the lad said at Kikkan's hesitation, "you might wish you had that torch later."

Kikkan nodded. "Come here." His tone suggested no argument would be welcome.

Weasel stepped forward and Kikkan took both his wrists in one hand.

"Don't make any sudden moves when this light goes out."

"Understood."

Kikkan took one final look at the boy before grinding the torch into a pile of dust that had gathered against the wall. The light flickered and died.

Instantly, they were engulfed in absolute darkness.

Kikkan's grip tightened on the boy's wrists.

"Wait," Weasel pleaded. "It will take your eyes a moment to adjust, but believe me the light is there."

The seconds ticked by and Kikkan could feel his heart racing. He peered with all of his might into the blackness. He was reminded of his old hut back at the farm of Duncan Kerr. But even the darkest nights in that foul pit did not compare to the utter nothing he now experienced.

"Wait," the boy pleaded.

A few more heartbeats passed, and then Kikkan thought he saw something. Dimly, at the edges of his vision, was a very slight glow. He waited, and the more he waited, the more the illumination grew. It was feeble at first, methodically increasing in intensity. The light never got so bright that Kikkan could see clearly, but it was sufficient to avoid lethal obstacles that had fallen by chaos or by design.

"Do you see?" Weasel asked.

"I do."

Releasing the boy, the former slave walked over to the wall. The light seemed to come from the surface, from some kind of strange substance growing along the tiles. Kikkan grasped a sample between his thumb and forefinger and gave an experimental rub. The substance crumbled with a sensation of heat, leaving a bright streak of bluish light to stain his fingers.

"It's remarkable," Kikkan said, turning back to Weasel.

His words echoed down the tunnel.

"Weasel?"

No reply.

The boy was gone.

Chapter 14: Humanitarian Banquet

Valeria entered the large house and made every attempt to hide her awe at the opulence on display. In the presence of Janus and Orion, she became keenly aware of her own stature. The two men seemed larger than other human beings, and she felt tiny by comparison. She had the disquieting sense that Orion could see right through her. The young woman clenched her hands at her sides and made an effort to push the debilitating thoughts away.

I can handle them.

I can handle anyone.

She repeated the mantra, but the nausea she felt indicated the words lacked their usual power.

"May I take your shawl, miss?" a voice asked. Valeria looked up to see a young man dressed in a smart black suit and wearing white gloves. Something about the gloves disturbed her. Valeria glanced at Janus, and saw her companion slip off his cloak without protest, so she followed suit.

Orion walked ahead, gesturing at the walls. "Forgive the disorder of my home, this banquet was thrust upon me and I didn't have time to prepare. You understand."

"Your home is as spotless as ever," Janus replied.

Valeria nodded her agreement.

Orion led them through a long hallway, past a dozen or so rooms, and finally into a garden behind the estate. A score of tables were set among the rose bushes, and slender trees sprouted up within the enclosed area. A brick pathway meandered through the grounds, and there was even a white picket bridge across a winding stream.

The tables were covered in peach-colored cloth that extended down to the ground. Chairs adorned with similar fabric surrounded the tables. Elegantly dressed men and women sat chatting with each other. Valeria felt as if she had stumbled into a different world; there was more luxury here than she had ever imagined.

At Orion's arrival, a hush fell upon the gathering and everyone looked up.

Valeria experienced a flush of trepidation, for it seemed that all the faces swiveled to look through her.

"Friends, I present you Janus and . . . companion," Orion said with a flourish.

The introduction produced a quiet muttering accentuated with the occasional chuckle.

Orion cast a glance at Valeria and smiled.

"Here is a place for you," he said, moving toward a table with eight of its ten seats already occupied. "Unfortunately, I won't be able to accommodate seating the two of you together."

Valeria looked toward the back of the garden, where several tables stood completely empty.

"Here you are," Orion said, gesturing at a chair.

"Thank you," Valeria replied, sitting.

Orion patted her shoulder and nodded at Janus, who had taken a seat across from the young woman.

"Now I shall take my leave. Duty calls," Orion said. The words caused Valeria's new table companions to titter. Orion inclined his head and sauntered off.

Valeria watched him go, then turned to regard the people surrounding her. To her right was a black-haired, middle-aged woman with an hourglass figure. The woman appeared to have had some sort of enhancement applied to her face. Valeria had seen the white cream that the wealthy merchants of San Borja sometimes used, but this wasn't the same. This woman's face had not been painted, but there was an unnatural shine that made her skin appear almost artificial.

"Hello," Valeria said.

The woman scowled, not deigning to reply. Instead, she turned to her neighbor and whispered something before looking back at Valeria. The two cackled loudly.

Valeria glanced at Janus, but her escort faced in the direction Orion had gone.

A moment later, another of the white-gloved attendants appeared. He carried a pitcher, and made his way around the table to serve the guests.

Valeria watched as red liquid poured into crystal glasses. When the attendant arrived at Valeria's place, the black-haired woman reached out to stop him.

"That's not for her," she said.

The servant paused.

The black-haired woman withdrew her arm and went back to her mumbled conversation, ignoring Valeria.

The servant returned Valeria's empty glass to the table and stepped away.

Valeria folded her hands and waited. She listened to the mumbled conversation around her and picked up the occasional word, although the context was lost in the chaos of overlapping voices.

"Common . . . low-born . . . disgraceful . . ."

When Valeria grew tired of listening, she glanced at Janus, but the large man sat immobile. He only moved to brush servants away when they offered him something.

As the minutes passed, Valeria's terror transformed into a deep, seething rage. The sensation provided comfort. Rage had always served her better than fear.

Finally, the lights dimmed by some unknown trick, ushering in a welcome darkness.

A metal utensil rang out against a glass and the chaotic jabber fell to a whisper. A man stood at the head of the front table. He wore a red suit with a different cut to anything Valeria had ever seen. His blond hair was curly but neatly cropped, and he smiled as he stood and gestured to the crowd.

"Tonight we have gathered to honor a great man, a humanitarian," the speaker said. "In the chaos of our daily lives, it's easy to forget that there are others in this world who are not as fortunate as we. Our own problems blind us to the difficult situations of others. But the man I'm about to introduce is dedicated to personal sacrifice for the goal of helping those who have less. He is known to offer his services as a surgeon and restore broken, suffering individuals to full strength. He possesses an almost magical ability to heal, and his willingness to selflessly share this gift with children is nothing short of saintly. We've all witnessed his tireless, heroic acts and enjoyed the benefit of his generosity. But above all, his greatness manifests in the way he accepts everyone he encounters as an equal."

Valeria felt furtive glances thrown her way which she ignored and kept her attention on the speaker.

"I present you with the living embodiment of all the greatest human qualities. Our dear Orion!"

"I'm going to kill him," Orion growled playfully as he stood. The words struck Valeria as misplaced, but then she realized Orion wished to convey that he didn't like all the attention.

Orion made his way to the front, smiling and shaking the hands of people he passed. The eyes of every man and woman he acknowledged twinkled for him.

After an extended delay, the white-haired man finally came to stand before the curly-haired speaker in the red suit. The speaker shook Orion's hand, and presented him with a silver chalice mounted on a wooden platform. Orion hefted the prize with appreciation.

"It's embarrassing," he said, still staring at the chalice, "to be rewarded for simply doing what we know to be right."

The humble-sounding words evoked another round of applause.

"Thank you all for coming to honor me like this. I am truly touched." Orion's gaze turned toward Valeria's table. "I'd like to especially thank Janus for coming."

There were a few muffled giggles.

"I hope we didn't interrupt the diversions he had planned for the evening."

The women on either side turned to stare at Valeria with undisguised contempt.

"But the night is long, isn't it, boys?" Orion's words were met by a roar of laughter and applause. Orion lifted up his humanitarian award and shook it. "Thank you," he said, nodding and bowing. "I'm humbled to receive this; thank you, thank you."

The applause continued as Orion made his way back to his table. As he sat, a man stepped forward and whispered something into his ear. Instantly, the older man's demeanor changed. He gave one authoritative nod, then dismissed the messenger with wave of his hand. He sat contemplating for a moment, but then, ever so slowly, his face turned to regard Valeria.

Orion stood and marched over, hugging the shadows of the wall, though his movement drew the attention of the entire gathering. When he arrived, he leaned in close to Janus and put his hand upon the Seneschal's shoulder.

"The two of you must come now," he said. "I've been informed we have a visitor."

Chapter 15: Cold Reception

Quillion and Cole approached the towering gates of Fort Brinewater. They lifted their hands, palms outward, in a gesture of submission. To their left and right, a field stretched as far as the eye could see. Crumbling buildings framed the field on one side and a crude wall framed the other. Fort Brinewater sat in the middle; as ugly a building as Quillion had ever seen. The fort was a new construction put together with pieces scavenged from the decaying city. Glistening black liquid, still wet in places, coated the walls. The apparition of the fort provoked a flicker of doubt within Quillion, but it was too late to turn back now.

"Strangers approaching," a voice hollered from the wall, and Quillion and Cole stopped in their tracks. The sound of booted footsteps preceded the crank of heavy machinery and the gate cracked open.

The response perplexed Quillion. Prudence dictated the visitors be questioned from behind the protection of the fortress. What could be gained by direct approach? Unless they considered even basic parley an unacceptable show of deference.

Eight red cloaks appeared beyond the gate. They marched forward, grabbed Quillion and Cole, then marched them inside without saying a word.

Quillion swallowed a hard lump in his throat. The grip on his arm was rough; rougher than necessary.

The two northerners were brought into a large room with a floor of ceramic tile. Metal columns were placed about the room at regular intervals. The red cloaks guided Quillion to one corner of the room, Cole to the other. The two mercenaries were made to stand in front of large tables with boxes of various sizes and shapes laid out before them.

Still no words were spoken as the red cloaks set about stripping Quillion. Quillion knew resistance would invite retribution, but remaining submissive proved difficult. The pawing hands showed not the slightest concern for dignity, taking every opportunity to pinch and prod even when gentleness would have served the purpose with equal effectiveness.

The first thing the red cloaks removed were the two hunting daggers and camping hatchet the northerner carried. The red cloaks gave suspicious grunts as they set the blades aside.

Next, they loosened Quillion's belt and went through the various pouches he had slung there. Quillion carried coins from different districts, and these the soldiers distributed into individual containers on the table.

Someone stripped Quillion of his pack and sat in the corner rifling through its contents as others tore his shirt, boots and pants from his body.

The chill air bit Quillion's flesh as he stood naked before the red cloaks. They hadn't finished, however. Two of them grabbed Quillion's arms and pulled them wide, but by then Quillion had endured enough. He engaged his muscles, but the show of resistance set the red cloaks to action. One stepped up behind and wrapped a meaty arm around

Quillion's neck. The arm pulled tight against his throat and Quillion felt the flicker of darkness descend upon him. He tried to kick, but the soldier choking him lifted the mercenary's whole body off the floor.

Quillion gasped, and even in his wash of panic he realized he was being allowed enough air to remain conscious. His eyes flicked forward and he noticed a man standing before him. The man was older than the others with traces of a new beard. He examined Quillion with a thorough, appraising look.

The older man stepped forward and began pinching Quillion. Rough hands caressed Quillion's thighs, arms, and abdomen. Then the old man reached down between Quillion's legs and grasped his testicles tightly.

Quillion grunted and tried to twist away, but the man behind him only tightened his hold.

Eventually, the old man freed Quillion from his probing, but Quillion's skin had begun to crawl.

As a final insult, the old man reached up to Quillion's face. First, he opened both eyelids and examined Quillion's eyes, then he stuck his thumbs into Quillion's mouth and lifted the lips to have a view of the teeth.

Only then did Quillion understand.

I'm a piece of meat to him.

The old man took a step back, never engaging Quillion's gaze. He seemed about to speak when the one rifling through Quillion's backpack made a gesture.

Quillion glanced in that one's direction, just in time to see the agitated red cloak lift up a small medallion.

Despite the circumstances, Quillion allowed an internal smile, for this was his bargaining chip.

It was the medallion of Cassius the Seneschal.

The old man stepped forward and grasped the item. He lifted his hand and Quillion was dropped to the floor. But the old man said nothing. He only scooped up the medallion and marched from the room.

*

Quillion and Cole stood shivering, awaiting the return of their tormentor.

Quillion could see the detachment in the eyes of the guarding red cloaks, made worse by the fact that he understood their method.

Naked, shivering, pathetic, Quillion had been reduced to a shade of his true self. Standing there alone and powerless, he was less than human.

Quillion latched upon the memory of the slaughter in the market.

I've killed men like these.

The words floated through his mind and gave him a seed of strength.

I've killed others and will kill these as well.

The vow reinforced the remaining sliver of his autonomy, but Quillion didn't allow himself to straighten his back. The jailers wanted to see him bent and broken, so that's what he would give them. What would he gain by a premature show of defiance?

The door opened. The soldiers surrounding Quillion grabbed the northerner's arms and drove him forward, pushing him along before he could catch his balance, and delighting in the torment of well-placed jabs that kept the mercenary stumbling.

Quillion managed to right himself by crashing into the door frame, but again the red cloaks were behind, urging him on, with Cole and his own set of tormentors following.

The procession went down a long hall, then came out onto the wall itself. Guards standing by the battlements jeered as Quillion and Cole were paraded before them. Some threw pebbles or bits of food, and by the time the walk came to an end, the prisoners' bodies boasted a dozen blood trails.

They passed through another door, coming finally into a small room with a large window on one side. A short, squat woman of bland features sat at a table. There was a dimness in her gaze that concerned Quillion, for in that dimness he saw not only a lack of intelligence, but also a lack of any kind of human compassion. One such as her posed no threat on a level playing field, but here, in the heart of her den, Quillion knew she was inescapably deadly.

The medallion of Cassius the Seneschal rested on the table before her.

Quillion and Cole were pushed to a halt and the red cloaks closed the door behind them.

"You are accused of forgery and possession of an illicit item," the woman said, not bothering to identify herself. Quillion assumed she was the Captain Jesse Weasel had told him about. "The penalty for these transgressions is death by hanging."

"What's the penalty for disobeying the orders of a Seneschal?" Quillion replied.

A red cloak smashed Quillion in the back of the head with a closed fist. Quillion had anticipated the blow, but it still caused flashes of color behind his eyes.

The woman fell silent. Quillion bowed his head to avoid further provocation as she contemplated. As the seconds passed, the northerner was able to make some progress in unraveling the riddle of his current situation. He had seen her kind before; she would not engage him in true dialogue so as to not invite outside influence on her conclusions.

She needed control.

Very well, he would allow her control.

The woman continued staring at the medallion. She flipped the item over and over in her hands.

"What is the name of this Seneschal?" she asked.

"Cassius," Quillion replied.

Short answers, she'll try to catch me in a lie.

"Where?"

"Acheron."

"There are no Seneschal in Acheron," she said, her eyes narrowing in suspicion.

Quillion kept his head bowed. In his peripheral vision, he caught a glimpse of the view offered by the window. Eden-town appeared in the distance. The city seemed to form concentric circles as it descended down to the shores of a great body of water. "Cassius was in Acheron on a mission."

"What mission?"

"He sought a reader."

The two soldiers behind Quillion snorted. The woman lost her patience and smacked the table with her hand. The two soldiers fell instantly silent.

"What reader?" she barked.

"Adam Lockhart."

Quillion flicked his eyes over the woman's features as he said the name, but there was no sign of recognition.

"What's expected of you?"

"I'm to make a report," he replied.

"And your compensation?" Jesse sneered.

"A place for myself and my companion in the red cloaks."

This time, the guards standing behind him did not laugh.

The woman lifted the medallion from the table and tapped it on the hard wood a few times. She breathed heavily through her mouth as she considered. There was a slight grunt with every exhalation that grew increasingly irritating through ceaseless repetition. Finally, she made up her mind.

"Take these two to a cell." She stood and turned her back on the men so that she could contemplate the city. "Summon the Inquisitor."

Once more, the red cloaks grabbed Quillion and Cole and spun them to the door. As they were being pushed through, the woman called out again.

"Give them a blanket each in case they are telling the truth." After a moment's pause, she continued. "And prepare two stake poles in case they are not."

Chapter 16: The Writing on the Wall

The light was blinding.

Simyon awoke in a cell like nothing he had ever seen. He cracked his swollen eye a hair's breadth, yet even that let in a piercing agony that caused the young thief to grunt and lift his hands to his head.

The movement brought a different sort of pain. Every muscle resisted his call. The throbbing in his head echoed a raging anguish that coursed through every fiber of his being.

So the cowards beat me when I was out.

The words brought a surge of anger, and the anger gave Simyon strength.

No questions, no talking, just the grinding of flesh. After all, they are the masters; they know everything.

The beginning of a sarcastic chuckle came to life in Simyon's belly, but the movement was overcome by another wave of agony. Simyon exhaled and tried to command his bruised muscles to go limp. He had awakened after an unconscious beating before; he knew the drill.

He breathed, and for the first time he noticed the stench.

There was wetness on his face, and he lay upon clinging grime. Once he was aware of the filth, he realized it was everywhere. On his cheeks, on his fingers, in the moistness of his garments.

The chamber floor was covered in excrement.

Simyon breathed through his mouth and tried to push the revelation from his thoughts. First, he had to control the throbbing in his head. He couldn't waste time on fear or self-pity. Only the privileged could entertain such emotions.

The young thief steeled himself against the incoming assault, and then cracked both eyes simultaneously.

Agony pierced him. He experienced a blinding white flash, followed by the sensation of spinning. The room seemed to tumble out of control and Simyon clenched his teeth for fear of being overcome by nausea. The tumbling lasted for an indeterminate amount of time and Simyon began to pant.

Slowly, slowly, his eyes adjusted, and the white became tolerable. He forced his eyes to stay open against every instinct in his flesh. Every heart beat brought the stab of a thousand daggers into his bloodshot pupils, but he endured it, and, as with all things, time eased the agony.

The room revealed itself.

The ceiling and walls were white. The walls were made of an unfamiliar material that glistened. The ceiling was less reflective. It appeared to be constructed of a series of rectangular panels. Most of them were an unassuming white, but at regular intervals the panels lit up with blinding illumination.

So that's the source of the light.

Having taken in everything he could from his current position, Simyon attempted to twist his head. Again, the jolts of agony came, but Simyon fought to control them.

I can't make it easy on them. I can't quit.

As he turned, he saw a door; a standard size door made of iron. It shone in the blinding light. In the center of the door was a black window.

Simyon attempted to swing his arm beneath his body to lift himself up, but the movement was premature. A wave of nausea crashed over him, and he paused to regroup. The thief took a few panting breaths and tried to focus on something, anything, other than the wretched stench of the foul air.

He flicked his eyes back to the door. Scanning the frame, he noticed something at the top. A plaque hung on the wall. In simple, all capital letters was written: THE EXIT CODE IS ZERO, ZERO, FOUR, NINE, ONE.

Simyon's eyes widened as he glanced to the right of the door. His experience in the sewer did not fail him. There, embedded in the wall, was a similar keypad to the one that had bought him entry into San Aryan.

For a moment, Simyon didn't understand. He just looked from the door to the keypad and back again.

But slowly, ever so slowly, the sinister truth became clear. *This isn't a prison.*
This is an experiment.
They want to confirm I can read.

*

Orion ushered Valeria and Janus toward a set of double doors at the edge of the garden. Valeria resisted the impulse to move fast. If Orion planned malice, Valeria would meet her fate with dignity. She took slow steps, matching the gaze of anyone seated in the garden who dared to glower at her.

Quite a few eyes did meet hers. The high society guests of the humanitarian banquet seethed with resentment at Valeria's presence.

These artificial old hags can't control their men, and they resent me for it. Out of spite, she made eye contact with some of the fashionable dandies and began blowing kisses. As the men flushed, the women beside them trembled in fury.

Valeria marked the women's faces, focusing on skull structure rather than overall appearance. If she ever had the opportunity, she would repay their hatred. No disguise could hide where the cheekbones rested in relationship to the eyes. Only archers of great skill would dare to target the eyes, but that had ever been Valeria's preference. These soft judgmental elites would find it difficult to flash a superior glare with a cloth-yard shaft protruding from their skulls.

The thought pleased Valeria, and greatly served to allay her growing concern.

Orion and Janus waited as she passed through the double doors at the end of the hall. Orion gave her a bemused look as he bid the doors be closed. Two servants leaped to his order.

"We've acquired a remarkable specimen," Orion said, turning and walking with the expectation of obedience. Valeria attempted to follow at her own pace, but she was surprised when Janus grabbed her by the elbow and pushed her along. The Seneschal did not do so with overt malice, but the set of his jaw was enough to prevent Valeria from protesting. He was the closest thing to an ally she had.

They traveled along a hallway, then down a flight of stairs. Valeria was surprised by how fast Orion could move. For a man of apparent advanced age, he didn't exhibit any signs of shortness of breath.

They traversed a labyrinth of tunnels. The halls darkened and then lit up again with a strange source of light unlike anything Valeria had ever seen. Panels adhering to the roof emanated rays along with a soft buzz.

After a while, the three came to a long corridor. Set in the wall were a series of iron-wrought doors.

Orion turned and flashed his predator's smile.

"What I'm going to show you now will seem quite remarkable."

He pushed a button on the wall, only to have a large panel of the corridor disappear into translucence. The door itself remained opaque, but on either side, stretching off for several yards, there was an unobstructed view into the room.

The sorcery stunned Valeria, and she took a step back. But not only was she amazed by the gimmick of the disappearing wall, she was also startled by the figure lying in the filth in the center of the revealed chamber.

Her years of survival did not abandon her, and she gave no outward indication that she recognized the man. Despite the bruises and the swelling, though, she identified him instantly.

Simyon.

Valeria was momentarily overcome by a debilitating sadness.

"Are you all right, my dear?" Orion's smile extended from ear to ear.

"The wall," Valeria replied, "I've never seen such a thing. It gave me a bit of vertigo."

"Indeed." Orion looked back at the wall, rapping his knuckles against the transparent surface. "Amazing, isn't it?"

"Who is he?" Janus asked.

"Something we picked up on the perimeter. He must have slipped through one of the portals."

"Impossible," Janus snapped, "all the portals are sealed."

"Not to those who know the tricks."

"But how—" Janus stopped, his eyes widening in realization. The older man caught his gaze. Orion stood for a long while, as if questing for a piece of hidden truth.

"How would he know the tricks?" Janus asked, measuring every word.

Orion nodded. "That's the question, isn't it?"

"Can he see us as well?" Valeria asked.

"At the moment, no," Orion said. "However, I can make it so. Shall I?"

He reached out toward another button.

Valeria watched him stretch his arm with agonizing slowness to the indicated panel on the wall. Just as he was about to touch it, his fingers curled into a fist. Valeria turned to meet his gaze and her blood ran cold. He regarded her as he might a specimen upon a tray, and his expression indicated his suspicions had just been confirmed.

Chapter 17: Demons

Kikkan's muscles tensed at Weasel's disappearance. His was not a warrior's instinct. The warrior instinct was instilled artificially in civilized men through repetition, training, and war games. Kikkan had never known civilization. He was raised as a slave, with death never more than a hair's breadth away. He possessed survival instinct: the true warrior readiness professional soldiers aspired to acquire.

Warfare had never been a game to Kikkan.

The former slave's senses were on high alert; every sound, every smell, every slight flicker of a shadow suddenly appeared as an enemy.

The boy had led him into a trap, and he cursed himself for falling into it so easily. Now he must await whatever threat existed here.

Kikkan slowly reached back to grip the comforting end of the pipe protruding from his scavenged back pack. He did not wish to disturb the energy of his imminent space, yet he was keenly aware of the ripples sent out by his movement.

Something stirred in the near darkness surrounding him.

Many things.

As Kikkan's fingers wrapped around the familiar grip of his primitive weapon, he felt an overwhelming sense of calm.

Blood surged through his veins. His heart rate increased, engorging his muscles with physical power. A barrier that had been calcifying around his will began to crack and flake away.

Freedom!

Even now, the distilled essence of that most intoxicating drug sent him on an unparalleled high. The discrepancy between what he felt now and where he had been only moments before was startling.

Kikkan realized that during his travels with Quillion, he had allowed himself to slip into another state of submission. The persuasive northerner had the ability to cast a spell of compliance. Only now, in his absence, had that power become apparent. Quillion was clever as well, and Kikkan wondered how many times he had been duped into taking one of Quillion's thoughts as his own.

What strange new form of influence was that?

But in this moment of threat there was no time for reflection. The former slave brandished the pipe before him. The darkness seemed to gather. There was an ominous menace to the shadow. The dim luminescence did not stretch far. Kikkan squinted and peered before him, turning slowly so as to put a wall against his back.

What is out there?

Now, as he watched, the traces of movement became more apparent. The clues were so limited that his mind had difficulty deciphering the image. There seemed to be dancing reflections, tiny glossy surfaces that trapped and bounced the meager light that existed in this subterranean hole.

The images swirled before him and then his nostrils caught the whiff of a smell. The smell pierced his skull like a needle, jolting his brain and sending his memories back to a moment of horror from his youth.

The slave market.

The smell of sweat and urine and men cooped up in boxes left to marinate in their own filth.

But it was more than that. Kikkan had been exposed enough to recognize the scent of *Bliss* hunger.

Armed with a framework of expectation, Kikkan set about confirming the suspicion. The blurry lines in the darkness resolved themselves, and Kikkan suddenly understood what he faced.

Slaves, demons, wandering undead, skeletal, zombie-like beasts. People once, pitiful people, subjected to torture and discarded to survive in the near-darkness of their addiction.

These were even less functional than the creatures of Oshia.

They shuffled toward him, and in an instant Kikkan realized what had drawn them.

The *Bliss* . . . the cursed *Bliss* that Quillion had insisted they harvest and carry. What had Weasel said? In the depths, even the plastic could not hide the scent . . .

Why had Kikkan allowed himself to be hypnotized?

Never again!

The resolution, despite his circumstances, brought joy. Kikkan recalled his first moment of freedom once more.

Alone, hungry, uncertain, but free!

So easy to be seduced into surrendering one's autonomy.

Never again.

Never!

As the creatures approached, Kikkan could discern their claws. There would be no reasoning here; the drug he carried had worked them into a frenzy. For a moment, he considered relinquishing his grip upon his weapon to send his hand into his satchel. He must separate himself from the cursed package. But no, they were too close now; he must buy some space, though the price would be high.

A distended bag of flesh and teeth lurched forward and met Kikkan's pipe. The dim thud echoed horribly in the dark. In the hyperawareness of battle, Kikkan heard the sound of the threaded end of his weapon scratching against teeth, and the clatter of others as they fell to the stone, dislodged from the straining skull that had housed them.

Still the beast came on. Another blow, then another, and one more before the body dropped motionless to the ground. Kikkan felt the volume of his breath increase as he acted. Sweat beaded on his forehead and he swung his weapon in a wide arc to clear his attackers. The swipe connected twice on its trajectory, and now the creatures had learned enough to recoil.

Some deep part of Kikkan's mind recognized that these were human beings he was fighting, transformed into monstrosities and insane, disease-ridden, ravenous animals. The most human part of Kikkan even wondered as to the boy's safety—the presence of oblivion too near to permit Kikkan to dwell on such a small thing as betrayal.

Kikkan did not begrudge the boy his impulse to escape. In the moment of reckoning, Kikkan's chief concern was that the lad had not risked too much in his daring gambit.

The claws came again, more frenzied now, and Kikkan disposed of each. When his pipe connected with a scratching hand, he felt the bones collapse beneath the force of his blow. Whatever extended into Kikkan's sphere of influence he pounced upon and rendered useless. Hands, heads, legs and arms.

Yet the force ranged against him was a sea, and despite Kikkan's effort, the limbs came surging in. As he fended off an assault to his right, a claw pierced his defenses to the left. Kikkan felt the gnarled, disease and filth-ridden nails upon his bicep and turned with frantic determination to crush his assailant into a quivering pile. However, this allowed a surge to assault him from the other side, and Kikkan instantly felt the attack on his exposed flank.

The former slave roared in anguish and felt a surge of desperate strength flow through him. He crouched and exploded upward, pushing hard against the wall behind him with every muscle in his body.

The sea of corrupted souls was pushed away, and this time Kikkan did not hesitate to loosen his grip upon his weapon. He thrust a free hand down to his satchel and felt the plastic-wrapped package.

The claws lunged forward again, scratching him in a dozen places, but Kikkan made no effort to repel them. He swung his arm in a massive arc, sending the package wide and far into the darkness over the heads of his attackers.

Kikkan was instantly forgotten. The zombies crashed upon each other like a scourge of rats burrowing into a rotten corpse. They turned, rending and tearing one another, focusing on their chemical obsession.

Fearing any remaining scent, Kikkan lifted the satchel from his shoulder and tossed that as well.

His wounds pestered him as he backed along the wall, away from the throbbing mass. His foot stumbled into a puddle and Kikkan knelt down to wash his fingers of any residue that might have clung to his skin. As he retreated, he was aware of figures pushing past him in the dark. They paid him no heed now, seeking only to arrive at the drug orgy their senses had promised.

Kikkan's progress was slow, but after a moment, his back came into contact with a ladder. Kikkan climbed. He needed out of this foul place.

With every rung that dropped beneath him, the echo of

guttural feeding faded further. Silence rained down from above and Kikkan went in the direction of peace.

There could be no thought of searching for the boy, and that pained Kikkan, for he sincerely wished to assure himself of the lad's safety. The former slave had promised no harm would come to that one, and Kikkan wished to honor his promises. But survival must come first, and Kikkan needed sanctuary.

When he had put enough levels between himself and the creatures that he could detect natural light from above, Kikkan paused. Endless hallways filled with dust surrounded him, and trying a door, Kikkan stumbled into a room.

There were no windows, no furniture, and minimal debris on the floor.

Shutting the door, Kikkan collapsed in the entryway. The door opened only inward, and if an enemy should attempt an attack, Kikkan was confident the impact of the swinging door would rouse him.

As satisfied with his security as circumstance would allow, Kikkan collapsed into sleep.

*

In the hallway outside, a hooded figure stood in the shadows, observing. The figure had watched the giant fight and was impressed with both the man's strength and his ability to think on his feet. Few would have survived that altercation in the underworld. Then again, few would have been foolish enough to traipse about with a quantity of *Bliss* that could attract such a crowd.

The figure stepped forward to listen at the door. The sound of deep breathing echoed from within. Satisfied, the figure retreated to a more discreet observation point.

The arrival of this giant was an interesting development.

Chapter 18: Exposed

The wall disappeared.

Simyon had recovered enough to realize the observation was not a hallucination. The darker exposed corridor was a welcome change from the brightness of the glistening walls. Simyon squinted to make out what he could among the shadows.

He didn't recognize the first man. He was old but strong, and seemed unassuming enough. As Simyon took account of the others, however, his heart stopped.

Valeria! And the man who had accompanied her in San Borja!

The sight brought focus to the young thief's battered thoughts. Had he telegraphed the recognition through his facial expressions? Simyon looked back to the first man, only to observe that he had already begun to move.

Simyon rose to his knees, focusing on Valeria.

Valeria made a gesture – a simple street sign, something the other two men probably wouldn't be able to detect. But Simyon caught it.

Can you get out?

Simyon's eyes flashed back to the spot over the door. The words written there had been erased when the wall disappeared, but he could still remember the code. He blinked once.

Yes.

Valeria exploded into motion too fast for either Janus or Orion to respond.

Simyon heard nothing, but he saw the flash of a glass vial hit the floor, followed by an expulsion of vapor.

"No!" the thief cried, stumbling to his feet, though the action brought agony.

The deterrent!

Simyon had never seen a vial activated before, but he had heard stories. Valeria's profession had certainly given her opportunity to become adept at hiding the glass canister so as to escape detection in a cursory search.

The elderly man slumped, as did the Seneschal, but Valeria exhibited a tolerance to the effects of the gas. She lurched toward the wall, weakened but still conscious. She leaned against the transparent surface, her face beautiful in the cloud of yellow smoke.

Let it dissipate before you escape, she signed.

You've given yourself up, Simyon replied.

Count to one hundred, that should be enough.

Valeria, Simyon signaled, *I'm not sure I can carry you.*

But she was already out.

Outside in the hallway, the three figures collapsed in a heap.

Simyon struggled to his feet and reached toward the wall pad, but stopped himself. If he opened the door early, he too would fall victim to the fumes. Their chances of escape were already minimal, but with Simyon unconscious, the probability reduced to nothing.

He pulled back his hand and began a silent count.

Simyon knew he had rushed, but he reached up to the

keypad and typed in the code anyway. His frenzy was even greater than it was when he had pushed himself through his ill-advised pursuit into these forbidden corridors.

The metallic pad clicked under his touch. The numbers ran off in quick succession.

Simyon waited.

For a moment, nothing happened. Simyon swallowed a lump in his throat as he thought about the consequences of failure. What if the door didn't open? He had already made peace with the possibility that he might be gutted, but the fact that Valeria had exposed herself to a similar fate was more than he could take.

Certainly, it was possible that the note on the wall was nothing more than a sinister trick. After all, why should the door open? Perhaps, instead, a signal could be sent to indicate a prisoner had revealed his guilt.

The young thief's musing ended at the sound of a metallic clink. The door looked the same. Simyon tried the handle and a wave of relief washed over him as he felt it turn. He pulled the door open and stepped into the hall.

A wave of acrid air assailed his nostrils, dropping Simyon to his knees. He was still weak from the beating he had received, and the foul air caused him to vomit. Spitting, Simyon wiped his mouth with the back of a shaking hand and crawled over to Valeria.

"Valeria," he whispered, pushing her hair gently out of her face.

Looking upon her symmetrical features, he was again reminded of their youth together. He had watched her sleep often in the past, in the bowels of the city. Sometimes, like now, the sight of her had brought half a heart beat's worth of peace to his soul.

His jaw tightened and he put his hands beneath her

shoulders to lift her. She issued a low moan at the jostling, and Simyon was encouraged by the response.

"Come on, Valeria, we're going."

Strength came to him and he got her off the floor. She was light, but Simyon had been weakened by the beating. Bearing Valeria, he looked back upon his rivals and considered taking the time to slit their sleeping throats.

I should. I should. I should.

But by then, his thieves' alarm, cultivated over years of running, had begun to ring.

There's no time!

Simyon turned and picked a direction at random. Movement would save him. When in doubt, move.

The flickering light pounded upon his consciousness. His mind ached. The hallway seemed to undulate like a wave, an effect of the beating and the toxin still lingering in the air.

I need to descend to be free. Descend. Descend. Descend. Very well, the underworld shall have me after all.

Valeria groaned, and the sound somehow piqued Simyon's anger.

"You foolish girl, you gave yourself up," he growled. The hallway continued to stretch on for an eternity. The thief began to fear this was an impossible task. He couldn't get out. He was weak. He didn't know where he was. The others would soon rouse and call for pursuit.

"You gave yourself up, you gave yourself up," he whispered, surprised to feel tears rolling down his cheeks.

His pace slowed. What was the purpose of urgency anyway? He had no destination. He began to walk, taking enormous gulps of air.

The air was better here; at least that was something.

Simyon looked down on Valeria. Her face was still, like a porcelain doll. Her features calmed him, eased his frenzy, and allowed him to focus. As usual, he felt better in her presence.

Her lips moved in what seemed more than a random exhalation.

Simyon leaned forward, tilting his ear towards her.

"Chute," she said.

The word electrified Simyon. He remembered his youth, wriggling in the dark like a worm, feeding on the table scraps and discards the gods of San Aryan sent plunging to the depths.

He lifted Valeria, but she was already recovering. Her legs moved, bearing the weight Simyon could no longer fully support.

They resumed their progress, different now that they had an objective. The hallway didn't seem to stretch as far.

They stopped at a recessed panel against the uniform white. Simyon lowered Valeria to the floor and began to scratch at the metal. A mechanism in the middle of the plate deterred him, but Simyon had picked enough locks to know this one wasn't ironclad. It would be nothing more than a metallic tab designed to hold the door in position.

He dug his fingers into the metal, scratching and pulling against the upper left corner. That was the best point for exploiting weakness.

The metal did not yield. Simyon closed his hand into a fist and punched the panel. The punch bowed the center and the upper left corner bent outward for an instant before snapping back into place. Simyon punched again, this time attempting to catch the displaced corner with his other hand. The metal cut through his finger, sending a rivulet of blood down the white wall. Simyon punched again and again, finally managing to jam his flesh between the jagged metal and the smooth surface of the housing.

From there, it took only determination. Simyon pulled

and jerked, plunging his fingers further and further into the panel until he finally had enough purchase to put his full weight against it. He jerked back. The flimsy lock resisted once, twice, but not three times. With a pop, the door swung open, causing Simyon to tumble to the floor.

He regained his feet and lifted his head over the hole. A shaft descended into darkness. Simyon could smell the depths of the underworld wafting up from below.

How far up are we?

How far is the fall?

Simyon felt something brush his shoulder and turned to see Valeria standing beside him.

"How long until the others recover?" he asked.

Valeria shook her head, indicating he shouldn't worry. Then she closed her eyes to stabilize herself, obviously still in the process of expelling the toxin from her system.

"I am resistant to the effects," she said. "The others won't recover as fast."

Simyon nodded at the hole.

"Will the fall kill us?"

"Possibly, but death is a certainty here."

Simyon shook his head. "Why did you do it?" he asked.

Valeria turned to look at him.

"Why did you give yourself up? You were close to achieving what you wanted."

Valeria snorted. "Fishing for a compliment? You always were too sensitive for this world, Simyon. There's no time for getting sentimental, climb in and hold onto the ledge."

Simyon's expression turned quizzical.

"We'll brace ourselves against one another and control our descent," she explained. "Now get going."

Simyon obeyed. He climbed into the hole, supporting himself by holding the ledge and propping his legs against the opposing wall.

Valeria steadied herself and then climbed in as well, straddling Simyon.

Their perch was an embrace, dangling precariously over infinity. At the touch of her, Simyon felt himself smiling.

"It looks like the underworld will have us at last. We'll seek out the free cities in the provinces; I hope they're more than legend."

"We've raided San Aryan," Valeria replied, "the depths will embrace us as fallen gods." Then she leaned in and kissed Simyon passionately. When she withdrew, Simyon felt imbued with new strength. He eased the pressure off the leg that was keeping them aloft and the two slid down into darkness.

Chapter 19: Interrogation

The cell was small. A rough-hewn door with metal bars over a small portal sealed the only exit. Inside, Quillion and Cole could stand but not recline.

Guards stood outside. The two mercenaries huddled beneath rough wool blankets. Now alone, the two travelers said nothing for a long time. Their first thought was to collect themselves. They huddled beneath the blankets as best they could, avoiding the wet floor, and settled in to wait.

It was cold.

Quillion finally found his voice.

"I thought they'd separate us."

He spoke in a whisper, his voice hardly discernible from a stray wind.

Cole said nothing.

There was almost no light, but Quillion could see the center of the smaller man's eyes shine in the near dark.

"Do you want to know why?" he asked.

No response.

"I thought they'd separate us so they could interrogate us individually to look for flaws in our stories."

Cole let out a spiteful cough.

"Yeah, you think of everything, don't you?" he snapped. "Why didn't you anticipate that they'd strip us naked and hang us from the walls?"

The words painted images in Quillion's mind. All too clearly, he could see his lifeless body, limp and pitiful, hanging in the courtyard. Discarded, sacrificed, abandoned—for what?

Faced with the specter of that image, he had to wonder.

What was the purpose of ferreting away hours in secrecy, teaching himself? What was the value of honing skills; any skills? Self-betterment? Self-improvement? Stealing thoughts he was not meant to entertain? What would the sacrifice of his labors bring him in the end?

As always, Quillion pushed back against the creeping despair.

If fate would have him dangling in a courtyard, his knowledge would be lost, but his adversaries could not change that he had existed. Ripples of his labors would remain. Still, Quillion sought more.

"They haven't hung us yet," he managed to say.

The two fell silent. Cole huddled deep below the scratchy wool. The sound of water dripping echoed in the black.

"You're right," Quillion said after a while. "This is worse than I anticipated. Far worse."

His voice took on a kind of growl. A guttural noise, the sound a boot made when it was extracted from ankle deep mud. Cole realized Quillion was berating himself.

"Here I imagined I had constructed a lesson for Kikkan. That there was something to be gained by being here with these *people* . . ." Quillion coughed, then found his voice again. "Kikkan was right."

"About what?" Cole replied.

"He was right that it's better to die with a weapon in your hand *your* way. It's better to die in the midst of a fight, truly alive, than to lie down and submit. It is folly to allow yourself to be disarmed. No greater good requires contrived suffering. Why do we lament the cruel judgment of lesser men? Who are they? What does their opinion matter? Great ones elevate their fellows, they don't dismantle them."

"Right now, they matter because they're on the other side of that door," Cole said.

"The door will open," Quillion replied. "A thing cannot resist its nature."

"Neither can a man," said Cole.

Quillion opened his mouth, then thought otherwise and fell silent once more.

*

The next morning, the door did open, and Quillion and Cole were escorted out. They were led to a room starkly different from their recent prison. This room was neat and clean. The floors were polished and the walls were smooth and straight. In fact, there was not a curve or imprecise angle to be seen.

In the center of the room stood a table. On one side were two simple stools. On the other was a cushioned chair made out of worn leather.

Quillion pulled his blanket closer to his neck. He was still naked beneath it, and a night of leaning against damp stone had rendered his skin and muscles numb. But even the stool was an improvement from his previous lodgings, and he shuffled over to one as Cole made for the other.

"You will wait here," their guard, a muscle-bound red cloak brute, admonished. "Do not speak."

Quillion studied his surroundings. He pointedly did not look at Cole. Behind them, an odd panel of black glass took up the entire length of the wall. Quillion could see his reflection in its surface.

He was surprised how much strength could be sapped from a person simply by locking them in a hole for a night. Quillion's face was drawn and his eyes were sunken. The process of rendering him into an object less than human continued. Cole didn't look any better.

As Quillion peered into the glass, he realized something was strange. He thought he could see shadows moving behind his reflection.

A chill went down his spine, and he turned his attention back to the table.

Now was not the time for overt acts of rebellion.

Obedience was required.

A short time later, a noise came from the door. The metal of the release mechanism screeched. A rot entered Quillion's belly and spread to the back of his throat; he didn't even have to engage his willpower to keep from turning his head. Instead, he fixed his gaze upon the table.

The door finally twisted open and a man entered. Still Quillion did not look up, but the slow, methodical footsteps echoing on the floor reminded him of an indomitable force he had once come up against.

Cassius...

The weight of undeniable authority filled the air. Quillion realized he must be in the presence of Captain Jesse's Inquisitor.

The figure went to the other side of the table and pulled back the chair. He sat, and Quillion could hear the leather strain beneath this new arrival as he shifted his weight, seeking a position of comfort.

Then came silence.

The seconds ticked by and, despite his chill, Quillion felt a bead of sweat form on his forehead. He didn't move. He assumed an air of submission, his vision fixed squarely on the table. He did not look up, did not look to Cole to gauge his companion's opinion.

Quillion could see nothing but the new arrival's hands. Hands that were curled into fists placed palm down on the polished wood. His sleeves were black. He did not move, did not fidget, did not even breathe so that it was overly audible. There was not the slightest consternation in his demeanor.

Quillion waited, becoming increasingly uncomfortable as time passed. Without saying a word, the man before them reached into his pocket and retrieved Cassius's medallion. This he tossed onto the table. The symbol of the Seneschal landed with a clatter.

Quillion glanced at the object.

"Explain," the Inquisitor said.

Quillion cleared his throat.

"We were conscripted into the service of Cassius of Edentown several months ago while investigating the murder of a farmer north of Acheron."

"When exactly?"

"Autumn."

"What farmer?" the Inquisitor asked.

It took Quillion a moment to recall the man's name. "Duncan Kerr." Quillion could sense the man nod, but the northerner did not lift his gaze to regard the Inquisitor's features. A pregnant silence fell, and Quillion felt compelled to continue his account.

"At the time, we were in the service of Captain Tark of Acheron."

"How long had you been under this Captain Tark's command?"

"Several days."

The Inquisitor stiffened, so Quillion explained.

"We had recently been discharged from the service of Captain Elvet in Nirdeen."

"So you're a couple of mercenaries, then?" the Inquisitor asked.

"Soldiers, yes. We find employment where we can."

"But you switch captains with disturbing frequency."

Quillion did not reply. The man motioned for him to continue.

"Cassius was seeking a fugitive named Adam Lockhart who was rumored to be teaching peasants to read in the outskirts of Acheron."

"Did you find this Adam Lockhart?"

"We did."

"What is his current status?"

"Dead," Quillion replied.

"And Cassius?"

"Also dead."

"Really?" The question was asked in an emotionless tone that Quillion couldn't quite read. The northerner wasn't sure if news of Cassius's death invoked incredulity, satisfaction, or indifference.

"Yes," he replied.

"How did he die?"

"After Cassius dispatched Adam Lockhart, we were attacked by a horde of slaves."

"Slaves?" Again, the Inquisitor's tone was ambiguous.

"Adam Lockhart had escaped into Oshia," Quillion explained. "The slaves were in their zombie state. Lockhart got them riled up by putting the smell of *Bliss* in the air."

"So this horde killed Cassius?"

"Yes."

"What about this Captain Tark?"

"Also killed."

"I see. So only you two managed to survive."

Quillion didn't reply. As he recounted his story, he was acutely aware of how suspicious it sounded.

"Look at me," the Inquisitor said.

Quillion and Cole lifted their eyes to regard the Inquisitor for the first time. The sight of him caused both to gasp in surprise. The man's skin was an unhealthy gray and his sunken cheeks were lined with wrinkles. His eyes, however, were alert, and Quillion got the sense that they peered straight through his heart. The northerner recalled feeling the same sensation when being interviewed by Cassius.

The Inquisitor's eyes fixed on one man, then the other. The moment seemed to last forever.

"Did Cassius have any final orders for you?"

"Only to report on the death of Adam Lockhart," Quillion said.

"You've done that. And tell me, what was to be your reward for providing us with this information?"

"Only the chance to earn an honest living as a member of the city guard," Quillion replied.

The Inquisitor's demeanor did not change, but Quillion thought he saw the man's eyes sparkle. The image was gone in an instant, but the sight left Quillion queasy.

The Inquisitor stood and walked to the door. As he passed, he addressed the guards waiting there.

"Get them uniforms. I will inform Captain Jesse that she has two more recruits."

Then the Inquisitor was gone.

Chapter 20: Flight to the Outskirts

Valeria and Simyon began their new lives with an impact upon a pile of stone. Janus and Orion lay unconscious from the deterrent in the halls of San Aryan, and it would be many months before spring would come and bring the arrival of travelers from Acheron to the Outskirts of Edentown.

Simyon was expelled first from the chute and cried out in pain as he hit the stones, his leg twisting unnaturally beneath his body. Valeria's fall was broken by Simyon, and she emerged without serious injury.

"Are you hurt?" she asked. She assessed her own condition, lifting her arms to regard torn fabric stained with rivulets of blood. Bracing her arms and legs against the walls of the chute to slow her fall and left her body riddled with cuts and abrasions.

"Yes, but I don't know how bad," Simyon hissed. He attempted to stand, but his ankle gave out beneath him. He tumbled down, dislodging rocks that echoed in the darkness.

"Wait," Valeria said, casting about for something to use as a splint. After a moment's search, she pulled a metallic frame down from an image on the wall. This she bent into a U shape and affixed it to Simyon's foot with a strip of fabric from her dress. "Can you walk?"

"I must," Simyon said, "we can't stay here." He looked about, attempting to get his bearings. "We're beyond the wall, I think; these tunnels are too decrepit for San Aryan."

"It figures that they'd dump their garbage on their neighbors," Valeria replied. She kneeled to help Simyon stand. The young thief rose to his feet, grinding his teeth against the pain. After a moment, he nodded and they made their way into the darkness.

The chute led into a tunnel. Ankle-deep water flowed along the bottom.

"I have an apartment in San Borja, but I don't think we can risk going back there. The Seneschals will be seeking us," Simyon said.

Valeria nodded.

"I didn't anticipate I'd be traveling when I left this morning, or I would have worn something more appropriate," he continued.

"With winter coming, this is not an ideal time to relocate, but fate has a sense of humor," Valeria replied.

"There's nothing in your apartment you need to retrieve?" he asked.

She replied with no remorse. "Nothing that's worth the risk. Where should we go?"

Simyon inclined his head at an object in the distance. Valeria looked to see a ladder bolted against the wall. As they neared, Simyon grasped the ladder and wiped the wall clean behind the rungs to reveal a plaque.

"The W symbol is the direction that takes us away from San Aryan," he said, reading the plaque. "We'll look for something that branches off and climb when we're able. For now, we have to put distance between us and any pursuit. How long until our captors awaken?"

"Perhaps never," Valeria said.

Simyon looked at her with surprise.

Valeria shrugged. "The deterrent is toxic. If they're in poor health or regularly taking other drugs, there can be a reaction . . ."

"I never realized the deterrent might kill," Simyon said.

"If these dandies would behave themselves, then it never would. Maybe a few more bodies littering the street will serve as a reminder that the powerless sometimes have hidden claws."

"Beasts are inclined to reject such lessons."

"They cannot reject death," she said.

The two fell into silence as they shuffled through the damp, cold darkness. They passed a dozen more ladders bolted into the wall before coming to a place where the tunnels divided. Simyon indicated they bear right, and the farther they went, the more junctions they encountered.

After many hours, Simyon dropped to his knees and vomited. The retching echoed down the tunnel as the young thief coughed and spat.

"It's the pain, isn't it?" Valeria asked. "You can't walk all the way to the outskirts with a mangled leg."

"I must," Simyon replied, "or we risk being found."

"We climb the next ladder," Valeria said. Simyon tried to protest, but Valeria silenced him. "You're making too much noise. What good is distancing ourselves from pursuit if you howl loud enough to rouse a demon horde?"

Simyon thought for a moment before conceding the point. The two stumbled forward until coming to another ladder, which they elected to climb.

Minutes later, they broke the surface into darkness. Night had fallen, and it was difficult to judge how far they had traveled. Were they still within San Borja? Or had they passed all the way through to Bellfore?

They emerged into a street, and the thick covering of dust indicated little to no foot traffic in the region.

Valeria helped Simyon get to a nearby building. They forced a door, found a room, and crumpled to the floor in exhaustion.

*

The next morning, Simyon awoke more satisfied than he had felt in years. His ankle had swollen grotesquely and it throbbed with a dull ache, but none of that mattered. Valeria was beside him, sharing his warmth, nestled up against him in the shelter of the room. He felt as if he were home.

He pushed a strand of hair away from her face and her eyes fluttered open.

"I'm hungry," she said.

Simyon sighed. "I guess we'll have to get used to eating rat again. The fine plates of San Borja are lost to us, I'm afraid."

She smiled. "I've eaten worse, especially in my last line of work."

Simyon coughed.

"Rest easy," Valeria said, "I'll find something."

She stood, but Simyon was reluctant to release her hand. "Is it not better that we go together?"

Valeria shook her head. "You'll slow me down too much with that ankle."

"But . . ."

"But nothing. I intend to survive this and you've already caused me enough trouble." She winked, which took some of the edge off her words. "Don't worry, I'll be back."

Saying nothing else, she pushed through the door and was gone.

*

The day passed and night fell.

Simyon was massaging his ankle and growing increasingly worried when Valeria returned. She slipped in the door like a shadow, so completely changed that Simyon at first concluded he was under attack. He sat up with a jolt and pressed himself against the wall, only to have Valeria ridicule him with mocking laughter.

"Be still, Simyon. We got lucky; this place is almost completely deserted."

Simyon nodded. Gone was the elegant gown Valeria had been wearing, though the travels through the tunnels had left little remnant of the vision she had been at the Vine. Now her outfit was practical. She was dressed in uniform black sweater, pants and boots. The clothing was dusty, but overall in a good state. On her hands she wore fingerless gloves, with a leather brace along her left forearm.

"Where did you go?" Simyon asked.

"I climbed this building to get some elevation. At first I was discouraged, for this zone is completely covered in dust, but then I saw something useful off in the distance."

"What?"

"The symbol of the white bird on a red field."

Simyon nodded. There had been such a building near San Borja when they were young. It was one of many symbols that indicated a place where useful items could be found.

"It was a fair hike, and the windows were broken, but the journey proved profitable." She tossed Simyon a bag, which he opened. On the top was a sheathed dagger on a belt. Beneath the dagger was a folded outfit similar to Valeria's.

"I think it will fit," she said.

"I don't think I'll be able to get my feet into these boots for a while," he replied.

"One is better than none." Valeria smiled. "But that isn't the best part." She stood and went to the door to retrieve an item she had left outside. Winking, she pulled another bag into the room. Pulling a zipper along the bag's edge, she flipped open the cover to reveal an unstrung recurve bow and a quiver of arrows.

Simyon let out a low whistle.

"I told you there was nothing in my apartment that couldn't be replaced," Valeria said with a satisfied smile.

"That's a formidable weapon," Simyon conceded.

"I had to tear that building apart to find it. The roof had collapsed in the back and I spent the afternoon excavating the destruction. I found these things sifting through dust and debris. At first I was concerned there were no bowstrings until I found some encased in plastic beneath a fallen wall."

"Have you had the opportunity to try it?"

Valeria gestured back at the pack she had tossed to Simyon. He reached in again and discovered a plastic package. Confused, he opened the wrapping to reveal half of a cooked rabbit.

"Sorry I didn't wait to join you," Valeria said, "but I was famished."

Simyon didn't begrudge her. He bit into the still-warm meat. Subsisting on rat would have to wait another day.

*

Over the next few days, they traveled. Simyon's leg left him in great pain, but the fear of pursuit drove him on. They stopped infrequently, and only when Valeria insisted he rest. The more distance they put between themselves and San

Aryan, the more comfortable they felt. The outer districts were less populated than San Borja, and they found it easy to avoid patrols.

They didn't pause at the Brinewater wall but instead descended beneath the surface and found a tunnel that emerged deep into the outskirts. The weather had grown cold, but the sound of voices drew Simyon and Valeria to a gathering of children playing in the streets. Noticing them, one approached.

"Hello, I'm –"

Before he had a chance to finish, Valeria loosed an arrow. The shaft caught the lad's sleeve and pegged it to the wall behind him. The other children scattered.

"We're not in the mood for games," Simyon said. "Don't try to con us."

"You're from the inner city," the lad replied.

"And you're a little weasel looking to make a coin," Valeria snapped.

The lad paled.

"We heard a rumor of a free settlement in this district," Simyon said. "We can be useful to such people and intend to settle there. Take us to them. Do as you're told, and you might get that reward after all."

"But if you think to betray us," Valeria warned, brandishing her dagger, "you'll lose your ears . . . Weasel."

Chapter 21: Lucid Nightmare

Janus awoke.

His eyelids fluttered, letting in brief bursts of blinding light.

Something was strange. His awareness was scattered, blurred.

Where am I? What's happening?

He felt a tickle over his right eye and tried to reach up to scratch, but found he couldn't.

Am I restrained?

He attempted to lift his head and found that his head would not move, either. His eyes fluttered, and Janus realized the motion was involuntary.

What's happening?

His heart rate accelerated; he felt the palpitations in his chest. Janus became aware of a shrill artificial beeping that seemed to match the pounding in his breast. The noise sounded like the chirp of a bird, only more metallic. Janus strained to turn his head toward the sound, but still he could not. He was paralyzed.

Suddenly, as if drawn by the metallic sound, a face came into his field of vision.

Orion.

"Ahhh, eye flutter, that's unusual," Orion said. He used a tone more appropriate for addressing a chair than a man.

Orion reached down and opened both of Janus's eyes wide, peering into each before allowing the lid to snap shut again. The light streaming down from the ceiling behind Orion was blinding.

"Don't worry, my friend," Orion said with a smile, "she didn't hurt us."

He patted Janus on the face. Janus heard the impact and saw his field of vision rock from side to side, but was powerless to resist. The rough texture of Orion's skin against his own sent shivers down his spine.

Orion turned away and Janus heard the sound of wheels scooting across tiles. He had seen Orion sit in a mobile chair before. There would be a tray of instruments nearby.

Am I on an operating table?

"Your companion didn't hurt us, but my, did she make us look vulnerable," Orion said with a laugh. His voice was muffled from having turned away, but Janus could imagine what the older man was doing. He must be perusing his selection of implements, deciding what tool would best suit his purposes.

A moment passed before Orion's head appeared in Janus's field of vision again.

"Imagine if she'd stabbed us in our sleep," he said. He made a gesture in the air. Janus saw he was holding a scalpel and wearing thin green, almost transparent, gloves. "She could have stabbed us unopposed," Orion continued, "or that thief we brought in might have. They're still missing, you know. Went down the chute . . ." Orion shook his head.

From where Janus lay, the view was strange. Orion seemed to be muttering to himself. He went about various tasks, but Janus couldn't turn to observe them. All he could see was Orion's eyes darting back and forth.

Those cold, blue eyes.

Orion pulled a pair of transparent glasses into place. On either side of the glasses shone a piercing white light. "She used some sort of toxin on us. I'm having it analyzed as we speak. It was pretty ingenious, but crudely distilled. I still have a headache . . . You, however, got the worst of it, probably due to your proximity when the toxin was released."

He began prodding Janus's abdomen.

"Thank goodness I recovered so quickly," he continued, "or I might not have been able to help you. You see, you're very close to death right now, my dear friend."

A flash of fear coursed through Janus's spine. Orion's prodding of his abdomen became more painful.

"Oh, don't be concerned," Orion continued, "there's plenty of time to fix you up. However, you are in need of minor surgery. You see, your appendix is inflamed. If it ruptures, I'm not sure I have the facilities to assist you."

Janus didn't know what the man was talking about, but his terror did not dissipate. The machine that echoed his beating heart began to sing.

Orion glanced behind him, then reached up and twisted a valve. There was a hissing sound and the chirping stabilized.

"There we go," Orion said. He patted Janus on the face once more. "Don't worry, old friend, I'll get you back together shortly. You won't feel a thing."

I feel everything!

Orion leaned in close and pulled down his mask. He smiled at Janus. "I'm not sure why I'm telling you all this since you're completely sedated. Old habit, I guess." He set his mask back in place, lifted his scalpel, and turned his focus on Janus's abdomen.

You do know! The words echoed in terrible silence in Janus's mind. *You know I feel this, this is a punishment; you know, you know, you know!*

The Seneschal's thoughts were cut short as the scalpel blade entered his soft flesh. The blade burned like ice as it sawed with precision through his skin.

Janus's mind echoed with a silent scream. The beeps on the heart machine erupted into a deafening cacophony, but Orion continued to cut away, apparently oblivious to the anguish he had unleashed.

Or, perhaps, the anguish compelled him.

*

Darkness.

A profound, eternal and terrifying darkness. Janus had only a fleeting awareness. He felt lost, disconnected. The essence of who and what he was seemed thoroughly scattered. Bits of him drifted together, pulled by some unknown sense of continuity, but no matter how many blind and questing parts encountered one another, Janus never recuperated the sense that he was whole.

He had been unmade and then reformed, as a weaker version of what he once was.

The violation shook him.

"Janus," a voice seemed to call from some unknown quarter. There was no direction. Only drifting space, void, and blackness.

"Janus," the voice said again. This time, a blurry form appeared in the distance. Janus found himself pulled to it. A light. Suddenly, the light erupted.

"Janus!"

All at once, the Seneschal became aware of pain. He could sense his eyelids again as they opened and squeezed shut. His throat was on fire; his mouth was dry. The opaque nothingness congealed into recognizable form, but Janus couldn't shake the awareness of purgatory.

That had been death.

Wherever he had awakened from was a place without dreams, without feelings, without a sense of self.

Complete and total oblivion.

So it is true – in death there is nothing.

The realization brought terror.

He opened his eyes and the blurry forms leering down at him resolved into shapes. Janus tried to call his limbs, but movement was limited and weak. The blurred form became a face, gigantic, godlike; hovering above him with a smug, supreme expression.

The terror built.

In that moment of weakness, Orion's features brought no comfort.

"So," Orion said, clearly recognizing the transition to lucidity in Janus's gaze, "how's my favorite patient?"

A tear formed in the corner of the Seneschal's eye. The weakness shamed him, but he had no power to control the response. All his armor had been stripped away, and his most precious core lay exposed.

"I felt everything," he whispered.

Orion looked confused. "What?"

"I felt everything," Janus repeated. "When you cut me, I was aware."

Within a haze of blinding light, Orion lifted his hand to his mouth. Even in his shattered state, Janus recognized an expression of sympathy, but the Seneschal was too disjointed to judge its sincerity.

"My god, Janus, I'm sorry." The gray-haired man sat on the bed and placed his hand on Janus's shoulder. The small gesture of comfort released a surge of involuntary gratitude. "I had no idea."

"I couldn't move."

"That was for your own safety. We can't risk reflexive muscle responses when we're performing surgery. A spasm could prove fatal."

The paternal touch upon Janus's shoulder helped the Seneschal center his thoughts. He was too weak for anger. How utterly destroyed he was, and Orion possessed so much power.

"I assure you, Janus, everything I did was to save your life. Our anesthesia is old, perhaps it has lost potency, but it was properly administered." As Orion spoke, he lifted his hand to Janus's head. "Without that surgery, you would have died."

They sat together for a moment, but the weight of consciousness began to tax the Seneschal. Janus felt his lids closing into a call of sleep more familiar and less menacing than the void he had so recently escaped.

"Rest," Orion said. "I'll need my best lieutenant in short order." He stood.

Janus felt himself fading. As the darkness washed over him, a question escaped his lips. "What of Valeria?"

Orion's face became unreadable. "The girl? What did you wish from her anyway? Surely there are sweeter pleasures to be found within the walls of San Aryan."

Janus replied in a delirious whisper, "I wished to experience something freely given."

Orion's eyes widened. He considered for a moment, then spoke with a smile. "Forgive my surprise, I see I underestimated the depths of your cruelty."

The statement perplexed Janus as he drifted back into sleep.

Chapter 22: The Edentown Library

Quillion slipped on the coarse and scratchy pants of his issued uniform. He pulled on the equally uncomfortable tunic, buckled his belt, and stood. When he moved, the fabric doubled into a point around his knee and dug into his flesh.

"You'll break it in in no time," Corporal Dag said, grinning at their predicament. "The cost of the uniform will be deducted from your first month's wages." Quillion already hated the man.

The northerner pulled on his new boots. They were a full size too big. He took an experimental step only to find that here too the stiff leather bent and dug into his feet.

Quillion recalled his old boots broken in by a thousand miles of travel. Their loss suddenly struck him as a great tragedy.

"What happened to our old clothing?" he asked.

"Burned," Dag replied. "You are red cloaks now. You must sever your connection to any other allegiance."

"There was an ivory pendant," Cole said. Dag's eyes snapped around to regard the smaller man. "I wore it on a leather cord around my neck."

"Destroyed," Dag snapped, "that's part of a past life you must forget."

Cole resumed dressing, but Quillion observed his companion had suffered a substantial wound. Before he could reflect further, Dag growled again. "Come on, I'll show you the grounds."

Quillion and Cole fell into step behind Dag as he marched from the room. "The red cloaks operate on a system of bells," Dag snapped. "When you hear the bell, you will respond appropriately. Failure to respond will be met with discipline, understood?"

"Yes sir!" Quillion and Cole answered.

"One bell means food, two bells mean assemble, three bells mean attack, understood?"

"Yes sir!"

In truth, they didn't understand at all. Where did they eat? Where did they assemble? Whom did they attack? All the vital information was left out. But the two mercenaries knew the omissions were intentional. The ambiguity allowed officers to dole out punishment on a whim.

"You will serve on daily patrol," Dag continued. "What do you believe is the purpose of this patrol?"

"The destruction of books?" Quillion offered.

Dag stopped so fast Quillion nearly crashed into him. The large corporal turned around to regard Quillion with a dim twinkle in his eyes

"You really are from the provinces, aren't you?"

Quillion said nothing, uncertain what Dag expected of him.

Dag shook his head and chuckled, then he resumed his march, thundering off in a new direction.

"C'mon!" he growled over his shoulder, leaving Quillion and Cole scampering to catch up.

They jogged through the corridors of Fort Brinewater. At first, Quillion was disoriented, but after a while he began to see that the structure was a hodgepodge of pre-existing buildings linked by zones of modern construction. The new zones were crude, and tended to resemble the stone dungeon where he and Cole had spent their first night.

They trended upward, and after a lengthy climb, Dag emerged into a small watchtower that overlooked Edentown.

"Behold," Dag said, his voice dripping with sarcasm, "the jewel of the world."

Quillion looked and gasped. He had finally been afforded a complete view of the city, and from this vantage point he could discern the enormity of Edentown. Buildings stretched out into the distance, a never-ending mass of decay, propped up with temporary supports that created a gross approximation of viability. Quillion could see people scurrying about, wiggling in the wreckage like maggots in rotten meat. There seemed to be a vast body of water in the distance; water stained red with the light of the morning sun.

It was a city in the throes of death.

Quillion felt his spirits sink. He clenched his teeth and forced himself to look again.

Curse you, Adam Lockhart, for urging us here! This place is a ruin. This cannot be the best the human race has to offer. Questing for your promised pupil is a fool's errand.

Quillion pushed the negative thoughts away; despair gained him nothing. He collected himself, cleared his thoughts, and attempted to regard the city with a clean perspective. Only then did he observe the fragments of prosperity amidst the omnipresent destruction.

Pockets of order slowly began to reveal themselves. Little more than wisps of coalesced logic that glowed like sputtering candles in the eternal night. His eyes darted along, resting for moments at the tops of more stable-looking buildings. He knew not what might compel his eye: maybe a lack of bowed or slanting walls; maybe a minute clean splash almost swallowed up by the overall soiled image; maybe a hint of something green . . .

Quillion couldn't say. But his curiosity was piqued and he had never needed more to nourish a secret ambition. He filed this overview of the city away in his memory for further reflection. Should he ever find the freedom to explore Edentown, he had identified several starting points.

"From here you can see every district of the city," Dag explained. "San Aryan sits by the water, then comes San Borja. After that you have Bellfore, Stoneforge, and Heights." Dag gestured at the indicated regions as he spoke. "At the foot of this wall is Brinewater."

"And beyond Brinewater?" Quillion asked.

"The outskirts . . . the ruins," Dag said, turning to regard the crumbling city behind them. Suddenly, he smiled.

"What's funny?" Quillion asked.

"What was it you thought you'd be seeking on patrol?"

Quillion didn't answer. He stared at Dag in confusion, attempting to decipher what the man found comical.

Finally, Cole jostled Quillion's arm and pointed to a spot just beyond the field that marked the border to the outskirts.

Quillion squinted in an attempt to make sense of the sight, then his eyes widened in horror.

As Quillion's realization became apparent, Dag roared with laughter. "Behold the library!" he said, pointing along the line of Quillion's gaze with a theatrical flourish.

A short way off, a soiled channel crossed the field. The channel stretched from a starting point somewhere within the outskirts and continued on into Brinewater and presumably beyond. A stream of mud ran down the center. Lining the walls of the channel were thousands and thousands of books.

"Books," Quillion gasped. "Where do they come from?"

"The people bring them," Dag replied. "We didn't even have to enforce an order. The books help with the smell; the peasants figured that out for themselves."

Quillion studied the channel. The books below the mid-point of the wall were yellow, water-stained, and bloated. Some, higher up, were open on their spines and pages flapped like surrender flags in the wind.

"There is a reservoir up in the high ground," Dag explained. "Twice a day, the water is released to flush through the network of channels. Look, you're just in time."

Quillion squinted. Off in the distance he caught sight of a wave of black water traveling down the channel. As the wave came closer, the water poured over the books, rising high on the wall before crashing down to stabilize at the mid-point.

The wave passed, leaving the channel half-full. A moment later, a terrible odor wafted over the wall. Quillion wrinkled his nose and turned to Dag. "Excrement?"

Dag roared with laughter.

"Yes! Everyone dumps their morning labors into the library. Connecting channels run throughout the city, but they all come out here. The reservoir's flush washes the filth away."

Quillion fought hard to swallow a gag.

Dag seemed quite satisfied as he regarded the slop-filled holding pond.

"I've heard stories of those who seek out books in the provinces, but I found the rumor hard to believe. As you can see, the population of Edentown is more advanced than our less cultivated country cousins. Rest assured that if any new caches of books are found, they'll end up in the library where they belong. Most would rather cut off their hand than even look at a book."

A state of shock descended upon Quillion. He cast about, looking for something to draw his attention away from the wanton destruction of the library. In the distance, Quillion caught the silhouette of a man scampering along the ledge of the channel. Without exactly knowing why, Quillion studied the figure.

The man was slender to the point of frailty and moved with jerks and twitches. He made his way along the ledge, stooping every now and then to scoop up a tome from the lapping waters, apparently impervious to the horrible stench. The figure peered at these books as he tottered awkwardly. Quillion thought he could detect the sound of incoherent babble, but the distance was too great to make any sense of what was said. Mostly, the figure tossed the books he recovered aside, always in the direction of dry ground. Sometimes he paused, and slipped a recovered item into a satchel on his hip.

"What about him?" Quillion asked. "That has to be an ordinal code violation."

"Oh, that's just the scholar," Dag said. The big corporal glanced around the watchtower until he found a loose stone. He made a cone with his hands and shouted, "Hey, Scholar!" before launching the stone into the air.

The scholar was too far away to be in any danger of getting struck. Still, at the sight of the men on the wall, he panicked and threw himself backward. The movement caused the scholar to slip on the shifting surface of soggy books, and he plunged knee deep into the slop. Still muttering to himself, the scholar made a slow and deliberate effort to pull himself from the water.

"What's wrong with him?" Quillion asked.

Dag shrugged, pointing his finger at his own head and spinning it in circles. "Who knows? He's not even worth the trouble of executing."

Quillion sighed. Ideas came so fast he didn't have time to formulate questions. He stood in silent contemplation. The gruesome image before him indelibly etched itself into his mind.

"Is the scholar always out there?" he asked.

"Yes," Dag replied. "Sometimes he falls in, and that gives us a chuckle. He's no threat. Beware the demons and the fathers of young girls, those are our enemies." Dag laughed, but then fell serious. "And beware the archer."

"A freeman?" Quillion asked, straining to disguise his interest. "I'd wondered if there were any."

"There are pockets of freemen scattered about, but they're disorganized and cowardly. The archer is a new development. All we know is that last winter the bodies of our brothers began turning up with arrows in their eyes."

Quillion opened his mouth to question Dag further, but at that moment, a bell began to ring.

Dag tilted his head. "Two bells," he said, when the noise had concluded.

"Assemble," Quillion replied.

Chapter 23: Thirst for Freedom

Kikkan awoke.

His back ached from pressing against the door, but otherwise he felt fine. Sitting up, he flexed his hands to help the blood return to his fingers.

He took a deep breath.

The room was peaceful.

It was silent outside after the insanity of the zombies' attack. Kikkan's thoughts settled. This fleeting glimpse of calm allowed him a moment of introspection. There was no feeling of judgment in the inanimate room. In his short life of freedom, Kikkan had killed many, yet the sun still rose every morning and the wind continued to blow through the buildings and trees. At first, the former slave had feared a greater power might object to the destruction of creation. Could Kikkan assume that the lack of consequence indicated approval?

No, that would be arrogant. Too many abominations went unpunished to believe any supernatural guardian coveted justice. Kikkan had seen the shade of the same irrational beast reflected in the eyes of his opponents. What caused that darkness to descend upon his fellow man? Was he, Kikkan, equally vulnerable to possession? Could the demon be sowing seeds within his psyche in the hope of one day claiming the former slave as a host?

The large man stood. He shook the aches from his muscles. He lifted his pipe for a moment and noted the fresh blood on the end.

Once more, he had killed.

The slaves he had destroyed were raging, mindless beasts, but the act still pained him.

Of all the creatures in this world, the ones who could most identify with Kikkan's life experience were those in that half-dead walking demonic state. With but a nudge, he might have shared their fate. It yet might be if he were captured and forced to consume *Bliss*.

The enemy could take a life, or do worse. Torment, destruction of self, annihilation of the spirit; none of these tactics were beneath the aspirations of his enemy. All Kikkan had to build his hopes on were the words and quest of a dying man.

His hands tightened on the pipe.

The quest sustained him, as did his strength . . .

Suddenly, the former slave was in need of an outlet for his frustration. He resented having again been forced to do battle with wretched creatures who had already been subjected to unspeakable torment. He preferred to punish the tormentors.

Kikkan felt that a righteous hunt might appease him. Pipe in hand, he braced his back against the wall and pulled open the door a crack to have a look around.

The hallway was empty. No tracks but Kikkan's marred the pathway to the room. Yet, there on the floor, Kikkan was shocked to see a small box filled with food.

He glanced left and right, but saw no one.

He returned his attention to the box.

The items were simple; some kind of cooked meat beside a mound of white-colored mush. Curious, Kikkan pushed at the box with his pipe.

The box moved a finger's length across the floor, silent except for the whisper of wood rasping against the ground.

Nothing else followed.

Could the food be poisoned? Laced with *Bliss* exactly as the former slave feared?

Possible, but such a trap seemed unlikely.

His opponents had never been inclined to trickery. They behaved with brute force and lies, as if the act of dominance itself held equal value to all other objectives. Allowing him to consume *Bliss* through subtlety was not their style. They would favor holding his mouth open and forcibly jamming the poison down his throat.

But still, consumption meant risk. Was it warranted?

Kikkan hefted his pack. He had supplies, but nothing that would last more than a few days. This urban jungle was a mystery. How did people sustain themselves? He would have to address the question of food eventually. When the consequences of his ignorance manifested, Kikkan would curse having shunned nourishment freely given.

He reached forward and clasped the box, taking one final look up and down the hallway before closing the door to his room. He pressed his ear against the crack in the frame, waiting for some outside indication that he had been observed.

Silence.

Shrugging, he dug his fingers into the mush and lifted the substance to his lips.

The food was bland, but not unpleasant. He ate quickly, then stood to listen before finally opening the door again.

Still nothing.

He set the box back on the floor and made his way down the hallway.

*

Kikkan climbed upward through the wreckage and the rust, through the broken bottles and the discarded refuse of the past. Up and up and up he went, searching for signs of life, driven on by his rage which, for the first time in a long while, had again been given free rein to burn.

He reflected on his last battle. The groping slaves in the darkness, mad for a drug that had been forced upon them.

Who had made them?

Stairwell after stairwell greeted Kikkan, and he raced ever upward until he broke through to the surface, and then continued to climb. He crossed an open street to the largest building he could see and scaled to the top. When the stairs ended, he pushed through a door and found a ladder. The rusty rungs bit into his hands and dust crumbled to the wind, but Kikkan didn't pause as he sought the heavens.

Finally at the top, with no higher ground available, Kikkan rested and scanned the horizon.

How did this world function?

How did the people live?

Where were the masters deserving of death?

The wind blew, and Kikkan had to grasp the metal framework he had climbed for fear of being swept away.

Below him, scattered like ants, he could make out the seething settlements of people. He knew he could sit and watch them for hours without knowing or understanding any more than a fragment of their lives. But he didn't have hours; the rage inside called for immediate action.

Find a target.

Kikkan hungered for a kill. Not a kill made in desperation or in self-defense; no, that was another aspect of manipulation. The former slave needed to act on his own decision. He longed to feel his labors contributed to the formation of a habitable world. He needed to set a plan in motion and see it through; something that was inspired by justice, free of the taint of dark influence or golden tongues.

This world was dominated by beasts who preyed upon the weak and subjugated them into oblivion. They used up the meager flash of divine spark that exists within all living things, and then discarded the dead flesh like a worthless husk.

Kikkan knew he only had to watch for a moment. A beast would make itself known.

And Kikkan would take him.

The longer he looked, the more he understood. Kikkan came to recognize the pathways taken to important points. He identified a market, and even a farm off in the distance. He saw the roads used to move between various establishments of commerce.

Still he looked, scouring the wreckage for a focal point to direct his anger.

In a short while, he had something.

A squat building stood some distance away. The top floor was flooded in an artificial light like Kikkan had never seen. Walls lifted up on all sides, obscuring the compound from the ground.

Why hide it?

There were plants in the corners, and a flash of blue in the center.

Water?

He watched.

Figures walked to and fro within the space. Most of them occupied, most with a purpose.

Except one.

That one reclined by the water, moving only to accept tokens from the others that hovered around him.

That one did nothing.

That one was the master.

Having seen enough, Kikkan took his bearings. Confident he could navigate, he began to scramble down the tower. When he reached the stairwell, he proceeded rapidly, stopping on occasion to check the changing appearance new perspective lent to his target as he descended.

From the surface, the building he had selected looked no different than any other. From the ground, it was impossible to know the emerald jewel that existed on the roof.

But Kikkan had marked the place.

Hefting his pipe from the bag, he trotted off with purpose.

Blood of recently departed slaves congealed upon his weapon.

It was time to add a master's blood.

They all bled the same.

Chapter 24: Duel

Dag led Quillion and Cole down to the courtyard. A large group of red cloaks stood in formation, and Captain Jesse stood at the front observing with glassy-eyed disgust.

A body of a red cloak hung from a pole in the center of the courtyard. Quillion became aware of the smell of decomposition and he tried to shift his focus elsewhere. His eyes darted about, by chance locking with Captain Jesse's. Quillion quickly bowed his head, but too late.

"You there!" Jesse screamed, and the low murmur of chatter in the courtyard died.

Quillion raised his head to find Jesse staring at him.

"Have you accepted your inferiority?"

The question had the ring of ceremony, and the assembled men tensed in anticipation of his response. The question itself made no sense. Inferiority to what? Inferiority to whom?

Never let a lesser person hold dominion over your sense of worth. If you doubt your own logic, you become vulnerable to oppression, violation, and control. Adam Lockhart's words, scrawled in the margins of a book from a different age.

"Have you accepted your inferiority?" Captain Jesse asked again, with more than a hint of rage.

"I have," Cole said, giving the obvious answer.

"Yes," Quillion coughed, "me too."

Jesse dropped her head and approached them like a flat-faced dog pestering a bull. She stopped just short of crashing into the two mercenaries and when she lifted her eyes to glare, her face was red.

"Inferior dregs is all I see. You're weak!" She pinched Quillion's arm. He was smart enough not to react. "You're weak! Both in the body and in the mind. Repeat!"

"I am weak both in the body and in the mind," Quillion and Cole said.

The immediate response seemed to drop her from her killing rage, but she continued to berate them. "Inferior! Unable to resist basic temptations, unworthy of making simple decisions!"

"We are inferior," the northerners repeated, "unable to resist temptations, unworthy of making decisions."

Captain Jesse stared for a long time, searching for signs of insubordination. Quillion wanted to laugh in her face. The woman was clearly a lunatic. He wondered how she had earned this post. What, beside the threat of punishment, compelled her soldiers to obey?

"Remember those words, repeat them when the bell rings," Jesse snapped. Then she returned to the front of the assembly. Lifting her voice, she addressed the crowd. "Let's see what these new recruits can do!"

Her tone dripped sarcasm and the assembled red cloaks laughed.

"Arm them," Jesse said, vaguely gesturing at Dag. Then she pointed at a large man in the crowd. The man saluted, and ran to the opposite corner of the courtyard to prepare himself.

Dag pulled Quillion and Cole to a small kiosk that housed a collection of wooden sparring swords.

"Take a shield and a sword," Dag said. "I hope you've picked up some skill with weapons in your travels."

Quillion swallowed. Humiliation and failure was clearly the designed outcome.

"Got any advice?" he asked.

"She's going to want to see you beat," Dag replied. "Show something, but go down when the time comes."

The instructions were absurd, but Quillion nodded. He turned to Cole. "Did you hear . . ." He broke off as he recognized a burning fury in Cole's eyes.

"What is it?" he asked.

"Didn't you notice?" Cole replied, low enough that Dag couldn't hear. Cole reached for a small shield. Quillion moved to help fix the item to Cole's arm.

"Notice what?"

"The Captain was wearing a leather cord around her neck," Cole said in a flat voice.

"So what?"

"It was my pendant, my ivory pendant."

Quillion finished strapping on the shield and removed a sword from the wall. He handed the sword to Cole, who made a few practice swings.

"What's the significance of the pendant?" Quillion whispered. Cole had never mentioned the item before.

Cole's face hardened. "It was my mother's."

Quillion didn't respond.

Cole stared straight ahead. Out in the field, a giant of a man stood waiting. The assembled red cloaks and Captain Jesse watched with mocking smiles. But Cole's eyes burned, and Quillion knew his friend was a more than capable warrior.

"Do you have anything else of your mother's?" Quillion asked.

"Only my heart and the blood it pumps," Cole snapped. "And I do not intend to see those gifts defiled along with my mother's pendant."

With that, Cole strode forward to meet his challenge.

Quillion reached for a shield and motioned Dag to help him while keeping his eye on Cole.

"Did you tell him what I said? Is he going to lie down?" Dag asked.

"Yes," Quillion replied, answering the first question. "And no," he continued, answering the second.

When Cole was five paces away from his opponent, he stopped and waited for a signal. The courtyard was a sandy surface and Captain Jesse sat upon a raised dais to Cole's left. To his right, the mass of assembled red cloaks broke ranks to form a circle around the combatants.

Cole's opponent was huge; perhaps the biggest man Quillion had ever seen. The red cloak was wreathed with unnatural muscle across his chest and biceps. The flesh twitched involuntarily, almost like that of a horse bothered by a fly. The warrior's legs were not nearly as developed as his upper body, however, and Quillion wondered if the inflated body was truly functional or just for show.

"Begin," Jesse commanded, giving no instruction on objective or how to yield.

Cole immediately dropped into a crouch. Quillion had fought beside the smaller man, but had never had the occasion to observe his skill from a distance.

Cole hefted his sparring sword with practiced ease. There was grace in his movements as he swayed from foot to foot, awaiting the giant's approach.

He did not have to wait long.

The giant stepped forward, swinging his trunk of a sword in a wild arc and eliciting a roar of approval from the crowd. Cole dodged rather than parried, skipping backward. The giant stepped forward again, swinging in another wild arc which Cole again dodged with little effort.

"Quit running, you coward!" came a cry from the assembly.

Quillion took his eyes from the duel to observe the red cloaks. The men stood like ravenous beasts fixated on the proceedings. They appeared angry. The battle was only two exchanges old and already they were bored. Only blood would sate them; they had no interest in evaluation.

Quillion felt a shiver of concern for his friend. He hoped Cole understood he had the crowd as well as his opponent to contend with. If the smaller warrior didn't do something soon, he might become subject to blindside attacks from the spectators.

Quillion returned his attention to Cole just as the giant lurched forward. As before, the huge man telegraphed his swing, relying on brute force rather than finesse to guide his attack. This time, the swing was rushed. Following the animus of the crowd, the brute was frustrated. His swing was rooted in his arms rather than supported by his trunk, and the result was a high assault that lacked balance.

Cole ducked and responded with a counter swing that smashed into the giant's knee.

The blow brought a resounding crack and the giant recoiled, but Cole had not finished. He jerked his sparring sword back and then brought the weapon crashing down again upon the same knee. The crack of the strike equaled the first and echoed across the courtyard. This time, the knee collapsed and the giant dropped, bending to support his weight on his other leg and offering Cole a new target. Cole obliged with two rapid blows to the other knee, and when that knee collapsed as well, Cole made a powerful overhand chop to his opponent's head.

The brute fell forward and lay motionless in the sand.

The fight was over so fast that the crowd didn't have time to assimilate a response. Cole took advantage of the confusion. He immediately thrust his sparring sword into the dirt. He kneeled and bowed his head.

"I accept my inferiority and pledge myself to your tutelage, Captain," he declared.

The surprised observers looked up at Captain Jesse to gauge her response.

"Gods," Dag whispered at Quillion's side.

Captain Jesse sat for a moment, her face vacant. She did nothing for a long while before finally lifting her finger in an ambiguous gesture. Quillion felt a flash of panic. *She's not leading, she's leaving the reaction to chance!*

At first, there was no response, then a few red cloaks came forward to pull the body of Cole's defeated foe away from the courtyard. Cole again seized the opportunity. He stood sharply, bowed his head in a respectful nod, made a military turn and marched over to where Quillion stood. Cole formally offered his sparring sword to Dag, who took it reflexively, then the smaller swordsman stepped into formation beside the bewildered corporal.

Well done, Quillion thought, appreciating how Cole had taken control even while projecting subservience.

Captain Jesse didn't object to the display, and after a moment she found her voice.

"Next," she cried.

At the command, another giant stepped forward. Quillion shook his head. The brute was almost indistinguishable from the last. Not wishing to provoke, Quillion marched forward and bowed to Captain Jesse.

"Begin," she snapped.

Quillion's heart raced; the captain's command brought an additional surge of adrenaline. The taste of bile was an acid burn at the back of his throat. He knew he wasn't Cole's equal as a swordsman, and he didn't like this situation at all. There was too high a probability of defeat. What was the point of an evaluation such as this? The duel was artificial, and the result meaningless. Quillion's true worth came from knowing how to avoid scenarios where the chance of failure was high.

But the crowd didn't know that, and if Captain Jesse did, she didn't appear willing to recognize it now. Maybe she simply enjoyed cultivating failure.

The brute waded in and Quillion knew better than to employ Cole's tactics. The first swing was fast and low. Quillion shifted his body to catch the blow on his shield. The impact was stunning. The force pushed Quillion back and instantly rendered his forearm numb. He struggled for a moment to pull his defenses together, but it was too late. When he looked up, he saw only the darkness of his opponent's weapon descending upon him, blocking out the sun.

There was an explosion of pain, and the fight was over.

Chapter 25: Ceremony

The approach turned out to be more complicated than Kikkan had anticipated.

First there was finding the building. Maintaining the proper heading on the ground based on what he had seen from above proved to be difficult, as distinguishing landmarks were hard to reconcile up close. Also, the distances were farther than he had realized. Kikkan soon found himself doubting his direction.

Eventually, the former slave came to the foot of a large structure with two white columns out front that he recognized beyond the shadow of a doubt. He stood across the street, scanning the windows for signs of life. There was no movement in any of the broken frames, but competent watchmen would know enough to remain still.

Kikkan glanced up and down the street. Unlike some of the neighboring blocks, there was little traffic here. Even the dust on the road was mostly undisturbed except for the scuffs of birds and rodents. Nothing of consequence had passed this way in recent time. Kikkan assumed any sentries that might exist would have grown complacent. The former slave pulled his metal pipe from the back pack and tightened the straps so his other possessions would not rattle. Taking two quick breaths, Kikkan sprinted into the street, half-expecting to be riddled with bullets or arrows.

He was met only with silence.

Arriving at the shelter of the columns, Kikkan paused to listen.

Looking back, he saw his line of footprints in the dust, but that was inconsequential. By the time they were discovered, he would be long gone. Or so he hoped.

He tried the door.

Locked!

Forcing it would be noisy, so Kikkan leaned back and assessed his options. Ten feet up was a broken skylight over the door. Kikkan snorted at the sight. What was the point of locking the door when other openings were left gaping to the outside world? He concluded that the area had probably not been fortified at all. Possibly, the door was jammed from decades of disuse. Any secure space likely existed further inside. The tall warrior slipped his weapon back into his pack and cinched the pipe in place.

Kikkan jumped, stretching to his full extension to grasp at the ledge. His fingers caught the dusty surface, but the hold was slippery and Kikkan fell back to the ground. Dusting off his hands, he tried again, and this time he got a good enough hold to pull himself up. Passing through the hole was awkward, but the former slave managed with minimal noise before dropping to the floor on the other side.

The room was dark. Kikkan waited as his night vision adjusted. After a moment, he could make out piles of old furniture stacked against the walls. Tiles had come loose from the ceiling, and cables hung down at random intervals. To all appearances, the place seemed abandoned. Kikkan drew his pipe once more, feeling comforted, as always, by its heft.

The former slave put his back to the wall and slid around the perimeter. The point of balance kept him from stumbling in the near darkness. He tried several doors before finding one that opened into a stairwell. Again putting his back to the railing, he began to climb.

*

The watcher observed Kikkan from a distance, laughing when Kikkan fell to the ground, grunting in surprise when the big man succeeded in making the leap.

"That's Lord Marion's sanctuary, stranger," the figure said. "Do you know what you're getting yourself into?"

The watcher considered, but didn't take long to arrive at a decision. The lean form soon detached itself from the shadows and set off in pursuit.

*

As time passed, Kikkan once again found himself doubting whether he had come to the right place. He had begun to consider turning around when he caught the whisper of muffled noise in the distance. He paused to listen, fully alert, and was rewarded by the sound of a cough.

The cough was close!

Kikkan trembled, realizing how near he had come to stumbling right into an enemy.

The former slave began to move again, slower than before, inching upward to avoid alerting the sentry to his presence. The stairwell was nearly dark. Kikkan held the pipe low along his leg to prevent the metal from flashing an errant reflection.

Up, up, up he went, his back hugging the wall. The closer he came, the clearer he could discern his enemy. There, with his back to the railing, stood a man, smoking. The guard kept the light of the ember cupped in his hand, but it flashed on occasion. Kikkan focused on the light as it moved down by the man's hip, then up to flare brightly as he took a drag.

The rhythm became repetitive as Kikkan continued to approach. Up, down, up down, inhale, exhale. Then, suddenly, the light paused in the air. Had the sentry noticed him? Kikkan didn't wait to find out. Adrenaline surged through the former slave and he exploded. He sprinted the last dozen steps and was upon the befuddled guard before the man knew what was happening. The sentry lifted his arm to deflect the descending blow of Kikkan's pipe, but Kikkan's assault shattered the bone and the strike connected with the sentry's vulnerable skull.

The body collapsed in a heap. Kikkan was left panting in the darkness on a narrow ledge before a heavy door. He became aware of noises, indicating the presence of a large gathering of people.

*

Kikkan cracked open the door a finger's width. Light flooded into the darkness of the stairwell. Outside, a crowd was in the midst of some kind of ceremony. The room had walls that came to just a little over Kikkan's height, but there was no ceiling and stars glittered in the night sky above. The opulence was staggering. Two groups of people had assembled, divided by an aisle. At the front of the gathering stood a man dressed in formal wear; beside him, facing the gathering, stood a figure dressed in the plain white robes of an acolyte.

Kikkan recalled the long hours he had spent in the metal shed on Duncan Kerr's farm enduring lectures from one such as this.

You must be obedient, obedience is rewarded in the next life. You must be docile, docility is rewarded in the next life.

Kikkan's fist tightened around his weapon at the memory. Everything the man had said had been a lie designed to entice Kikkan deeper into submission. There could be no greater traitor than an enemy who presented himself as a friend. Kikkan had long since resolved to violate every "you must" order the acolyte had drilled into him.

The appearance of a very young girl interrupted Kikkan's thoughts. She arrived at the far end of the room and everyone turned to look at her. From her height, Kikkan guessed she was little more than a child. She was dressed in an extravagant gown with a long train. Her face was covered in a veil, but her whole body seemed to shake as she was pushed forward by an elderly woman visibly frustrated by the girl's resistance.

The girl was being forced!

A man twice the girl's height and four times her girth stood waiting for her at the front of the room. He smiled like an animal perched upon a kill awaiting his human prize. This was not something Kikkan could allow.

The former slave scanned the assembly one last time. Servants stood in corners and in shadow dressed in identical uniforms, present among the others but designated as less than human and therefore invisible. Kikkan knew he would encounter no resistance from these. There didn't appear to be any warriors, and the merchants involved in the ceremony did not concern the former slave.

Resolved, Kikkan awaited his moment. The path of the bride came close to Kikkan's hiding place. The former slave waited, observing, taking one hurried opportunity to verify his conclusions. In the final frantic seconds, nothing arose to make him doubt.

The girl came close and Kikkan moved.

Pipe in hand, Kikkan pulled open the door with a jerk. Only then did he notice the two red cloaked guards standing on either side of the door. Their presence had been hidden by the narrowness of his observation slit. The crowd was so focused on the procession that they didn't even perceive Kikkan at first. The red cloaks reacted at the sight of the burly warrior, but Kikkan's weapon was ready and gave him the advantage. He swung hard at his first opponent, a black-bearded brute with crystal blue eyes. The pipe thudded squarely into the red cloak's face, dropping him in a heap. The delay of dispatching the first allowed the other warrior to draw his sword, but as Kikkan stepped forward to engage, he was surprised by the zip of an arrow which suddenly appeared, quivering, in the red cloak's shoulder.

The warrior winced, and Kikkan swung again, connecting with a blow that crushed his opponent's head.

By now, the crowd had become aware of the intrusion and panic ensued. Kikkan watched with regret as figures stood and pushed to escape; some trampling their weaker comrades in panic.

As predicted, the servants remained docile, too broken to dare to act on their own volition.

From the corners of the room, more red cloaks came. They charged, pushing through the surging crowd, but were slowed by the milling of the frantic mass. In an instant, Kikkan realized there were too many. He tightened his hands upon his weapon. This would be the end, but if so, Kikkan resolved to kill as many as he could.

Two red cloaks broke free and charged forward. Kikkan braced, but again came the arrows. Two black shafts sliced through the night, lodging in the neck of one warrior and the chest of the next. The red cloaks tumbled to the ground. This time, Kikkan had the opportunity to trace the arrow's direction, and his eyes came to rest upon a hooded figure standing upon the wall. The archer loosed two more arrows, which drove into the back of a fat man attempting to flee. Kikkan recognized the most recent victim as the man who had been awaiting the girl at the front of the room.

The hooded figure dropped down beside Kikkan.

"Come on!" said a female voice. "You might as well grab her." The hooded figure gestured, and Kikkan looked to see the young bride standing confused and forgotten as the masses fought for escape all around.

Kikkan reached forward and grabbed the girl, surprised that she did not resist. He swept her up and slipped back out the door. The archer loosed two more arrows into the throng and then skipped in behind Kikkan, slamming the door as she passed through.

The stairwell blocked out the chaos of the outside world. The archer dropped to her knee and pulled a length of chain from her satchel. This she wrapped around the door handle and a pipe that protruded from the wall. Pulling the length tight, she fastened the two ends together with a clamp.

"That will buy us some time," she said, then turned to the girl. The archer pulled back her hood to reveal features of such beauty that Kikkan found himself transfixed. The archer ignored the former slave's reaction and pushed aside the girl's veil to reveal the terrorized face of a young child.

"You will not be harmed," the archer said. The girl was listless and the archer's face tightened in sudden anger. She turned to Kikkan. "She's been drugged. They do that sometimes to ease the pain of consummation." To Kikkan's surprise, the archer leaned forward to embrace the would-be bride. The young girl accepted the comfort passively.

"Now you," the archer said turning her attention on Kikkan, "can you possibly comprehend how much trouble you've caused? What were you thinking?"

The words confused Kikkan.

"Slave owners must die," he managed to sputter.

"Oh, that's it?" the archer continued. "This isn't a case of seeing something you liked?"

Kikkan's head tilted in confusion. The archer gestured at the bride. All of a sudden, Kikkan realized what the archer was implying.

"No, the girl was being forced," he stammered.

"Her parents had arranged a union for her," the archer replied.

"With that pig at the front of the room? He wished only to violate her!"

"It would have been a legal joining under the blessing of the church!"

"I cannot forgive legitimizing the rape of a child through ritual ceremony. Any institution truly committed to acts of good should stand opposed to such abominations, not seek out ways to profit by them."

The archer snorted. "What do you know about violation, a powerful man such as yourself?"

The words piqued Kikkan's anger allowing him to regain his balance in the interrogation. His voice took on an edge. "Do you think I sprang from the womb fully formed? I was a child once, weak, and a slave. I have only recently claimed my body as my own. When I lacked development and muscle, my owners did with me as they wished. I would spare this girl such a fate."

The words silenced the archer. "So you saved her?" she said, after a pause.

"For the moment."

The archer still held the child in a maternal embrace. She turned to regard the girl, and suddenly the building tension in the small quarters seemed to evaporate.

"Ok then," the archer said, her voice resolved now instead of accusing. "We might as well see things through." She turned to face Kikkan. "Your actions were rash. I only let you proceed because you happened to be right. There were several in that room who deserved death; I knew one of them in a former life."

"Former life?"

"Too much to explain," the archer continued. "Just know we're discouraged from engaging in slaughter, as much as we may wish to." She winked at Kikkan. The action bewitched him.

The archer stood and extended her hand. Kikkan took it.

"I'm Valeria."

"Kikkan."

"Come on," Valeria said. "This place will be crawling with red cloaks soon. I have to get you below."

Chapter 26: Gruel

Quillion awoke to find himself on a bumpy cot in a shadowed room. Bunk beds stretched off as far as he could see in all directions. He was covered by a thick, scratchy blanket. His head throbbed and his throat was dry. He tried to work his tongue to get some moisture in his mouth.

"So you're awake?" Cole asked.

"Unfortunately." Quillion tried to sit up but nausea prevented him.

"Relax," Cole said, offering him a wooden cup. As Quillion took a long drink, Cole continued. "I outrank you now."

Quillion finished his drink and handed the cup back.

"Good for you; what designation did you earn?"

"Private first class."

"I assume they don't promote newbies that often?"

Cole nodded.

Quillion closed his eyes. "Be careful you don't make any enemies with your rapid ascension."

"We're to call each other Private now," Cole said.

"Certainly, the system couldn't tolerate a mass of soldiers clinging to individual identities. We must join the collective whole in pursuit of a common good," Quillion said.

Cole shook his head, not understanding the purpose of the brief rant. "How are you feeling?"

Quillion snorted. "I'll manage. What happened after I blacked out?"

"You didn't miss anything. Captain Jesse stood over your prostrate body and berated the rest of us for a while. Then they dragged you here."

"Did they have a healer look at me?"

Cole shook his head.

Quillion squinted. "Do you think that's because they don't have healers, or because they don't care?"

"The latter, although I don't know for sure whether they have healers."

"Perfect."

"Can you stand yet?"

"What's the rush?"

"I'm to take you to the mess hall."

"Food? Well, at least that's positive."

Cole's grimace suggested otherwise.

Quillion pushed back the blankets and swung his legs to the floor. He had been placed on the cot fully clothed. The dirt from his boots had muddied up his bed. He stood over the cot and put the bed in order. He didn't need to be told to keep his sleeping area tidy; that had been protocol everywhere he had served.

Cole helped with the task, then led Quillion down a hallway and through a large set of doors. Outside, heavy rain fell on the smooth stone surface of the courtyard. Their path took them by the sad, broken body hanging from the stake. Quillion observed the heavy raindrops driving into the gray flesh and tattered clothing. The corpse could do nothing to protect itself against the weather. How quickly the beauty of a man, all he knew, all he entailed, could be reduced to a tattered tapestry, incapable even of coming in from the wet and the cold.

Quillion and Cole made their way toward the yellow glow of a distant doorway. Cole entered with little objection, but as Quillion made to follow, a rough hand stopped him in his tracks.

"New recruit," a soldier said, "did you have a nice nap?" The soldier was taller than Quillion, with the same overdeveloped musculature common among the red cloaks.

"Some fancy swordplay for sure," said another man; this one had a bald head and a thick beard.

Quillion didn't reply. He had been stopped short of the cover of the door and water poured down on him from the heavens.

The two red cloaks awaited a retort. With none forthcoming, they appeared equally delighted simply to watch Quillion stand in the rain.

"What's the holdup?" Cole snapped.

The two turned on the smaller man in annoyance, but paused when they noticed the insignia on his arm.

"You're foolin'," one of them said, "you're not a . . ."

"I am," Cole snapped. "Should we head on over and discuss this with the section commander?"

The two red cloaks became uneasy. Cole decided not to push his luck. He reached between the towering brutes to grab Quillion's shoulder and pulled the stout northerner through.

Quillion said nothing, and the two campaigners made their way into the mess hall.

Inside, the room was loud with undisciplined men roaring with laughter as they stuffed their faces with what appeared to be porridge or stew. Quillion squinted at the main dish and discerned only that it was red and lumpy.

"Come on," Cole said.

They moved to a line forming along the back wall. Several enormous men stood beside large pots, scooping servings with ladles.

"New meat," one said as he shoved a wooden bowl into Quillion's hands. He then tossed the ladle full of food at Quillion, half-drenching the northerner with the contents. The server was more courteous with Cole, filling the bowl with care and even offering a sloppy salute.

Food in hand, they sat.

Quillion took a closer look at the food. He discovered it was more gruel than porridge. He lifted a spoonful to his nose and sniffed. Then he brought the concoction to his mouth to taste.

The acrid flavor forced him to fight back a gag.

The gruel was watery with an unpleasant mixture of flavors. Rancid meat provided the backbone with a heavy dosage of salt. Quillion assumed the salt had been added to drown out the more unpleasant flavors that might have been detected.

"You have to eat it all," Cole advised.

Quillion stared at his spoon and steeled himself against the nausea which still lingered in his throat from his latest beating. He took another scoop of the foul stew and choked the rancid mouthful down.

"What happens if I don't finish it?"

"Finish."

Quillion sighed.

He was all too aware that this food, in addition to its poor nutritive quality, likely contained some sort of drug that would effect a physical change.

Quillion clenched his wooden spoon. As he shoved the poison in, he reflected that perhaps living men could be reduced as easily as the dead.

Chapter 27: The One You Seek

Valeria led Kikkan and the girl below ground level and deep into the underworld. In the months since their escape from Orion's estate, she and Simyon had grown familiar with the subterranean labyrinth of tunnels and passageways. She and her charges traversed stairwells and scrambled down abandoned shafts. Occasionally, they stopped for rest, but the pauses were infrequent.

"You're pushing the girl too hard," Kikkan said at one rest point.

Valeria looked over to see the girl leaning against a wall, panting. Her wedding dress was soiled by the grime of their descent. Valeria approached her. "What's your name?" she asked, kindly but with authority.

"Allie," the girl said, stumbling over her own tongue. Her movements indicated that she was still intoxicated and she seemed to be growing more lethargic. "Allison . . . but I'm called Allie."

"What did they give you before the ceremony?" Valeria asked.

"A drink," Allie said, her voice slurring. "I don't know what."

"Who gave it to you?" Kikkan asked.

"My mother."

Kikkan tilted his head and looked to Valeria for an explanation.

"The sedative makes young brides less troublesome on their wedding night. She'll be asleep in an hour," she said.

Kikkan nodded.

Valeria kneeled.

"Allie, your dress is too cumbersome. I'm going to trim some away with my knife, is that all right?"

"Yes," Allie said.

Kikkan snorted. "She'd probably agree to anything right now."

"That's the idea."

Valeria slipped her knife from its sheath and cut the dress at mid-calf length. The archer gathered up the trimmings and stuffed the material into a satchel.

"Why are you keeping it?" Kikkan asked.

Valeria eyed him. "I don't want to make it easy for anyone who might try to track us. We should be going."

Kikkan looked at Allie again and saw that the girl was almost asleep on her feet.

"And her?"

"Can you carry her?"

"Yes."

"Then you have my permission." Valeria slipped her dagger back into its sheath and trotted off into the dark. Kikkan scooped up the girl and followed.

*

The deeper they went, the darker it became, until suddenly the glow began to return. Kikkan had seen the luminescence before, but the mystery still troubled him.

"What is the source of that light?" he asked, keeping his voice hushed out of respect for unseen dangers.

"Who knows?" Valeria said. "I've lived in the near dark all my life, including half a year here in the outskirts, and not discovered any answer. All we seem to have is evidence of a past filled with wonders, and no knowledge of how they function."

"I have some knowledge."

Valeria stopped and swirled on Kikkan in the near dark. The whiteness of her eyes and her teeth stood out, and Kikkan realized she regarded him with a mocking smile.

"Are you a master of the craft, then?"

"The craft?"

Valeria laughed, loud enough that the echo made Kikkan uncomfortable.

"You can't know much if you don't know what 'the craft' is." She gestured at a wall. The shadows could not hide the scrawled markings.

"There," she said. "Some say those random scratches contain insight. What do you say?"

Kikkan squinted. He hadn't recognized the markings as letters in the darkness and the grime, but as he looked closer he was startled to recognize the presence of words.

"Enjoy," Kikkan read.

Valeria swung on him.

Kikkan shrugged. "It says 'enjoy.'"

"Enjoy what?"

"I don't know, that's all I can see. Perhaps there is more hidden under the filth."

Valeria assessed Kikkan for a moment, her manner changing considerably.

"You have pleasing features," he said finally.

Valeria snorted. "Is that all you can think of? If we aren't killed by the red cloaks tonight, they'll probably have us in a week or so. Then there are the demons to consider."

"I've fought them off before," Kikkan replied.

"Yes, I saw. So you know how dangerous they are."

Kikkan exhaled. "I've been living on borrowed time for months. If I can survive another year as a free man I will be grateful, but if it's only another hundred breaths, I'll take that as well. What would be the point of desiring more life if I did not appreciate the moments I already have?"

The words did not displease Valeria. "You're a strange one to find wandering the cursed streets of Edentown."

"I didn't come here by accident."

"Oh, really? Do tell what brought you." Valeria resumed walking. Kikkan hefted the girl, who was sleeping soundly in his arms, and followed.

"I was sent."

"Sent by whom?"

"Adam Lockhart."

Valeria turned on Kikkan with a new kind of fire in her eyes. "Where did you hear that name?"

"I had the honor of being his student for a few months in Acheron."

"Student . . ." Valeria said. "What did he teach you?"

"The craft."

"What else?" The way she asked made Kikkan think she might have known the answer already.

"He bid me seek a thief in Edentown with a star-shaped birthmark behind his ear."

"Oh, and he specified that this 'thief' was a man, then?"

Kikkan was about to respond in the affirmative, but stopped. *Had* Adam indicated his pupil's gender? Could this

Valeria be the one? A shiver of excitement slid down Kik-kan's spine.

"Do you have a birthmark behind your ear?"

Valeria smirked. She lifted her hand to her hair and tilted her head to reveal . . . nothing. The procedure was repeated on the other side.

"Sorry, Kikkan, I'm not your salvation."

Kikkan nodded. "Not the one Adam Lockhart spoke of, anyway."

Valeria heard the words, and the darkness hid her smile.

*

The three finally came to the mouth of a long tunnel. Here, they found the going easier. The near darkness contin-ued, but there was a glow of light in the distance.

Kikkan sighed at the sight. The darkness had been weigh-ing on him.

Figures waited in the distance. Valeria stepped in front of Kikkan and put her fingers to her mouth to issue a low whistle.

The distant figures, silhouettes against the light, formed up at the sound and came running.

"Declaration!" shouted a voice.

"Valeria."

"Who is with you?"

"The giant of the surface that Weasel mentioned."

At the boy's name, Kikkan's head snapped round to re-gard Valeria. She felt the look and shrugged.

"I never said we didn't know about you."

Kikkan might have reached for his weapon were it not for the girl in his arms. But he felt protective, and he held her sleeping body close.

"Weasel was briefly in my custody for reasons beyond my control. He escaped me, however."

"I know," Valeria replied. The silhouettes of the approaching men grew larger. Kikkan felt a sense of urgency to explain.

"I did not treat the boy unkindly."

"If you had, you'd already be dead," Valeria said as the men arrived.

The first stepped forward. He wasn't as tall as Valeria, but he had an athletic build and there was a keenness to his eyes.

"Report," he said.

"We crashed a wedding and stole the bride."

"Damn it, Valeria, you draw too much attention."

"It wasn't my doing, Simyon," Valeria replied, "it was the giant's idea. He says he was sent by Adam Lockhart."

Simyon turned to look at Kikkan with an expression of shock.

"What Valeria says is true," Kikkan said. "I am the last student of Adam Lockhart. With his dying breath, he bid me go to Edentown to find a man with a star-shaped birthmark behind his ear. Are you this man?"

Simyon stood still for a moment, his body trembling.

"Please, I must know," Kikkan urged, "are you this man?"

With a shaking hand, Simyon reached his hand up to pull his hair back from his ear, first one side, then the other.

There was nothing but smooth white skin.

Kikkan dropped his head in disappointment. A shocking emptiness flooded him. Valeria's awareness had made the escaped slave hopeful, but now he had to wonder if he had been manipulated. Perhaps Quillion was right after all? Perhaps Adam Lockhart had been nothing more than a deranged fool.

It certainly appeared that where the quixotic old scholar was involved there existed only riddles and mystery.

"Come," Simyon said, rousing Kikkan from his dark reverie, "we have much to discuss."

Chapter 28: Orders of Separation

A beam of sunlight came in through the eastern facing window and woke Janus. He gazed at the rays for a moment, observing as dust motes lit up in brilliant flares. A strange sensation spread through him, like the first instant of slipping into a hot bath. He breathed deeply, and the feeling was gone.

Don't steal time.

The words echoed through him. One of a thousand mantras that had been drilled again and again and again.

Duty above all.

Sacrifice now, success later.

Merit will be rewarded.

Janus put the thoughts away and slipped from his bed. The floor was cold on his bare feet as he stood and tried to stretch. His surgery had been many months ago, he should have been completely healed; yet a nagging sting persisted. He reached down to touch the scar Orion had given him.

For your own good.

To save your life.

To make you whole.

He thought of Orion to keep his thoughts from Valeria.

What has become of her?

Stop.

A servant approached with robes, and Janus slipped into them. He didn't utter a word, but gestured that he be led out. The servant spun on her heel and set off at an accelerated pace. Janus followed.

On a normal day, Janus would have been busy. Training in the morning, followed by whatever assignment he was working on.

But that would not be the case this morning, as it had not been the case yesterday.

Since the surgery, Orion had kept Janus's schedule open.

"Take some time to recuperate," the white-haired man had said.

Recuperate.

Contribute, or be left behind.

At first the furlough was welcome, but lately anxiety had set in. Orion had little patience for tasks left undone.

Janus arrived at the small table where he took breakfast. The table was outside, on the top floor of one of the higher buildings in San Borja.

From his seated position, Janus could look down at the streets. His apartment overlooked one of the busier thoroughfares, and already people were out at work. Janus watched them, wondering as always how they sustained themselves living like rats in the gutter.

But sustain themselves they did, and that made their lives of some value. The Seneschal wondered how many of them had hope for the future. Did they achieve satisfaction rearing their children on rat meat? When wealthy merchants offered to buy their mature boys and girls, did the street people sell them with a sense of pride and achievement?

A servant set a plate before Janus. The plate contained a nice presentation of two eggs and a portion of bread.

Janus lifted a fork. His musings had left him without appetite, but he wouldn't waste the food. He cut into the eggs.

"How's my favorite patient?" a voice said from the patio entryway.

It was Orion. Only Orion could enter as he wished unannounced.

Janus stood and extended his hand. Orion pushed the hand aside and came forward to wrap Janus in a firm embrace.

"Come now, Janus; after all we've been through together, you're like a son to me," Orion said, smiling.

Janus smiled as well. "Are you hungry?" The Seneschal lifted up his hand to alert one of his servants.

"No, no, no," Orion said, but Janus instructed the servant to bring a similar plate of breakfast. The white-haired man continued, "You look strong as ever, how are you feeling?"

"Good," Janus replied.

"Residual soreness, tightness, any pain at all?"

"No," Janus said, shaking his head to emphasize the point. "I'm ready to resume my duties."

"That's the spirit," Orion said, slapping Janus on the shoulder. The friendly blow reverberated down directly into Janus's scar.

"We've had a development," Orion continued, becoming serious.

"What?"

"Shots have been fired over in Brinewater."

"Shots? Gun shots? This was in a report?"

"They sent a man with a description of the wounds," Orion explained. "That the wounds were caused by gun shots is my assessment."

Janus shook his head in surprise. "Casualties?"

"Red cloaks."

"Who is in command up there?"

"Captain Jesse," Orion replied. "She's a Chandwick."

"As in General Chandwick?"

Orion nodded.

Janus snorted. "Is she any good?"

"She's working through a two-year placement," Orion replied. "The family wanted to give her a playground for a while and Brinewater can't be made worse than it already is."

Janus nodded. "Any witnesses to the shooting?"

"Ha!" Orion barked. "Nobody admits to being there."

"Typical."

"They killed a slave as well."

Janus didn't see the significance. Orion observed the the Seneschal's confusion and elaborated.

"The slave was a cage alarm. The attackers overdosed him with *Bliss*."

That *was* noteworthy.

"Were they sending a message?"

"By shooting people and overdosing slaves? I think it's safe to say they were . . . although what that message might be is up to interpretation." Orion paused, and gave Janus a paternal look. "Well, do you think you're ready?"

Janus didn't hesitate. "Absolutely."

"Good!" Orion clapped his hands together. "Good, good, good. Now, don't go and get yourself shot, I don't want to have to stitch you back together again."

"I don't want that either," Janus admitted.

Orion laughed, then saluted Janus. Janus returned the gesture, but Orion had already headed back out the door.

Alone again, free from tension, Janus let out a sigh.

He looked down at his table.

Orion had not touched his eggs, and Janus's were only half-eaten.

The tall man stood and took the two plates to the edge of the building and began scraping them off into the street. He watched as the bits of food drifted through the air, swooping this way and that before landing in a pile on a slab of concrete.

Maybe a person would find them before a demon or a dog.

If it was a person, Janus knew that chewing his soiled table scraps would be the singular sensory experience of their life.

He turned away, not wishing to have the improbability of his romantic vision confirmed. The dog had a far greater chance.

Chapter 29: Bodies in the Street

Quillion, along with two other men, approached the corpse in the courtyard. Quillion suppressed a gag as he neared. The body had developed an odor so pungent that the removal command had finally been issued. Quillion found the stench unbearable even from the barracks, but as he moved closer, the smell became acidic enough to elicit tears.

Glancing to his right, Quillion didn't need to be informed that the men selected for this duty were the bottom dwellers of Fort Brinewater. Two brutes named Jakko and Bas stood beside him. Quillion had observed them during his time with the red cloaks. Jakko's face was generally plastered with a dim-witted smile, although his proximity to the stench contorted this expression to a grimace of disgust. Bas expressed his displeasure through a furrowed brow, and his sunken eyes were only visible as points of light in the shadowed center.

"Quit dallying," Corporal Dag cried out, "Captain Jesse wants this filth removed immediately." Cole stood beside Dag, tasked with supervision rather than assistance.

Quillion glanced up at the body. He had to remind himself that the thing hanging there had once been a human being. The stench prevented him from pursuing any philosophical musings, but he felt a sense of deep sadness.

Jakko and Bas stepped forward. The pole was thick, and the two of them struggled to find purchase. They strained against the weight, jostling the pole. The movement caused droplets of clear liquid to rain down from the body above. It spattered upon all three straining men. Jakko and Quillion immediately doubled over to vomit, while Bas leaned against the pole and gagged.

"Quit stalling!" Dag cried.

Quillion glanced up at the body and had an idea. "Can you bring a mallet and a spike?"

"Why?" Dag replied.

Quillion had to suppress his annoyance. Even with the declared urgency, the idiot corporal needed to have everything explained. "We can't get hold of the pole. I want to nail a spike into the base so that we have something to grab."

Before Dag could deny the request, Cole trotted over to the smithy shed. He returned with two spikes, which he gave to Quillion. Quillion took the items with a nod of gratitude as Cole returned to his assigned spot beside Corporal Dag.

Pounding the spikes into place produced another shower of repugnant clear liquid, but a few moments later, Quillion and Jakko were straining against the lodged spikes. Bas stood behind them with his hands high, and as the pole lifted, he guided the heavy object to the ground.

Quillion stepped forward and attempted to pull the corpse's arms from where they had been spiked. The flesh was like the soil of a swamp, and as he pulled on the arm, the skin and muscle disintegrated into slime in his hands. Quillion was barely able to stifle his continued gags as he wrestled the body free from the spike. The three men managed to slide it onto a piece of canvas.

"Drag that piece of trash outside," Dag commanded.

Already, the canvas showed signs of moisture soaking through as Quillion, Jakko, and Bas lifted. They half-walked, half-shuffled toward the gate with Dag and Cole trailing. Outside, they made their way past a dozen vacant streets before coming to a vast pit. Here, they rolled the body in and watched as it tumbled down the side.

Beside the edge of the pit was a mound of white powder and a shovel. The powder gave off a strong but not unpleasant odor. Guessing the purpose, Quillion grabbed the shovel and tossed a couple of scoops on the body.

With the chore completed, Quillion regarded the pit. The walls were littered with canvas-wrapped bodies all covered in powder. Flies buzzed so loudly that Quillion could hardly hear himself think. The northerner shook his head.

How do they not see? Advancement is an illusion; this pit contains the only fate the red cloaks will ever know. Yet they persist, loyal to the corrupt captain.

Task complete, the group of five returned to Fort Brinewater. Sergeant Keene awaited them in the courtyard. The sergeant examined their handiwork and prowled around like a caged animal, his trademark grin plastered across his face. The staking pole still lay where it had fallen. At the group's arrival, Keene barked a question. "Who hammered that iron stake into the post?"

"That one," Corporal Dag said, pointing at Quillion.

Keene's face wrinkled up in a sneer, and he shook his head. "The idea was too good to have come from him."

Corporal Dag coughed. "The order was mine, the newbie simply performed the task."

Keene nodded. "Get that pole out of here, then come with me; there's been a slaughter in the risers."

*

The risers turned out to be a group of tall buildings some miles within the outskirts. Sergeant Keene led Dag, Cole, Jakko, Bas and Quillion to join with a group of four men who had been left on site. By the time Quillion's group arrived, the murder scene had already been cold for a day. The killing had taken place during a ceremony on one of the higher levels, but the detachment Keene had left had brought the bodies down to street level for disposal.

"Six kills," Keene said. "Four of them red cloaks."

Quillion regarded the dead. The situation would have been easier to assess had he been able to observe the bodies in the context of the battle scene. Removing the corpses to the street was the equivalent of discarding a major portion of the available evidence.

"Where did they fall?" he asked.

Keene swiveled on him. "I don't remember granting you permission to speak, Private."

"Permission to speak, sir."

"Denied."

Keene took a step closer to Quillion. "You had a fair chance to show what you're made of back at the assembly and you got your skull caved in. Don't think you can talk your way into higher standing now."

Quillion said nothing.

"Troop, listen up," Keene barked. The men snapped to attention. "The private here," he gestured at Quillion, "has volunteered to report to Captain Jesse on this matter."

There was a cheer from the group. Keene chortled.

Quillion approached the bodies and Cole walked up beside him. "When are you going to learn to shut up?"

Quillion snorted. "This is the way it is with thugs: assign an impossible task and revel in the imminent failure. You can't escape that through courtesy. I suspect the red cloaks have become accustomed to laboring in the shadow of one of their number hanging from a post in the courtyard."

Cole's voice dropped to a whisper. "We need to leave."

"Not yet," Quillion replied.

Quillion kneeled to have a closer look at the bodies. Arrows protruded from four of the victims. He studied one of the shafts, which was made of some extremely lightweight material Quillion had never seen. He shifted his examination to the first body that had not been felled by arrows.

The corpse was another red cloak. The head had been caved in by a blow of tremendous force. Quillion kneeled in closer and was able to discern thread marks inside the wound.

Blunt force had done this. Quillion had seen its like before.

"Kikkan," he muttered to himself. "Our paths have crossed again." He spoke the words in a whisper even Cole did not hear.

Chapter 30: The City Beneath

"We're at an impasse," Simyon said. He stood in the low light of the hallway, at the ready but not aggressive. Kikkan didn't begrudge him his demeanor; after all, it was Kikkan who had marched, uninvited, into Simyon's home. Considering the circumstances, the man was actually quite reasonable.

The former slave looked down at the still-slumbering face of the girl he held in his arms. He felt an obligation to ensure her welfare.

"What will become of this one?" he said, indicating the girl.

"What will happen if you place her with us?" Simyon asked, guessing Kikkan's meaning. "She will have to work if she stays here. We barely get by, truth be told."

Kikkan tensed at the words.

"What do you want me to say?" Simyon snapped. "Of course she'll have to work. Would you prefer me to lie to you?"

"You'll force her?"

"Could anyone force you?" Simyon replied. "I've never found force to be an effective motivator."

Kikkan relaxed.

"It won't all be work," Simyon continued, turning to gaze upon the girl. "We'll teach her, train her to defend herself, and make no requests that she surrender anything she would not freely give."

Allie stirred in Kikkan's arms. The former slave pushed a strand of hair from her face.

"I do not intend to turn her over and be on my way," he said. "I would observe for a time."

"Not unreasonable," Simyon replied, "but you'll have to live by our rules."

Kikkan felt weary. He could only nod. Valeria noticed his defenses drop and stepped forward.

"I can take her," she said, lifting the girl.

Kikkan didn't resist. He watched Valeria take Allie and disappear into the shadows.

"You've killed red cloaks?" Simyon asked.

"Yes."

"How many?"

Kikkan shrugged.

Simyon became contemplative. He judged his words before speaking. "I've found it's counterproductive to slaughter the grifters. Left alone, they are directionless bullies who occupy themselves with strong drink or rough sex. But when attacked, they have shown an aptitude for organization, and if a Seneschal should come to lead them, the situation would grow precarious for us."

Kikkan replied with humorless laugh. The lecture reminded him of Quillion's words upon entering the fringes of Edentown.

"So you would advise me not to kill them?"

"It might not matter, you may have already killed enough."

Simyon gave Kikkan a final, evaluating look, but his mind seemed to be made up. He sighed, shook his head, and then made eye contact with the former slave.

"Come, I'll show you how we live."

Simyon led Kikkan through a labyrinth of tunnels hidden within the depths of the underworld. As Kikkan glanced around, he saw people occupying themselves with various chores. Their tasks were mainly foreign to Kikkan's experience, but he observed a few engaged in mundane activities such as cleaning or organizing rooms.

"Valeria and I have been here since last winter," Simyon said.

"Are you the leader of these people?" Kikkan asked.

"We are a collective of free people. We don't have a leader, but I do have influence. We seek only to live our lives and not draw the attention of the red cloaks or the Seneschals."

"Are there many fighting men?"

"Yes, but our numbers are limited. Our warriors are too valuable to risk in needless scuffles with red cloaks."

"Valeria doesn't seem to agree," Kikkan said.

"Valeria has a strong sense of justice, but we must also consider the needs of the weak."

Kikkan nodded; again, he had heard something similar before.

"There are hideaways like this scattered throughout Edentown," Simyon continued. "Every person has a job. We don't have the luxury of allowing people who are not useful to stay."

"What then becomes of such people? Are they exterminated?" Kikkan asked.

Simyon threw him a distasteful look.

"No, we *find* their purpose. In fact, we have succeeded in finding purpose even among those *you* have discarded."

The words confused Kikkan. In response, Simyon pushed open a door to reveal a small room occupied by a single man seated at a table.

Kikkan gasped. The seated form seemed little more than a skeleton covered by a thin layer of skin. The man had the look of a corpse so long deceased even the worms had abandoned the prospect of probing the flesh for sustenance. Yet the body was animated. There he sat, scribbling with his back turned to the door. Points of bony vertebrae stuck through the flimsy garment he wore, and Kikkan wondered how the unsupported spine could keep the heavy head from lolling from side to side. Almost as shocking was the fact that the figure openly engaged in the act of writing. A stack of blank parchment sat to his left, and to the right sat a stack covered in tiny black letters. In addition to the scrawl of words, there were also images drawn upon the pages. The images were precise, with no hint of errant or doubtful lines. Gazing at the man's work, Kikkan immediately sensed that the pages were genuine; that this was a copy of some other text which had perhaps been lost. Instinctively, Kikkan glanced behind the man's ears in the hope of finding the goal to Lockhart's quest, but again his search produced no result.

"Kikkan, I present you Aramis."

The skeleton named Aramis tilted his head. Ever so slowly, he placed his writing utensil down on the table and turned.

Seeing the man from the front was no less terrifying than Kikkan's previous perspective. Aramis's face was drawn tight against his skull. His lips were peeled back in an involuntary, perpetual smile, and his eyes, surrounded by the gaunt cheeks and hairless scalp, were unnaturally large.

Aramis stood. He took a few shaky steps to stand before Kikkan, regarding him with a piercing gaze. Then he looked at Simyon.

"This one has tasted *Bliss*," he said.

Kikkan's eyes widened. The only ones who developed a scent for *Bliss* were those who had consumed the foul drug themselves.

"When you were young, correct?" Aramis continued, turning back to Kikkan. Kikkan nodded. "But they took you off it early. You were lucky."

Aramis made his way back to his seat to resume his mysterious labors. "He's clean," he muttered.

On instinct, Kikkan reached into his pack and withdrew the tattered copy of 'The Demon Haunted World.' He handed it to Aramis.

The skeletal man reached forward to take the item, his head tilting in curiosity. He lifted the book to his face and squinted to read the cover, his already garish features breaking into an even wider grin. "Somebody's playing games with you," he said, offering the book back to Kikkan. The former slave took the proffered tome with a shaking hand.

Simyon gestured for Kikkan to follow and the two men left the room, closing the door behind them. In the hallway, Kikkan tried to recover as he stuffed the book back into his pack.

"Who was that?"

"A reclaimed man," Simyon said.

"Reclaimed from what?" Kikkan's voice quivered with suspicion.

"*Bliss,* of course. He was one of those raging demons you find in the depths. We've reclaimed few, but Aramis is different. He's the first to manifest an ability to write and recall things from the old world. Who knows how many more like him are out there, fighting and dying in the underworld? How many demons have you slain, Kikkan?"

Kikkan's hands began to tremble.

"I thought they lost their humanity when they became monsters. I . . ." The former slave was caught short at the enormity of the revelation. "They can be brought back?"

"Yes," Simyon said, "if you have the care, the time, and the inclination to do so. The question is whether the effort is worth the cost."

Kikkan's face screwed up in confusion.

"The process is dangerous," Simyon explained. "We had to dedicate two men to watching Aramis through the first month and a half of the procedure. After that, there was a period of listlessness during which he was too weak to move or feed himself." Simyon paused. "That's the stage when most of them perish in the wilderness. You won't find wolves or dogs willing to supply a man with nutrients from an eye dropper."

They arrived at another room. Simyon opened the door and gestured for Kikkan to enter. Inside were a bed and a small desk.

"You must be tired," Simyon said. "You may rest here. You are welcome to lock the door if you feel unsafe, but you have my assurance that you will not be harmed. I will post a guide here who will accompany you when you wake. Consider what you have seen."

Kikkan could only nod.

Simyon extended his hand, they shared a brief shake, and then Simyon left the former slave to his thoughts.

*

Back in his own quarters, Simyon rebuked Valeria. "How could you let him assault Lord Marion's sanctuary?"

Valeria raised her brows. "Have you had a look at the man? I'm not sure any of us could have stopped him."

Simyon paced back and forth, veins bursting in his forehead. Rarely had Valeria seen him so angry.

"And I'm sure it was coincidence that this was the wedding of Lord Marion's child. He was one of your regulars at one time, was he not?"

Valeria stiffened. "Are you jealous?"

"Jealous that you put an arrow in the back of one of your old tricks? I don't think jealous is the right word. Don't you see how you've endangered us?"

"Lord Marion was a beast who deserved to die," she replied. "I don't deny I enjoyed sending him on his way."

Simyon smashed his hands down on the table. "At the risk of everything we've achieved!"

Valeria gave a remorseless shrug. "We've cowered long enough. You know as well as I do that we have the men to launch an attack on Fort Brinewater. It's time the scourge of red cloaks was eliminated."

Simyon pinched the bridge of his nose with his thumb and forefinger. "We lack the resources for war. We don't even know what weapons they have. Don't think for one second the red cloaks are the worst of our enemies. What happens if a troop of Seneschal turns up?"

"I don't think they work in troops."

"Be serious!"

Valeria did not back down, but she didn't push the issue further. An uncomfortable silence descended.

Simyon cleared his throat. He knew the archer well enough to know that screaming at her would not change her position. "There's already a lot of heat from that slaughter in the slave's market. Now with this . . ." Simyon's voice trailed off. "Captain Jesse has eliminated the last of her enemies beneath her command. She'll be looking to execute an outsider this time. Now is not the time to act."

Valeria rolled her eyes.

"We'll lose, Valeria!" Simyon snapped. "Would you have me turn over that girl you liberated? I'm sure every conscripted beast infused with serum at Brinewater would love to have something as young and innocent as that to play with for a time." He saw he had scored a point; Valeria's eyes flashed.

"Or we could give them Weasel," she retorted, "his voice hasn't changed yet; they probably wouldn't even notice the difference. Weasel admires you; he'd probably appreciate the opportunity to acquire your limp."

Simyon felt his cheeks flush with anger but he battled for control. He counted twenty breaths before speaking.

"I don't want to give them the girl, or you, or anyone, but what happens if we pick a fight we can't win? Who will be left to provide protection?"

There was no change in Valeria's combative demeanor. "What do you suggest?"

"Fort Brinewater needs to be appeased. We have to give them somebody."

"Who?"

"Kikkan."

"No," Valeria replied. "His strength is too great an asset."

"He's not one of us yet," Simyon said. "Taking him will cost the red cloaks dearly, enough that they'll lose their taste for vengeance. His sacrifice will buy us time. Maybe in a few months we can . . ."

"Months!" Valeria cried. "Years, decades, lifetimes! Lies! It's been the same story since we escaped San Aryan. It's been the same story since I've known you. Hiding in shadows, huddling from the unknown enemy."

"The enemy is real."

"The enemy is killing us without showing his face."

Simyon threw himself into a chair.

"We have to do something," he said. "The red cloaks will not rest without blood. I do not wish to submit to their judgment as to whose and how much will be spilled."

"You're right," Valeria admitted.

The concession surprised Simyon.

"We must face them, but let's do so with at least the hope of some kind of victory. I find the idea of leading Kikkan to a certain death distasteful. He deserves better than betrayal."

"Betrayal is the way of the world; we can only chose when and where," Simyon replied, but now there was affection in his voice. "I remember a woman who betrayed a man only for the sake of a childhood memory."

"Yes, and don't think she hasn't often wondered if she chose correctly," Valeria said.

A flash of pain crossed Simyon's features. Seeing this, Valeria kneeled beside him and put her hand upon his shoulder. "Let us strive to be better than the world, and chose survival only when we must."

Simyon wasn't sure if she had agreed to go along with his plan or not. But she didn't appear to be openly resisting him. He had learned with Valeria that passive acquiescence was the most he could hope for.

"Ok," he said, "but if forced, I will choose my survival . . . and yours."

Chapter 31: Whispers in the Library

A bend of the putrid, septic pool known as the library meandered several blocks away from the site of the wedding massacre. Sergeant Keene forced his men toward the library, taking great delight in the discomfort the stench brought on the troop. Eventually, he grew tired of the game.

"No more complaining," he declared, "or I'll order you to camp in the slurry."

"Yes sir!" came the reply.

The men set up camp and the cook prepared the rancid stew that had become the staple of Quillion's life. Even after a few days of such sustenance, the northerner had started to feel a change in his body. He had lost some sensitivity in his fingers, which had also started to swell, though not yet to the bulbous, unnatural proportions of his fellow red cloaks. His feet, too, had swollen, which had the advantage of improving the fit of his oversized boots. He wondered how long it would take to outgrow the gear.

The trail cook slapped a ladle full of stew into Quillion's bowl and the northerner spun away before the man could offer a second. Quillion found a chunk of broken concrete to sit on and tried to focus on anything other than the multiple assaults on his senses. The smell of the library, however, and the taste of the stew sent his stomach rolling.

Quillion steeled himself against the nausea, knowing he would be beaten if he protested at the food. He stared off into the distance in the direction of the library. The river of septic waste was still. Quillion's questions about the mechanism for how the waterway was flushed had fallen on deaf ears. The red cloaks didn't know, or didn't care. From his current vantage point, Quillion could discern the piles of books left out to rot, tomes open on their spines.

Movement in the distance roused him from his reverie and he squinted. A figure stood on the fringes of the water, kneeling and gazing upon the wreckage, sifting through the muck at frequent intervals. It was the one Dag had named the scholar.

Quillion observed for a while and came to a decision. With an intense effort, he forced down the last of his food, then stood and presented himself to Sergeant Keene.

Keene did not look up at the northerner's arrival. The brutish sergeant reclined with his legs upon some refuse and his back against a brick.

"Commander?" Quillion asked.

Keene failed to acknowledge the address. He stared vacantly, his face plastered with its ever-present mischievous grin. Quillion waited for his salutation to be recognized, but after a moment the northerner elected to make his request anyway.

"Permission to question the man scouring the library," he said. "He's in sight of our current position, and he might have seen something of the massacre."

Keene grunted.

Ambiguous orders were the norm. Quillion saluted. "Thank you, I shall return shortly."

Quillion made his way toward the edge of camp. His movement provoked no small amount of attention. Cole trotted up to him.

"What are you doing?"

"I'm going to interrogate the scholar."

"Are you crazy? You know as well as I do they're just looking for an excuse . . ."

"I have to," Quillion said, "there might not be another chance."

Bas sat at the camp border. As Quillion approached, Bas gave no indication that he recognized his laboring partner from the courtyard.

"I've been given permission to interrogate the man in the library," Quillion declared.

Bas didn't look up. He shrugged and resumed his meal.

Quillion turned to Cole. Cole shook his head.

"I'll be right back," Quillion said.

"Stay in sight," Cole whispered.

*

After a short jog from camp, Quillion soon stood near the scholar. The terrain was soft beneath his feet. The pages of books rotted like flesh beneath the acid bite of city sewage. Every step was a dagger into Quillion's soul as he felt spines bend and pages slip like flesh ripped from the bone.

The scholar grew tense at Quillion's approach, like a wild animal accustomed to being hunted. But a certain air of defeat hung about the man, as if he had lost faith in the usefulness of flight. When Quillion neared to within a few steps, the scholar surprised him by speaking.

"Are you to be my tormentor today?" A series of random vocalizations and garble followed the coherent sentence.

Quillion couldn't decide if the query was directed at him, so he stopped to observe, making no reply. A moment later, he understood that by 'tormentor', the scholar had been referring to the books at his feet. Periodically, the scholar stooped to grasp a tome, flicking off clinging pieces of filth with a brush of his hand.

"Tormentor, tormentor . . ." the scholar said, his voice drifting to a whisper.

The man was rail thin. Quillion was reminded of the slaves of Oshia. Could a quest for knowledge be equally as debilitating as an addiction to *Bliss*?

No, that's the red cloaks talking again. How have they managed to infiltrate my mind with their thoughts?

The scholar opened the book he had gathered and focused on the contents. Instantly, his body went rigid. Quillion was impressed by the outward projection of concentration. The scene lasted only a moment, however, and the scholar closed the book with a scowl. Finished, he didn't throw the book away, but placed it gently on a high spot out of the filth. Moving on, he grazed like an animal along the sloped bank, seeking some mystery with a purpose Quillion could only guess.

Satisfied that the man was not at all spooked by his arrival, Quillion advanced. The closer the northerner got the more of the soft muttering he could hear, but less and less made sense. The word 'tormentor' was repeated most often.

When he was close enough that the scholar could not have failed to see him, Quillion spoke.

"What are you looking for?"

The scholar didn't pause in his strange movements, but neither did he respond.

Quillion moved closer still.

The scholar twisted his head and lifted his arm as if anticipating a blow. Quillion froze. Dropping his voice, he spoke once more.

"I have no wish to harm you. What are you looking for?"

The scholar said nothing. With a trembling hand, he reached down to the muck and extracted another book. He cleaned it off. He reached up to adjust his thin glasses, leaving a smear on his cheek, before staring at the pages with that same, almost inhuman intensity.

Quillion waited until the spell was broken, then he dropped his voice to a whisper.

"I have been sent by Adam Lockhart to learn the secret language of numbers. Do you know this language?"

The query elicited a startling response. The scholar's eyes flicked to Quillion, and for a moment he locked gazes with the stout northerner. The connection lasted only an instant, but in that flicker of time Quillion sensed the presence of far more lucidity in the scholar than might have been expected.

Without a word, the scholar resumed his random searching.

"Wait," Quillion said, but somehow the scholar stopped him. He made no overt motion, but something about the shift of his balance indicated to Quillion that he should listen. The scholar spoke, the words again spilling out in gibberish. Long combinations of syllables that Quillion had never heard placed together before. Long extractions of sounds that might have meant something in an age when complex thinking abounded and masterful ideas could be expressed in language.

Then, all at once, some of the vocalizations became recognizable.

"You do not know the enemy . . ."

Quillion perked up, but he didn't speak, not wanting to interrupt.

"You cannot know what they are capable of. They exist in a world we dare not consider."

The scholar drifted away from Quillion. Quillion mirrored his movement, attempting to stay within earshot but not wishing to startle the man.

"A good person cannot think as they do . . . they are at a disadvantage . . . the enemy cannot be anticipated . . . most would shy away in terror at the depths to which they willingly descend . . . you'll cross over to darkness before you understand."

An edge had entered the scholar's voice, and Quillion stopped his pursuit in the hope of easing the frail man's consternation.

"Their strength of purpose comes from a lack of conscience . . . their advantage has brought about an age of stagnation . . ."

The scholar bent at the waist and began pawing at the earth. Quillion grew concerned; was the man having a seizure? His motions were random, filled with jerks and stops. Suddenly, there was the shriek of metal, and the scholar disappeared from view.

Startled, Quillion ran forward. There, set on a concrete platform extending just above water level, was a black tunnel leading straight into the ground. A heavy capping plate sat haphazard in the opening. Quillion could hear the sound of the man descending a set of metal rungs.

For a moment, Quillion felt the temptation to follow. Instead, he reached down and fit the cap back into position, sealing the tunnel and obscuring the scholar's escape.

*

Quillion knew he was in trouble as he approached the red cloak camp. Though he had been barely out of sight and just on the fringe of earshot, the men had gathered to watch his return. Cole stood beside them, his jaw set.

"Sergeant Keene," Quillion yelled as he neared, "I wish to report that my interrogation of the scholar yielded no useful information."

He continued walking, but he was already close enough to see the sergeant's smile.

"Private," Sergeant Keene said, "you are accused of attempted desertion and are subject to a field punishment of my choosing."

Quillion didn't reply, but the nausea returned.

"What shall it be, men? Arrows? Clubs? Socks and rocks?"

The last option elicited a cheer and Keene grinned.

"Socks and rocks it is. Bas and Cole, restrain the private."

Bas jumped forward at the order. Cole hesitated, but Quillion threw his friend an almost imperceptible nod indicating he should proceed.

Bas secured Quillion's right arm and Cole secured the left. Meanwhile, Keene and the others set about scouring the ground for stones. Some of them withdrew extra socks from their back packs. Others sat and removed one of the garments they already wore. A few didn't have socks and made do with small pouches. Soon, the whole troop stood ready, hefting their makeshift weapons.

Keene stepped forward. "Thank you for supplying us with worthy entertainment this evening," he said.

"Sir, I asked your permission before breaking the circle."

"I did not grant it," Keene replied. He turned to the group. "Two cycles, men! Chest then choice." Keene turned and struck Quillion across the chest with the wool-bound stones.

Quillion felt as if his heart had stopped. The blow left an ache that burned all the way to the back of his throat. He didn't have time to recover before the next strike was upon him, then the next. When the whole troop had gone through, Quillion was barely able to stand.

"Not so tough, is he?" Keene bellowed, to a roar of approval. "Although we knew that from the courtyard. It's good to discover the limitations of our allies in the calm of camp rather than the chaos of battle, is it not?"

"Yes sir," came the reply.

The men came through for the second cycle. Quillion heard the blows rather than felt them. There was only so much pain that would register. He didn't even know who was striking him until Keene's voice echoed out a final time.

"Cole, take your pleasure," the brute commander said. "Put him out for the evening."

Quillion lifted his head. He was prone on the ground now, with no recollection as to how he had gotten there. Cole stood above him, a bulging sock hanging from his hand. The smaller man looked down with remorse.

Then the makeshift bundle of stones swung.

The last thing Quillion heard was a roar of approval.

Chapter 32: Seneschal Provoked

Janus decided to walk.

Too long had he been cooped up in the confines of his apartment; too long since he had felt whole. The straps of the leather pack upon his shoulders felt good, as did the heft of the sword at his hip. The sun on his face and the wind in his hair created the illusion of freedom, and that too lifted his spirit.

In San Borja, he was known, and the sea of humanity lining the streets parted at his approach. He enjoyed the same reception in Bellfore. Yet by the time he entered Stoneforge, the landscape had changed considerably.

The people still scurried at his approach, but they lingered under cover to watch him. Janus could feel their eyes staring from the reclusive shadows of crumbling structures.

Moving on through the long stretch known as the Heights, the people were different still – more rat-like, less human. Their clothing became rougher, threadbare; the glint in their eyes more desperate.

Do not contemplate the ugliness.

The words came back to him from years ago.

Think of pleasant things. Never forget how fortunate you are.

The lessons had been well taught, reinforced with strap and club when necessary. Still, in the midst of a sensory orgy of stench and poverty, the darkness could not help but penetrate.

Finding places to camp was easy. A room could be fortified with the locks and chains he carried. Maybe not so well as to keep enemies out forever, but certainly sufficient to create a racket should there be an attempt to disturb him.

Yet disturbances were few. Even if his appearance did not strike the same terror here that it did at home, they knew him for a predator.

The lesser animals would not attack.

After days of travel, Janus came across a woman skinning a puppy next to a barrel fire. She looked up in silence as he approached. Janus wrinkled his nose. The woman's face was stained with dirt. Only the depths of her wrinkles flashed white as her expression changed.

Oddly, Janus felt greater sympathy for the puppy.

The woman slipped a metal rod into the tiny creature's slack jaw, then fastened the skewer with a thrust that sent the pointed end exploding from the tiny animal's behind. Thus affixed, she placed the meat over the fire to roast, turning one end absently and keeping her eyes on Janus as he passed.

There were times when Janus wondered if poverty was cultivated simply to provide the privileged an ample supply of playthings; entertainment to fill the vast and monotonous hours of recreation. Even gods had to contend with boredom, after all.

From a second floor window, Janus caught sight of a young girl staring at him provocatively. As he looked, she lifted her leg onto the ledge so that the fabric of her skirt fell away on either side. She had caught the scent of wealth, and that smell overrode any concern of inherent danger.

He considered tossing her a coin out of charity, but habit compelled him to gaze up and down the street. He observed a dozen more windows sliding open in response to his apparent interest.

The Seneschal turned back to the street before him and resumed his march.

The residents of San Aryan often remarked that the fringe peasants deserved their fate, as they were lazy, immoral, and too incompetent to work their way to a better life.

Slaves cannot labor their way to freedom.

Another lesson, but from a different teacher.

*

Arriving at a more populous area, Janus met a patrol. At the sight of the patrol, the locals retreated behind slammed doors. There were four in the group; large men in plain pants and tunics with red cloaks slung across their backs. They moved with the confidence of lords.

Carts had been left abandoned, loaded with the wares of desperate sellers who had retreated to hidden alcoves. Many of the street vendors had managed to escape with their property, gathering up the corners of blankets and sprinting off with their products jingling in the center of makeshift bags.

Those who were trying to peddle vegetables did not have the luxury of encumbered escape. Faced with the choice of protecting their goods or sprinting away unscathed, they chose flight.

The red cloaks approached the quiet carts and sifted through the abandoned items. Janus watched as they took a bite or two from various vegetables before tossing the items into the street. He crossed his arms to observe further, when one of the red cloaks saw him.

"Hey, you," the man yelled, pointing with a half-chewed radish.

Janus acknowledged the gesture with a nod.

"Shouldn't you be running?" the red cloak said. The quip elicited a chuckle from his companions.

Janus shook his head. The governed never gave him trouble. But emissaries of local authority blustered and growled; unwilling to relinquish power, even for an instant.

Janus stepped forward.

"Who are you and where are you from?" the first red cloak said, anger replacing mockery in his voice.

"I am a Seneschal from San Borja, here to investigate an incident in Brinewater. Are these the borders of Brinewater?"

"Yes," the first man said, his tone still defiant.

Janus advanced until he stood an arm's length away.

"Are you under the command of Captain Jesse?"

"Yes," the man snapped again.

"Well, take me to her."

The soldier hesitated, but Janus's patience had run out. The red cloak had been foolish to allow him to get close. The Seneschal sprang into action, reaching out with both arms. He grasped the back of the red cloak's neck in one hand and the man's right arm in the other. Taking advantage of his forward momentum, Janus drove his knee into his adversary's abdomen. The red cloak folded in half and Janus drove his opponent's head down to the concrete.

Janus felt the man go limp, and he kneeled on the body.

Only then did Janus regard other three. The assault had been so violent and so fast that the muscle-bound brutes hadn't reacted.

They use the serum in Brinewater, Janus remembered, *the serum slows their thinking.*

"Grab this one," Janus ordered, pointing at the prostrate body, "and take me to Captain Jesse."

The brutes were dullards, but the previous lesson had been clear. They hopped to obey the Seneschal's order.

Janus walked behind them as they led the way, attempting to hide a smirk.

There was a dull ache in his knee that felt surprisingly good.

He felt more alive than he had in a long time.

*

A short while later, Janus stood at the gates of Fort Brinewater behind the red cloaks he had met on the road. Three carried the unconscious body of the fourth.

"Identify yourself!" came a voice from the wall.

The closest red cloak answered as he had been instructed.

"We are in the company of Janus of Edentown, a Seneschal who seeks audience with Captain Jesse."

The declaration caused quite the buzz. Janus hid a smile as the sounds of heated debate floated through the air. Eventually, the gate opened.

Janus stepped into the courtyard. To say that he was unimpressed would be an understatement. To his eye, the place was a slum. Pockets of trash strewn about the wall were outdone only by the uniform filth that clung to the walls.

The men, too, appeared to lack discipline. Everything about them struck Janus as repugnant and slovenly, from their slack-jawed expressions to the way they moved. The red cloaks milled about like preening beasts. They meandered, rather than marched, dropping their hips and rolling their shoulders with every step.

Captain Jesse arrived from the far corner in an explosion of energy. A door slammed and there she was, bathed in sunlight, squat legs churning and amber eyes sparkling with anger. She was a flurry of motion, gesturing to all the men in her presence and hollering reprimands in a transparently inflated show of diligence.

"Hector, that wall needs to be clean, does that look clean to you, Hector?" she howled, even stopping to face the focus of her anger, bending slightly at the waist to bring her teeth closer to the man.

Hector stood with his head bowed.

"Answer me!"

"It doesn't look clean, I will clean it," Hector said, having the wherewithal to grasp a bucket.

Janus noted that Jesse's voice provoked a group of lounging men to scatter like a pack of rats in the presence of a cat. The captain berated a few more as they scurried off, then came to present herself to Janus.

"These men are like dogs and deserve to be beaten," she said.

"Beat them then," Janus replied, "you have that authority. Maybe they'll learn to salute your arrival rather than flee."

Jesse coughed, her face paling a shade, but she was smart enough to snap her heels and salute.

"Captain Jesse Chandwick of Fort Brinewater," she barked, formally presenting herself.

Janus nodded at Captain Jesse's declaration while gazing beyond her. "Where is Commander Marcos? Is he not stationed here?"

Captain Jesse cleared her throat. "Commander Marcos was executed for insubordination several weeks ago."

Janus fixed Jesse with an angry stare. Jesse squirmed under the gaze. When she couldn't take the tension, she spoke up. "I trust my men escorted you adequately."

"They did not," Janus replied.

"My apologies, they'll be dealt with."

"How?" Janus pressed.

"I'll put them on underground patrol for a month."

"Lashings would be better."

Jesse's eyes widened. "Five?"

"Ten," Janus snapped, "today. Starting with him," Janus pointed to the unconscious one, "and include the one you called Hector, this place is filthy."

Jesse nodded.

"As you command. It is an honor to have a Seneschal visit us at Brinewater."

"Yes," Janus snapped, "it is."

Chapter 33: The Mysteries of Oshia

Kikkan awoke in the morning in the hold of the free-men and opened the door to his small quarters. A man sat in a chair outside. He was of middle age and physically well-built. He looked up at Kikkan standing in the doorway and stood, extending his hand.

"Hello, my name is Darrik. Are you hungry?"

Kikkan shook Darrik's hand and nodded at his question. "My name is Kikkan."

"I know. Walk with me."

As Darrik guided Kikkan through the compound, he started up a friendly conversation. Kikkan recognized that it was something of an interrogation, but the former slave didn't object. The denizens of this place would naturally harbor curiosity.

"You're new to Edentown, correct?" Darrik said.

"Yes."

"Why did you come to this cursed place?"

"The whole world is cursed, I think," Kikkan replied.

Darrik snorted. "We've all heard stories of the wonders of faraway lands. Tell me truthfully; is it worse where you come from than here?"

"I come from slavery," Kikkan said. "The deepest, foulest, blackest hole you can imagine is a sunrise by comparison."

Darrik said nothing.

The odd pair arrived at a small room. A man with a greasy apron sat on a stool beside a large kettle. Darrik gave the man a coin, then offered a bowl which was filled with unrecognizable slop. Darrik proffered the bowl to Kikkan along with a spoon, and guided him to a place at a nearby table.

"I owe you for the food," Kikkan said.

Darrik shook his head. "A meal is a small courtesy." Before Kikkan could protest further, Darrik continued. "You're fortunate, we don't always have food. Luckily, the traps were full this morning."

Kikkan stirred the mixture in the bowl. A piece of meat came to the surface. He caught the morsel on his spoon and brought it to his mouth. The flavor was salty.

"Your arrival has caused something of a sensation," Darrik said. "I've rarely seen Simyon this agitated. It will be interesting to see what comes of it."

"Simyon said he's not in charge here," Kikkan replied.

Darrik chuckled. "Well, technically he's not, but we've certainly been a more organized community since he and Valeria arrived." Darrik got serious. "Simyon is a valuable man, he's given us hope. Some of us even think under Simyon's leadership we might be able to take on the red cloaks."

Kikkan noted Darrik's enthusiasm for the idea as he scooped up another spoonful of stew. The former slave was about to question the man further when he looked up to see Simyon approaching.

"I see you've met Darrik," Simyon said. "Very good." He sat down at the table beside the two men. "Is the food to your liking?"

Kikkan nodded. "I'm grateful."

Simyon regarded the former slave, then took a deep breath. When he spoke, it was as much to Darrik as Kikkan. "I've thought the matter over and concluded we have to anticipate a response from Fort Brinewater. We need to make haste to the surface."

"Excellent," Darrik replied. "It's about time we took the fight to the red cloaks."

"I don't wish to fight," Simyon said, "but it may be our hand has been forced." He turned to Kikkan. "Will you accompany us?"

Kikkan locked gazes with Simyon. He did not observe overt deceit in the smaller man's eyes, but he realized Simyon had left some things unsaid. Marching into a fight with a troop of freemen contained inherent danger, but they had fed Kikkan and offered him a place to rest. It didn't take him long to decide he could do worse than to die in the defense of such as these, particularly if his participation bought a place for the girl, Allie, among them.

"I will," he said.

*

The group of freemen selected for the surface party was small. Valeria insisted on joining Kikkan, Simyon and Darrik. Also present were two men named Colton and Miles. Colton was a stout fellow, older than Darrik, with short-cropped white hair. Miles was a thin-faced youth of slight build. To Kikkan's surprise, Weasel was also a member of the group. He approached Kikkan with a mischievous smile.

"No hard feelings about before," he said, extending his hand.

Kikkan enveloped the boy's fingers in his massive grasp and squeezed hard enough that a flicker of concern crossed

Weasel's face. Then Kikkan smiled and released his grip. "I see now there's more to you than I realized."

Weasel rubbed his hand against his leg and laughed nervously. "Any word from your friends?"

Kikkan shook his head in the negative.

"They're probably dead by now," Weasel muttered before wandering off to finish his preparations

Their journey started with a descent instead of the climb Kikkan anticipated. Simyon was secretive about his purpose, but the others appeared mindful of an unspoken task. They stopped at random intervals and directed Kikkan to close and brace doors, or seal off hallways. Kikkan came to understand they were clearing a corridor from the underworld to the surface, but its purpose remained a mystery.

They emerged near the risers where Kikkan had met Valeria and Allie. The wind through the buildings made the former slave reflective, and he thought about the girl. Before he had left, Kikkan had observed Allie sitting with a group of children close to her own age. She had not appeared to be in overt distress, but Kikkan did not truly know what to hope for her. Then again, what could anyone hope for?

A day's walk brought them within sight of Fort Brinewater. Simyon selected an observation building, and the troop climbed to the roof. The chosen structure was taller than the others, affording them a clear line of sight to the distant gates.

"Here we'll be able to watch their movements," Simyon said as he settled in to wait. "Let us hope for no activity."

*

As time passed, the group's nervousness of being on the surface gradually faded into boredom.

Simyon held a pair of cylinders to his eyes and crouched behind cover to peer at Brinewater.

"What is that thing?" Kikkan asked, referring to the cylinders.

Simyon offered the item to the former slave. "Be careful, these are heavy but fragile."

Kikkan took the proffered object.

"Look through this end," Simyon said, gesturing to two soft, black circlets with points of light in their center. Kikkan lifted the item and looked. What he saw made no sense. There was only a blinding blur of harsh white and pink light. Furthermore, the image bounced and shifted erratically.

"You have to hold it very still," Simyon said, reaching over to secure and direct the cylinders. Kikkan looked again, and this time he could make out familiar images. He saw a wall, and windows.

"What is this?" he asked.

"A spy glass, it allows you to see across great distances."

"How?"

Simyon shrugged. "A mystery, more of the miraculous industry of a forgotten age."

Kikkan paused, for Simyon's words echoed the lessons of Adam Lockhart. Simyon caught Kikkan's quizzical expression and laughed.

"In my youth I had a teacher, a woman." Simyon closed his eyes, falling into memory, opening them a moment later after a jolt of recall. "Madeline, that was her name, although I mainly referred to her as 'master.' They all like to be called master."

Kikkan turned to regard the horizon. He felt troubled and couldn't understand why. In a flash, it came to him—the name! He recognized the name.

"I knew a woman named Madeline," he said.

"Everybody has a name," Simyon replied.

"No, she was in the company of Adam Lockhart. She berated me for . . ."

Simyon turned to look at the former slave. "For what?"

Kikkan collected himself against the unpleasant memory. "In my quest for freedom, I killed my master and his wife. Madeline objected to the assassination of the woman."

"Ha!" Simyon barked. "That does sound like her, always claiming a moral high ground." He took the spy glass back from Kikkan and resumed his observation of Fort Brinewater. "The privileged commonly dismiss impoverished suffering as self-inflicted. It's a coping mechanism against conscience which makes possible a life of leisure. Those born to a life of ease must dehumanize the lowborn or be compelled into their service."

"Compelled," Kikkan asked, "by whom?"

"By themselves," Simyon replied. "Compassion is the only weapon capable of fending off the darkness. Slave owners and red cloaks are among those who are conditioned to reject the most essentially human impulse. As a result, over time, they are rendered into beasts."

"Are these more of Madeline's lessons?"

"No," Simyon said, his face turning serious. "I figured that out myself. What happened to Madeline?"

"I left her in Oshia," Kikkan admitted. "I think she went there to die."

"Hmmm," Simyon exhaled, "a person like that doesn't go to die. The Madeline I knew clouded herself in purpose and mystery. Her lessons always stopped just at the point where they started becoming useful." He let his voice trail off.

Kikkan followed Simyon's line of sight. Fort Brinewater rose up in the distance. The building was a hive of activity.

Men crawled around on the ramparts, bustling with directionless industry.

"What else did Madeline teach you?" Kikkan asked.

"Nothing of value," Simyon spat. "Only how to read."

Chapter 34: A Worthy Adversary

Quillion fought to focus. The piercing light of early morning caused his head to spin.

"Shhh," Cole hissed, handing his friend a water skin.

Quillion drank, but said nothing. He was having too much difficulty maintaining his equilibrium to engage in niceties.

"Rest for another hour or so, but be ready to march when we break camp," Cole advised.

The idea of marching provoked an earthquake in Quillion's stomach.

"I'm not sure I can walk."

"You have to," Cole snapped. "Don't think for a moment they won't slit your throat and leave you behind."

Quillion knew Cole was right. The stout northerner leaned back and tried to will his shattered body to mend.

The morning was cool and the sun's rays created long shadows on the husks of the decaying buildings. One man sat awake, guarding the camp. Quillion wondered what he was there for. What did this group fear? Who was out there?

The enemy of my enemy is my friend.

Memories were more discernible than the objects scattered beyond the reach of his arm. The chicken scrawl handwriting on the pages of 'The Demon Haunted World' flashed before his eyes.

Curse Adam Lockhart and his riddles, Quillion thought, *he sent us to our deaths by urging us to Edentown. If I ever recover that book, I'll burn it.*

Yet even as the spiteful declaration manifested, Quillion knew it to be untrue. Even now, he could not free himself from the call of those ancient pages. Even with all the hardship pursuit had brought him.

"Awaken! Present!"

The voice was Keene's.

Quillion gritted his teeth and lifted himself to a standing position. He moved into formation and sought out Cole. Cole was smart enough not to throw his arm around his travel companion, but he provided a firm shoulder Quillion could brace against when necessary.

Keene went up and down the line, stopping in front of Quillion to smirk.

"Looks like you got the worst of it yesterday," he said to scattered chuckles. He leaned forward. "Don't lag behind."

Quillion had no retort. The northerner was broken now. To make matters worse, the sacrifice had won no appreciable gain. His miscalculation in seeking out the red cloaks was colossal. The knowledge of his error, as much as the beating, threatened to steal the last of his strength.

Keene turned and began his march.

"Come," Cole urged.

Quillion hissed in air and willed himself to move, thankful that the troops of Brinewater did not bother with the discipline of a tight formation.

The men marched in silence except for the noise they created by kicking stray pieces of scrap from their path. The sound of tin cans rattling on concrete echoed on the surrounding walls.

The first few steps were the most difficult for Quillion. His head felt like a half-filled bucket of water, listing violently in every direction but the one he willed. Soon he resorted to the old trick of sending his mind away, and then it was merely a matter of placing one foot in front of the other.

Fort Brinewater is not far.

He let the words echo in the darkness of his thoughts.

Fort Brinewater is not far.

Never did Quillion contemplate what arrival would mean—that it was as likely they would put him to work as let him rest. The northerner fended off tendrils of despair and made himself move. All the while, Cole walked beside him, never reaching out but always willing to push with his shoulder when a boost was necessary.

*

Cool air and shadow came to replace the heat and light of day, and it was with an overwhelming sense of relief that Quillion found himself before the black gates. When he stopped marching, he swayed, standing upright through an incredible force of will. The gates opened, and once inside the courtyard, Quillion almost allowed himself a sigh of relief.

Then he saw Captain Jesse.

The woman made no effort to hide the direction of her attention. Her eyes fixated on Quillion like the gaze of a predatory bird. She crossed the open space, and stood in front of Keene.

"Report."

"Ceremony slaying," Keene said. "The archer was involved."

"The archer," Jesse sighed. "We've tolerated that one long enough."

Keene nodded. "There were signs of another. Someone capable of wielding a blunt instrument with enough force to cave in skulls."

Jesse nodded in Quillion's direction. "And him?"

"Attempted desertion," Keene smiled. "I've made him responsible for resolving the slaying."

"Good," Jesse replied, "there's better discipline with a corpse in the yard. But the investigation will have to wait. We have a visitor, and he'd like to have a word."

"Visitor?" Keene asked.

"A Seneschal," Jesse said.

Quillion's head snapped up. Jesse laughed.

"My, that got his attention, didn't it?"

Keene laughed.

Quillion took a deep breath. Indeed, the news had startled him, but not in the way Jesse imagined.

Quillion had endured audiences with Seneschal before. They were cold, calculating and brutal, but they were also capable of recognizing an asset. That was more than Quillion could say of Captain Jesse or Sergeant Keene.

*

Quillion sat at the table, still disoriented. His swollen eye throbbed, as did his lip, and he found it difficult to swallow. The taste of blood filled his mouth. In the pane of glass that lined the wall across from him, Quillion could see his own reflection.

The sight evoked a humorless snort.

He looked like one of the demons now, little more than a bag of meat. Captain Jesse's effort to transform him into something less than human was nearing completion. Any person, no matter how great, could be deconstructed in this manner. What a base and revolting tactic. Appeals to kindness, compassion, love, fell on deaf ears when the pleas were made by something that resembled a creature rather than a man.

Appeals to reason succeeded even less frequently. Ignorance enticed, understanding deterred. Surrender was easier than defiance. Quillion's resolve had been eroded like a stone beneath the sea. The eternal wave had worn him down one infinitesimal splash at a time. His spirit was broken; he was uncaring. In his mind, he could see his body tossed into the air, the head lolling like that of a discarded doll: fluids spilling, entrails scattered. The complexity of all things reduced to mush and dust and refuse and dirt.

Take the coveted thing you call victory. Chaos stacked to order is easily toppled back to its natural state. Violate the unguarded soul as you violate everything . . . you, the faceless, orderless brute; irrational, unreasoning, entitled, lazy . . .

In the depths of his surrender, a mocking smile split Quillion's lips.

But none shall ever say I bore the banner of the enemy. At least I did resist . . . that small victory I claim.

The door opened and in walked a man wearing the uniform of a Seneschal.

Quillion registered the man's physical similarity to Cassius. Normally, that alone would have been enough to send surges of fear down his spine. But in his numbness, Quillion could only observe.

The Seneschal sat down.

"My name is Janus, and you are Quillion?"

Quillion nodded.

"There have been some disturbing events recently," Janus said. "I am hopeful that you'll be able to provide some insight."

"I once knew a man like you," Quillion said.

The interruption caused a change in the Seneschal's expression. Quillion was emboldened.

"Like you, he was powerful, confident and capable. Yet even he had no response as the bullets tore through his torso."

Janus looked startled. "You know of bullets?"

Quillion snorted. "Yes, I know a lot of things. I know of bullets, I know of letters, I know of words and I know of numbers."

"You admit this, though you know such knowledge is forbidden?" Janus didn't appear rattled, but Quillion had not finished.

"I know that you know of all these things as well. I've been interrogated by a Seneschal before. Tell me, did you hear of that interview by direct consultation, or were you handed a written report?"

"Why do you say this," Janus asked, a hint of surprise entering his tone, "when you know the penalty for such talk?"

"Would you believe my claim that I was pledged to the service of Cassius of Edentown if I did not make such statements?"

Janus nodded. "Very well, let's proceed. Did you kill Cassius?"

"No," Quillion replied. "No, I couldn't have killed him, as you can see I lack the strength."

"Did you kill the red cloaks in the market north of here?"

"Don't pretend you care about them," Quillion replied, "you know as well as I do the red cloaks only exist to torment the wretched."

"Answer the question," Janus said.

"No, I didn't."

Janus clenched his jaw and nodded slowly. "Well, who did?"

Quillion smiled. "He's out there. He's strong. He won't be reasoned with and he won't be bought. He's the one who is giving the red cloaks and Captain Jesse so much trouble."

"Who is he?"

"He is Adam Lockhart's pupil."

Janus paled slightly. "You know of Adam Lockhart?"

"Wasn't that in the report?"

Janus tapped the table with his fingers. "What do you know of Adam Lockhart?"

"Lockhart told us to come to Edentown. He told us to find the literate thief."

"The literate thief? Who is that?"

Quillion laughed. "A phantom, a ghost, a delusion of a deranged and dying old man. Lockhart told us of his former pupil in Edentown; a man who was versed in the language of numbers. Lockhart said this one could teach us, but he didn't know where he was. He didn't know what he looked like. I call him 'the literate thief,' since he's probably scrounging in the gutters, furious that the promises of power from his secret knowledge resulted only in desolation."

"How were you to recognize him?"

"He has a distinguishing mark."

Janus's face tightened. Quillion noted the response.

"What is the distinguishing mark?"

Quillion blinked away the bleariness that continually crept into his vision. He wanted as clear a view as possible of the Seneschal's reaction.

"The literate thief has a star-shaped birthmark behind his ear."

Janus nodded and looked away.

Has he heard of this person before?

Are they looking for him?

Does he exist?

Quillion's own curiosity surprised him. Deep, deep down, he suddenly felt a flicker of hope.

"Did you tell anyone else of this?" Janus asked.

"No."

Janus continued. "You know the man who killed Cassius?"

"Yes."

"Would you give him up in exchange for your own life?"

"Yes."

"So easily? You must not know him all that well."

"I traveled with him for many months, he was my companion and ally," Quillion replied.

"Yet you'd sacrifice him to save yourself?"

Quillion laughed, and there was real humor in the noise. "I've long since found it more prudent to trust an admittedly dishonest man than one who praises his own virtue. A man who admits dishonesty demonstrates he's at least capable of some form of truth. There's no reason to believe that the man who claims virtue will tell you anything but lies."

Janus's eyes widened.

"You know this already, don't you?" Quillion said. "Honestly, aren't you tired of the deception? Doesn't it make more sense for there to be only one set of rules that we all live by? One truth? Don't you find maintaining the duality exhausting? One set of rules for the powerful, and one set of rules for the weak, so you never have to hold yourself to the same standard as those you rule. What happens when you slip a rung? Did you ever think of that? Does it not weaken us to enforce a belief system we know to be false?"

Janus said nothing. He pushed himself away from the table.

"Who is the warrior who killed Cassius?"

Quillion looked down.

"He is an escaped slave from Acheron who uses a simple pipe as a weapon."

"What is his name?"

"Kikkan."

Janus walked to the door, but paused. "You condemn this Kikkan to death?"

"No," Quillion replied, "I'm not in a position to condemn anyone."

Janus considered. "Get some rest tonight," he said, "you'll be marching with me in the morning."

A flicker of a smile played across Quillion's lips—that was the result he had hoped for.

Chapter 35: Leap of Faith

The gates of Brinewater cracked open and Kikkan, Simyon, Valeria and the others turned as one to regard the swinging doors. Light poured through the crack in the wall and grew more blinding as the gap grew wider. The illumination was no more than a trick of the sun, but something about the sight sent a shiver of disquiet down Kikkan's spine.

Instinctively, the former slave slipped his pipe from the knapsack that hung perpetually on his broad shoulders. The weapon grounded him, recalling his first evenings of freedom, huddling in an abandoned house a day's run from his former master's estate.

"So they are coming," Simyon whispered. Somehow, the tenor of his voice cut through the ominous air that had gathered. Kikkan exhaled. "One, two, three," Simyon said, lifting his spyglass to count, "four, five . . ." He stopped short and pulled the glass away from his eyes to squint into the distance before pressing the object back against his face. "Something strange," he said, "there in the center."

Kikkan looked, but could make out no more than a dark shape. Still, that was enough to bring back the feeling of disquiet that had been slowly ebbing.

"May I look?" he asked.

Simyon handed him the ancient glass, the smaller man's attention fixed on the former slave's reaction to the new development. Kikkan took the glass and peered through the eye hole as he had practiced. He scanned the group and could see that there were many. "What is the count?" he asked.

"Twenty," Simyon replied, "plus a—"

"Seneschal," Kikkan finished. The former slave couldn't see Simyon's reaction, but the commander of the underground flicked a glance at Valeria.

"You know of the Seneschal?" Simyon asked.

"Yes." Kikkan lowered the glass to look at him. "One pursued me in Acheron."

"And his fate?"

Kikkan lifted the glass again. "I split his head open." He indicated the pipe with his free hand.

"You've killed a Seneschal?" Valeria asked, with as much awe as incredulity in her voice.

"He was wounded," Kikkan replied. He continued to scan the group, and paused as he encountered something else familiar. The man was a swollen mess, but he recognized him anyway. Beside him walked the other, lending support.

Quillion and Cole.

"What is it?" Simyon asked, noticing a new tension in Kikkan's stance.

Kikkan lowered the spyglass and returned the item. His eyes met Simyon's. Should he tell them of Quillion and Cole? What had Weasel disclosed to Simyon about Kikkan's companions?

In a flash, Kikkan decided. The two northern sellswords marched with the enemy. When the battle began, Kikkan did not need the status of his former friends slowing the reactions of his current allies. Quillion would be granted a chance to explain himself if the opportunity presented, but not at the risk of Kikkan's well-being.

"Nothing," Kikkan said as Simyon lifted the weight of the glass from the former slave's hand. "Nothing at all."

*

Janus smiled as the troop stepped beyond the gates of Brinewater. He fell back until he was walking alongside Quillion. The stout northerner did not welcome the Seneschal's presence, but Quillion was hardly in a position to protest. He had mended enough on two nights' rest to stay upright, but the majority of his body throbbed in agony. In his current state, Quillion knew he would be at a disadvantage in a fight, and that a fight was inevitable. Still, this fate was preferable to whatever torment Captain Jesse might have planned.

"It feels good, doesn't it," Janus said, "to return to the wilds?"

Quillion twisted a skeptical, swollen eye to regard the Seneschal. Janus caught the glance, and his handsome features hardened.

"I won't be much good to you when the battle begins," Quillion said.

Janus nodded. "But I had to bring you. You know that. What's waiting for us out there, Quillion?"

Quillion closed his eyes and tried to will his headache away. "Death."

"Death awaits us all," Janus replied.

Quillion noticed Sergeant Keene glancing up at them from the back of the group. His expression alternated between spite and resentment.

"Take us to the market where your fellows were slaughtered," Janus barked to the men at the front of the column.

"Keep your eyes on the terrain; I expect we'll draw swords before the day is done."

"You're overly confident, aren't you?" Quillion asked. Sometimes words escaped his lips before his brain had a chance to intervene.

Janus locked eyes with him, and he returned the stare.

"What good are swords against bullets?" Quillion asked.

"What good is an educated mind against a club?" Janus replied.

Quillion winced. Something about the sentiment cut him to his essence.

"You've mistaken my meaning," Janus continued, noticing how Quillion crumpled. "The educated mind does win."

With that, Janus picked up his pace, leaving Quillion to wonder.

*

"The market," Simyon said as he watched the movements of the troop. "That is the route they're taking." He turned to regard his small contingent. "We'll set up an ambush in the narrows. Weasel, go and prime the corridor."

Weasel gave a sharp nod before jogging off. Kikkan didn't know what the order meant, but the others seemed to tense at the command.

"We'll take the high road," Simyon said, then turned and made his way toward the stairs leading down from the roof.

Kikkan was about to follow when he felt a light touch on his arm. Valeria stood beside him. Something about her demeanor compelled Kikkan to pause.

Miles and Colton tossed Valeria disapproving looks, but their will was nothing compared to that of the lethal archer.

Her glare alone sent them scurrying, leaving her and Kikkan to follow behind the main group.

"They'll arrange for you face the Seneschal," Valeria whispered.

"I do not fear the Seneschal," Kikkan replied.

"You should," Valeria said, "a lot can happen in battle. Be mindful. You have my word none of my arrows will strike you. I can make no other guarantees." She gestured that he fall into line before her, and Kikkan did so, impressed by her ability to command.

Kikkan appreciated the opportunity to contemplate Valeria's words beyond her physical sphere. Walking alone, he received fewer spiteful backward glances from the men loyal to Simyon.

What had the archer meant? Betrayal?

Kikkan regarded the freemen with a new perspective. As they scurried through the wreckage and debris on their way to the narrows, Kikkan's concerns lessened. Simyon's men were awkward, barely able to keep their feet beneath them. The former slave had little doubt he could dispatch them all with minimal effort. In fact, Kikkan wondered what use they would be in the fight ahead.

Six against twenty. Twenty plus a Seneschal, which could probably be considered a doubling of the enemy's strength. Kikkan considered Simyon. That one seemed clever; he reminded the former slave of Quillion to some extent. Kikkan doubted Simyon would send them into battle without a plan for extraction. Correction—Simyon would have a plan for *Simyon's* extraction.

Up ahead, Colton slipped in the stairwell they were navigating and caught himself against the wall. He snapped an angry glance at Kikkan, as if the former slave were somehow responsible for the misstep. The flash of undeserved contempt brought realization to the former slave.

Kikkan was the extraction plan. He would be left to battle while the others slipped away.

One against twenty-one.

The former slave nodded to himself. Oddly, he felt little resentment. Rats, too, fled at the approach of the wolf. Simyon and his band of pathetic weaklings were right to fear him. But what of Valeria? Kikkan didn't need to glance back; he could feel her presence. That one was not afraid to bring death duly deserved. He had seen her arrows fly at the wedding, consequences be damned.

Could she be counted on?

The truth would be revealed in battle. Cowards fled; traitors struck. There was no use in fretting over a mystery soon to be revealed. Kikkan would keep his wits about him, and save strength to punish those who proved false.

The former slave had just arrived at his conclusions when he came to a ledge where Simyon and the others had gathered. A cable was affixed to the wall. Simyon gazed up to see the line was attached to the top of the adjacent building.

"These cables allow us to traverse the streets without descent," he explained. He gestured at a trailing rope that was affixed to the cable. "After I have crossed, pull the cable back with this." He hauled the cable until it was taut, gripped it tightly, and stepped off the ledge.

The distance to the other building was not great, although Simyon still lost a floor of elevation in the swing. As Simyon's feet touched the floor on the opposing structure, he released the cable. Immediately, Miles began hauling in the rope to bring the cable back. A moment later, Miles had joined Simyon on the other side.

"Keep your feet in front of you," Valeria said. "If it looks like you're going to strike a column, brace yourself with your legs."

She held out the cable to Kikkan and he gave it an experimental tug. Would it hold him? He was larger than the others.

Kikkan made a loop to put his hand through. A kernel of doubt grew in the back of his mind. Unwilling to allow the negative emotion more strength, Kikkan stepped out into space.

Wind whistled past Kikkan's ear as he swung across the gap. He had resolved not to look down as he launched, but look down he did. It was strange to see the world below him, and nothing around for support but the extra length of cable and the knot of the trailing rope below. At the last moment, Kikkan looked up to see Simyon reaching out. Kikkan lifted his feet, noticing there was a danger he would strike the opposing floor. Simyon caught him.

"Well done," Simyon said.

Kikkan smiled. "That . . ." he said, surprised at how quickly all his tension had evaporated, "was fun."

Chapter 36: The Burden of Leadership

Quillion marched in silence. His body ached in dull discomfort. Better still, he was able to think again. The mechanisms of his mind twirled, not at their usual speed, but with a significant acceleration over what he had experienced the last few days.

The Seneschal's presence changed the dynamic of the red cloaks. Some semblance of order had been restored to Captain Jesse's mob. Quillion wondered how long Sergeant Keene and the others would stay in line. Inevitably, they would test the warrior. How many would Janus the Seneschal have to kill before comprehension dawned upon the dim red cloaks?

One?

A dozen?

All of them?

Quillion could only hope for the last. The red cloaks were stubborn.

The northerner glanced around. The streets led into a collection of buildings that had been constructed very close together. Even as he made the observation, Quillion recognized the danger. His head was on a swivel, moving back and forth across the horizon, but suddenly he stopped.

There!

His heart filled with a swell of hope. In the fog of the last few weeks, he had almost forgotten, but the appearance of the enormous red and white sign rising up helped recall his stashed asset.

The gun!

Chance had brought him close; the opportunity could not be squandered. It would take only a distraction. Was he fit enough to run? Could he slip away? Could he find the hiding place in time?

If it came to a battle of blades, Quillion was lost. His strength was not sufficient. But with the gun in his hand . . .

Resolve settled over him.

Death was a certainty along his current course. The time had come to correct his heading.

*

Kikkan crossed another chasm on a hanging cable. His landings were softer now, and he stood on the ledge holding the cable away from the side of the structure so it couldn't catch on any obstructions below. Valeria stood with Miles and Colton on the ledge across the span. Kikkan nodded at her to begin hauling the rope, but the archer shook her head. Kikkan was confused.

"They aren't joining us," Simyon explained.

"Why not?"

"Valeria is going to seek higher ground. The troop of red cloaks is approaching the narrows. They'll pass below."

"You still haven't told me how you intend to defeat them," Kikkan said. "They outnumber us significantly."

"I'm only here to orchestrate this battle," Simyon replied, "not fight it. There's too much risk in fighting." The leader of the freemen kneeled beside a column overlooking the ledge. Weasel arrived on the street below. Simyon whistled to get the boy's attention, and a moment later the lad stood beside them.

"It's done," Weasel said, "the scent is in the air. They'll be gathering soon."

Simyon nodded as Kikkan's face darkened in suspicion. Contemplating the street, Simyon pulled two sealed bags from the chest pocket of his jacket. The bags were made of plastic, and appeared to be filled with white powder.

"What's that?" Kikkan asked, knowing the answer all too well.

Simyon cast him an apologetic look. "We kept the corridor open to the underworld for a reason."

"It's *Bliss,* isn't it?" Kikkan asked with disgust. "You've ground it to powder." He turned to Weasel. "You're the one who collects it. Is this why you approach every new visitor to Edentown? In preparation for moments like these?"

Simyon offered Weasel a small packet. The lad maintained a wary eye on Kikkan. Darrik, too, scrutinized the former slave. The pantomime was almost amusing to Kikkan. If the large freeman felt like dying, he was welcome to try something.

"Go to the high point and loose this if the frenzy ebbs," Simyon ordered Weasel. "Then take the shaft below. Use your best judgment and be careful. This is not a game."

Weasel nodded, snatched the packet and ran.

"The powder has already been put out, Kikkan," Simyon said, turning back to the street. "Once the scent is in the air, the demons form a pack. This whole operation depends on timing. What does it matter, anyway? How many demons have you killed?"

"Things are different. Now I know they can be reclaimed," Kikkan said. "You're not herding animals, they are people. Who knows what knowledge is lost when their skulls are cleaved? What happened to your belief that human beings must embrace compassion?"

Simyon set the remaining bag of powdered *Bliss* on the ground and stood. He wore a frustrated expression. "What choice do I have? You and Valeria slaughtered everything in sight, consequences be damned. You conceived this battle, and now you dare to lecture me? How about shouldering your share of the responsibility? I'm not a god, I'm a mortal trying to clean up your mess. We cannot stop the battle, we can only hope to minimize the sacrifice. Does that enrage you? Then pull that pipe from your pack and end my suffering! I'll thank you for it."

The raw emotion in Simyon's face gave Kikkan pause.

There might have been a time when Kikkan would have rejected Simyon's words on principal alone, but the former slave had seen too much in recent months. He recalled Quillion's admonishment from their camp on the outskirts of Edentown. The former slave had to admit that Simyon's position was not without reason, though the realization made him sick. Sympathy caused the muscles in the large man's face to ease. Simyon, too, relaxed.

The leader of the freemen kneeled and slipped a thin glove over his hand.

"Don't let any of this powder get on you or you'll be pursued," he said. Reaching in to grab a handful, he scattered the dust into the air. The particles sparkled like diamonds in the sunlight. "The demons will quest for the scent. When I drop the remaining contents, the horde will feast."

"You're sure they'll come?" Kikkan asked.

"They'll come. It's inevitable. We save the ones we can and the others fight our battles."

"The others save you," Kikkan corrected.

"Yes."

"Then you must revere their sacrifice by acting with honor," Kikkan said.

Simyon's jaw tensed, but whether the expression indicated annoyance or resolve, Kikkan couldn't tell.

Chapter 37: The Uncertainty of Battle

What is Janus thinking? This is a perfect spot for an ambush, the Seneschal should know better.

Almost, Quillion thought of speaking up. His survival was on the line as much as anyone's, and the northerner did not make a habit of cowering in terror and submitting to the poor judgment of others. A week ago, he would have spoken, but the events of the last few days had slowed his tongue.

It didn't matter if he was right; it didn't matter if his opinion might save lives. They only cared that he show obedience. To doubt his captains was arrogant, reckless, foolish.

Lies!

As Quillion walked, he scoured the walls for escape routes and cover. A flutter of motion in his peripheral vision caught his attention, but when he turned to get a better view, he saw nothing. The motion had come from several stories up, and as Quillion stared, he noticed an unusual number of dust motes catching the sunlight and drifting slowly down. A pit began to harden in Quillion's stomach and he drifted closer to the cover of the walls.

He took a deep breath, licked his lips, and paused.

There was a flavor there; a flavor he recognized from the wilds of Oshia.

Bliss.

Quillion pulled his hood over his head and tightened his cloak around his shoulders. Cole noticed the action, and Quillion gave the lean swordsman a silent urging to follow suit. Cole did as he was bid.

Quillion felt his heart rate rise.

Somebody's here, they're dropping Bliss on us, that can only mean . . .

The stout northerner cast furtive glances to the left, right and behind. He peered deep into the shadows, mapping the terrain, preparing. He recorded everything in a combination of heightened awareness and desperation.

Then, in the distance, the shadows came to life.

"The enemy is upon us!" Quillion shouted, diving into an alcove as the street erupted. Arrows and stones rained down from above, and a cloud of dust enveloped them. Already, the taste of *Bliss* the northerner had caught on the wind began to alter his perception. In the sudden, desperate confusion, Quillion saw little, but he could make out wild eyes, rending claws, and flashing, feral teeth.

*

Kikkan watched the chaos unfold. A horde of demons came sprinting down the street, following the corridor up from the pit of the underworld, called by their unnatural longing. The demons moved fast, kicking up a cloud of dust which enveloped the unsuspecting red cloaks. There came a crash, and Kikkan turned to see a large structure of metal and stone topple down upon the troop's flank. He looked up and caught sight of Valeria loosing arrow after arrow into the fray.

The former slave's eyes darted back to the front of the column. He hefted a stone and sought out the Seneschal. The demons moved like a uniform beast, raking the red cloaks with the frenzy of addiction. Kikkan identified the dark one, but the man moved impossibly fast and dove into the lower floor of the building where Kikkan crouched. The Seneschal's action was more than reflexive.

Had he anticipated the ambush?

Kikkan didn't have time to contemplate as there were plenty of red cloaks in need of slaughter. The former slave sent his stone hurtling below. He found satisfaction in the thud of impact, though not equal to the pleasure gained from the reverberations along his pipe at the delivery of a death blow. The large warrior did not waste time in lament, knowing he would have his share of hand to hand combat before the day had ended.

Simyon and Darrik were busy sending arrows down into the confusion, and Kikkan scrambled to launch stones and topple stacks of cinder blocks into space. A sheen of sweat broke upon his brow, and as he wiped the traces away, he again caught sight of Valeria across the corridor. The speed with which she drew and launched arrows was something to behold, but suddenly she paused. Amidst the din of battle, Kikkan could not make out her words. But he saw her point and then turn to run.

Kikkan saw several red cloaks break off from the main group and go running down a corridor that paralleled Valeria's heading. Had others escaped? Did Valeria run in flight or pursuit?

A cacophony of screams mixed with snarls, coughs, and roars. The dust cloud rose, momentarily obscuring Kikkan's view. The former slave glanced at Simyon, and realized Valeria's retreat had not gone unnoticed.

"Valeria!" Simyon called. "No!" But Valeria was gone. Hysteria seemed to overcome Simyon, and he and Darrik erupted into action. Simyon slung his bow on his back and grasped the cable to swing out across the chasm.

"What are you doing?" Kikkan asked. "You'll give away our position!"

Simyon ignored Kikkan's words and readied himself to swing. Kikkan reached up and grabbed the cable, stopping it.

Simyon's eyes met those of the former slave. Kikkan could see it was madness rather than betrayal which had overcome the leader of the freemen. The former slave opened his mouth to speak, but his words were halted as Darrik came at the large warrior, swinging a heavy club. Kikkan released Simyon's cable and caught the club in the air. Immediately, Simyon launched himself to the adjoining building.

For a moment, Darrik contested Kikkan's hold on the club. The former slave gazed at the smaller man with contempt.

"Don't be a fool," Kikkan demanded. "The Seneschal entered our building; do you wish to face him alone?"

Kikkan was surprised when common sense prevailed. Darrik released the club and took a step back. At first, he reached for his bow, but Kikkan shook his head. Darrik settled for the stones and turned his back to Kikkan to resume launching projectiles at the battle below.

Kikkan backed away, tossing Darrik's club to the ground and drawing his pipe. Reaching the stairs, he turned and sprinted down. He would deal with this minor altercation later; for the moment, he had a Seneschal to kill.

*

An explosion of falling stones covered Quillion's retreat into a small alleyway between buildings. The space was narrow, and the northerner could only fit sideways. Cole followed.

"Quillion!" came a shout from behind. It was Corporal Dag. "Stop, coward!" Quillion continued his progress through the small space. Back in the corridor, Dag howled back into the growing chaos. "Keene, Quillion's fleeing!" But the words were drowned out by the explosion of battle. Dust rolled through the alley, followed by screams and the ring of blades.

Quillion looked back to see three red cloaks push into the alley in pursuit.

"They're following us," Cole shouted.

"That was inevitable," Quillion replied, hoping he could stay ahead of the group in his weakened state. Achieving the end of the alley, he pulled his cloak from his shoulders.

"Drop that," he said, gesturing to Cole's own cloak, "it has been doused with *Bliss*."

Quillion threw the garment into the alley and began sprinting in the direction of the building with the red and white sign. His head throbbed with every footfall and he had to utilize all of his concentration to maintain his balance.

They created quite a gap as their pursuers squeezed through the last tight section, but all too soon the sound of pursuit could be heard.

Quillion ran, though it felt as though he were pushing through water. He knew he had no time to search, so his direction must be precise. Scouring his memories, he tried to recall the exact shape of the door. But the light was different now, and nowhere he looked did the lines seem to accord with his memory.

Where is it?

A familiar structure rose up before him. Could that be . . . ?

The boots echoing behind seemed to be gaining.

There was no time to doubt. Quillion dove through the door, knowing an error would doom both him and Cole to death.

Chapter 38: Unexpected Meeting

Simyon felt it again: the strange tightness across his chest; a fearful acceleration of his heart; the frantic pull of desperation. Valeria had gone! What was she doing? Where had she fled to this time?

He could keep the episodes under control when she went on patrol, out of his sight. There were always tasks available to hide the trembling in his hands, always ways to distract himself from thinking about the void that was left when she was absent.

Yet in the fever of battle, his most essential emotions rose inexorably to the surface. The adrenaline of the fight accelerated his thinking, and when she turned and ran, Simyon lost control.

All at once, he realized his mistake. All at once, it was clear.

Valeria had never intended to follow Simyon's battle plan. She had her own agenda. She wished to deal Fort Brinewater a crippling blow; there was no telling what risks she would take to achieve this end.

Simyon landed on the ledge above the turmoil in the street and sprinted up to where Valeria and the others had taken position. Footprints in the dust indicated the direction of their retreat.

Simyon scampered to the edge of the building. A narrow alley was all that separated this structure from the next. Valeria's group had crossed over. Without a second thought, Simyon leaped across the minor distance.

He tried to gain some clue from his sense of hearing, but the only sounds were those of the raging chaos below. Valeria had rushed on.

Whom was she pursuing?

What had she seen?

Simyon sprinted, not really knowing what he intended to achieve.

This woman will be the death of you, his inner voice admonished. Simyon nodded to himself.

That, he already knew. He was hers. Worst of all was that she knew it, too.

*

Kikkan found the stairs and began his descent. He knew danger waited below, but he kept glancing behind to make sure Darrik had no ambitions to slip a dagger in his back. The former slave dropped down several levels before he turned all his focus forward.

He could not take the Seneschal lightly, even at the risk of being struck from behind.

Kikkan slowed.

The element of surprise was on his side, and the former slave would need every advantage.

It was true that Kikkan had slain Cassius of Edentown, but that adversary had been sorely wounded. Still, Kikkan had grown in strength and skill since the encounter, and he felt he had a reasonable chance of overcoming whatever new terror he would meet.

A few turns of the dusty stairwell later, Kikkan passed through a door hanging haphazard in its frame. In the remaining moments he had before the fight, Kikkan doubted he would find a better opportunity for ambush. The former slave crouched against the wall. He took stock of his position while attempting to recover his breath and calm his thundering heart.

Between the shadows and the door, Kikkan hid. He gazed through a crack to observe the stairwell.

Could he spring from here and land a blow before the Seneschal saw him?

Perhaps.

Was the distance too far?

Maybe, but on short notice, this was the best trap Kikkan could construct.

He crouched down, pipe in hand, and waited.

The din continued below, voices cried out in agony along with the thud of metal striking flesh. The noise was terrible. So much evil went unpunished.

A noise on the stairwell interrupted his thoughts. Kikkan peered through the crack and his blood froze. A shadow made its way up the stairs. A black, athletic figure climbing smoothly, reaching out with a white hand to grab the rail and pull itself upward.

Kikkan tightened his grip.

The shadow paused. The figure had been about to turn and continue the climb when he swung to face the door where Kikkan crouched.

"Are you there?" the shadow said.

Kikkan did not reply, dejected that his ambush had been perceived.

"Are you the one they call Kikkan?"

The sound of his name unnerved the former slave. What powers did this one have to identify him?

"Are you the student of Adam Lockhart?"

Kikkan did not wish to endure further provocation.

"I am," he said, and the sound of his own voice increased his resolve. He stood, pushing the door open. Now that he had gained his feet, Kikkan realized that he towered over the Seneschal. There was nothing to fear from this one. *Nothing to fear . . . nothing to fear . . .* "One of us shall go and one of us shall stay," Kikkan said, his hands tensing in preparation.

"Wait," the Seneschal replied.

Kikkan lifted his pipe to shoulder level and braced his feet against the wall. He would not lose to a trick.

"Wait!" the Seneschal said again. "My name is Janus, and I would talk to you."

"What do we have to talk about?" Kikkan snapped.

"I am holding no weapon," Janus said, lifting his empty hands.

"That's your mistake."

"It's not a mistake, it's an order. You see, I knew Adam Lockhart too."

Kikkan's face screwed up in confusion. He had the distinct sense that something strange was about to happen.

"You were tasked with hunting him?" Kikkan snarled.

"No," Janus said, and in a lightning fast motion, he pulled back his hood and turned his head sideways. "Adam said you'd be coming. He told me to find you. Do you see?"

Kikkan squinted, then all at once his eyes widened.

There, nestled within the Seneschal's black locks, was a distinctive birthmark in the shape of a star.

*

Hoping against hope, Quillion pushed through the door. He risked a quick glance back as he entered and his heart sank.

Their pursuers had closed the distance. He had run out of time.

"Can you hold them, Cole?" he yelled.

Cole grunted, drawing his sword.

The door opened to a narrow room, so at least Cole would have the advantage of engaging them individually.

Quillion sprinted in without giving his flank another thought. It wouldn't matter anyway if he was wrong. Cut down from behind or cut down from the front; what was the difference? Quillion focused all of his attention on his surroundings.

Was this the right room?

Despair crept in. He cast about. Passing a wall of lockers, he felt a tingle of encouragement.

Perhaps . . .

Then, turning a corner, his eyes fell upon his objective. The sealed pipe extended from the wall. Yet with the sight of the hiding place came the clang of crossed swords.

Quillion dove forward and scratched at the sealed cap. At first it didn't turn, but Quillion applied all his strength and with a shriek, the cap came loose. The stout northerner spun the cap until it fell from the pipe. Quillion's hands quested inside the tube.

The grip of the gun felt good on his fingers and Quillion sprinted back into the hallway.

Cole was upright but giving space. Dag was upon him, driving Cole back with overhand blows.

"The coward has returned," Dag howled, seeing Quillion enter. Four men stood behind the grim corporal. "I'm going to enjoy dismembering the two of you."

Quillion stepped forward, reaching the gun past Cole's right shoulder. Dag lunged as Quillion pulled the trigger, and the corporal's head exploded with the full force of the blast.

Cole winced in pain and dropped to his knees at the gun's report, but Quillion didn't have time to check on his friend. The red cloaks behind Dag recoiled in surprise, not understanding how their moment of triumph had turned into defeat.

Quillion pulled the trigger again, then again, and two more red cloaks fell to the ground. The last two tried to escape. They sprinted toward the door. Quillion took aim and shot the fourth in the back. But the fifth made it outside.

The northerner leaped over Cole, hoping the swordsman had not sustained any serious injury. Arriving at the door, Quillion saw his target sprinting off down the street. He had only one shot remaining. He took the time to stabilize himself and aim.

The northerner pulled the trigger a final time. The explosion sounded, and the fleeing red cloak crumpled to the earth. Quillion let loose a sigh of relief just as a black arrow thudded into the crumpled red cloak corpse at the door. Quillion dropped to his knees and fought to discern the arrow's source. He did not have far to look. There, in the dusty, abandoned street, stood a man holding a bow. An arrow was nocked but the weapon was not drawn.

"Explain yourself, red cloak," the man said.

Quillion sighed and slouched down into the dirt. The adrenaline from his most recent battle was fading, causing him to crash. The stress of the last few weeks, the marching and the beatings all caught up at once. Quillion knew he had no more tricks left to play.

"I'm no red cloak," he said simply.

"You marched with them," the stranger replied.

"As their prisoner. Look at me!" Quillion lifted his face to the light. "I've been beaten to within an inch of my life. I've just killed five of them."

"Who are you?"

"My name is Quillion. I came to Edentown in pursuit of a man with a star-shaped birthmark. My companions were the swordsman Cole, who lies behind me, and a giant named Kikkan, a former slave."

"Kikkan?"

"Yes."

"Kikkan never mentioned you," the archer snapped.

A ray of hope flashed through Quillion's despair and he found himself laughing. "No, no, he wouldn't have. What about a boy named Weasel?"

The archer advanced to stand before Quillion.

"Weasel told the story of a pair of fools who marched to their deaths," he paused for a moment. "How can I trust you?"

Quillion sighed. He lifted the gun with his thumb and forefinger so that it dangled in the air.

"You saw the power of this weapon?"

"Yes," the man said.

"Then take it. Use it on me if you have no trust. But know I seek only to kill red cloaks."

The man reached forward and took the item. Quillion smiled and slouched back against the door. There was a moment of quiet as the northerner awaited some kind of further attack. When none came, he was emboldened.

"My friend is inside," he said, "he sustained an injury. Might I check on him?"

The man nodded. He was examining the gun, turning it over and over in his hands.

"I can show you how it works," Quillion said. "May I ask your name?"

The archer paused and lifted his head to make eye contact. "My name is Simyon."

Chapter 39: Crawling

Valeria put her shoulder against the decrepit structure and pushed. Miles and Colton did the same. The massive artificial boulder of stone and metal tipped, slowly at first, then gained momentum as gravity took hold. Valeria watched the object fall, quickly gaining speed before crashing into the back of the column.

"Damn!"

Toppling the mass had taken too long. She had hoped to crush the troop's spine rather than clip the tail.

Her frustration was eased by the screams from below. Instantly, her bow was in her hand, arrow nocked and launched. She was higher than any of her companions and had a superior view of how the battle unfolded.

The knot of demons rolling down the street was both beautiful and terrible. Such power remained in the tormented limbs of those pitiful beings. Valeria could even detect the motes of *Bliss* still flashing in the air. The demons' shining eyes were fixated on those particles as well. Their claws came up and dug into red cloak flesh, yet never once did the crazed eyes divert from the focus of their prize.

Valeria saw the Seneschal move like a shadow and disappear under the cover of the building; gone before she could loose an arrow.

"Damn!" she said again, picking a new target and launching a shaft. The red cloaks faced away from her, so she aimed for the neck rather than the eye. She picked the ones standing in confusion at the center. It must be hell down there; terror at the front, walls on all sides, the clamor of battle ringing in their ears.

Valeria smiled.

They had chosen to be terror merchants, yet they squealed like piglets when the tide turned against them. Valeria felt no pity as the bowstring slipped from her finger again and again. Any that survived would resume their duties of pestering the weak; better to gut them now.

A crash got the archer's attention and she looked down to see a group of red cloaks demolish a wall and go scrambling through the rubble.

"Kikkan!" she howled, pointing. The large warrior saw her, but Valeria knew he could not hear. She gestured again, but the escape point was obstructed from Kikkan's view.

Valeria decided in an instant. She slung her bow over her shoulder.

"What are you doing?" Miles asked.

"That's Sergeant Keene slipping away. I can't allow that."

"We can't leave the others," Colton protested, "we can pursue Keene when this battle is in hand."

"It must be now," Valeria snapped, "come on!" She turned and sprinted across the building, jumping a ledge and then to the center where a stairwell would take them to ground level. Colton and Miles could do nothing but follow. They knew the archer. When she had her sights set on prey, she could be diverted only by a kill.

At ground level, Valeria once again readied her bow. Miles and Colton did the same. The three crossed the street, behind where the wreckage had cut off the red cloak retreat.

More demons came, called by the lure of *Bliss*. These were the weaker ones, however; those that didn't have the strength to sprint in pursuit of their calling. Instead, they crawled, pulling their broken bodies along the ground, tearing their flesh upon exposed rocks. Valeria stepped over rubble and watched as the pitiful creatures reached out for her. Some of them had their heads buried in the sand, licking the pavement for particles that had fallen to the ground. Valeria clenched her jaw and moved on.

She knew her actions to be reckless, but the opportunity could not be missed. The liberty to deal out much-needed death came infrequently, and she would not squander the opportunity. She knew the time would never be right for Simyon to aspire to attack Brinewater. His pragmatism bordered on cowardice. All the while, he urged her to endure the trespass of glutinous thugs whose lives did little more than sully the very air she breathed.

One's skin can only crawl for so long. Valeria had changed since their arrival at the outskirts, though Simyon had fooled himself into blindness. The evening kills had brought her peace, and there had been many, many more than even Simyon realized. Through her hunts, she had discovered the truth: the red cloaks were weak, they could be toppled.

Yet it was Simyon the freemen followed, not her. The people were as weak as he; that was why he could influence them. He told them what they already thought.

Very well then, if she could not push them, she would push Simyon.

The thief of San Borja would pursue her; she knew that all too well. She would go all the way to Fort Brinewater this very day if she must. The time was now! One way or another, her life spent cowering in shadows must end.

"Ambush!" Colton cried in terror.

Valeria looked up to see seven red cloak brutes come crashing at them through a window. Shards of glass blew out across the street as Valeria lifted her arm in defense against the cutting edges. She had walked right into their trap.

Valeria loosed her arrow, which found a target without delivering a fatal wound. The red cloak drove forward, slashing with his sword which lodged into the wood of her bow. Valeria kicked the man in the chest, swinging her bow, which, weakened by the chop of the blade, exploded into splinters across the man's face. Her opponent howled, reeling, buying Valeria some space.

Miles and Colton did not fare much better. Even as she watched, a red cloak plunged a sword into Colton's chest. Miles struggled with another, arms locked in battle.

Valeria reached into her vest and threw a glass vial to the ground at the feet of her enemies. Yellow vapor erupted. The red cloaks surrounding Colton's body lifted their hands to their faces and coughed. Valeria took a deep breath as she pulled her long dagger from the sheath at her hip. She dove forward, plunging the blade deep into a flailing man's neck.

In close quarters, the deterrent might have saved her, but out in the open the wind carried the poisonous gas away. A few red cloaks retched and one fell, but the rest remained dangerous and among them was Sergeant Keene. Valeria recognized him as he stepped forward to fasten Miles in a headlock. The red cloak sergeant placed a wicked-looking dagger against the young man's neck.

"You cannot be the archer," Keene said, "you're a woman."

Valeria stood with her dagger at the ready.

"Put it down," Keene said. "Put it down and your friend will accompany us to Fort Brinewater."

"If I refuse?"

"He'll stay here," Keene replied, and he jerked on the dagger. A rivulet of blood ran down the young freeman's neck.

"You'll kill him either way," she said.

Keene laughed. "You're right." He pulled the dagger in a sharp jerk, sending a spray of blood into the air. Valeria dove forward, slashing her dagger across Keene's forehead. Keene absorbed the strike and lifted up the freeman's body as a shield. Valeria's second slash drove into Miles's corpse and Keene drove forward, pushing Valeria off balance and knocking her down. From there, she was quickly overpowered. Her skin crawled, worse than before. The feeling of helplessness, present after such a prolonged absence, was almost too much to bear.

"I'm glad you happened along," Keene said, "otherwise this outing might have been a total disaster."

Chapter 40: Opportunity

"May I check on my friend?" Quillion asked again.

Simyon was indecisive. He glanced out beyond Quillion into the distance as though he were in the middle of a desperate pursuit and every passing second pained him. The sound of heavy footfalls drew Simyon's attention and he turned to see a man approaching.

"Darrik," Simyon called out in relief. "What news?"

"Chaos," Darrik replied. "The main group is still back there struggling with the demons. I'm not sure where Valeria and the others went; we have lost their trail."

"Did Weasel get away?"

"I don't know," Darrik replied.

"Damn!" Simyon said. "And Kikkan?"

"Off to fight the Seneschal."

"That will be a good fight," Quillion offered. "He's already dispatched one."

Simyon looked back at the stout swordsman and considered for a moment, but now he made up his mind. Urgency did not leave time for lengthy contemplation.

"We better check your friend," he said. "We cannot linger here."

Quillion nodded and gestured at the bodies. "The clothing of these dead ones has been coated in *Bliss*. How long before the demons come?"

Simyon seemed startled at Quillion's precise observations, but he didn't waste time with questions. "Soon."

Quillion pushed open the door. Simyon and Darrik watched Quillion as he moved toward Cole. The lean swordsman lay prostrate in the hall.

"Cole," Quillion said, nudging the man. To Quillion's great relief, Cole groaned.

"What happened?" Quillion asked.

"I don't know," Cole replied. "The explosion of that weapon hit me like a roundhouse to the ear."

Quillion squinted in the shadow and saw a trickle of blood running down Cole's cheek.

"Come on, friend, the demons will be here soon."

Cole nodded, and allowed Quillion to help him regain his feet. The two stumbled back to reunite with Simyon and Darrik.

The brief calm that had seized Simyon at the appearance of Darrik was quickly evaporating, replaced by frantic energy.

"Come on," he snapped, and then set off. Darrik brought up the rear, urging the two former red cloaks on. To Quillion, the configuration seemed a needless risk. As far as the freemen knew, he and Cole were enemies, assassins, or worse. True, he had just slaughtered five red cloaks, but a man who slaughtered his fellows could not be considered trustworthy. Quillion could see a fire was burning within Simyon; some kind of mania that pushed him to make frantic choices. The northerner noted opportunities would be forthcoming.

They went at a run. As the buildings flew by, Cole leaned in for counsel. "What's happening?"

"We're in pursuit of someone," Quillion replied.

"Who?"

"I don't know."

"Kikkan?"

"I don't think so, it seems he's off fighting Janus."

Cole snorted. "That will be a good fight."

"That's what I said." They settled into silence.

Within the cover of the buildings, Simyon stopped periodically. He crouched to the ground before standing and picking a direction. He led them to a stairwell and flew up like a man possessed. After several flights, Simyon came to an abrupt halt. He was pensive. In the brief reprieve, Quillion again turned to Cole.

"You were doing well in the red cloaks," he said, "why did you come with me when I broke away?"

Cole gave him an incredulous glance. Then he turned his attention back to Simyon.

"I've marched with you long enough to know you always have something up your sleeve."

It was Quillion's turn to be surprised.

"You give me too much credit. Never have I made such a sequence of poor decisions as I have these last few weeks."

Cole gave a humorless grunt. "That may be, but I've observed you execute a lethal strike from a prone position. I don't fear a man facing me with a sword. I fear the man who can kill me unobserved from the shadows two days before I even think to attack."

Cole's words disturbed Quillion; he didn't want his friend operating on false assumptions. "There's no larger plan, Cole. I try to survive from moment to moment, like anyone else."

"That's where you're wrong," Cole replied, "there is a larger plan, one that you contribute to without even knowing."

Before Quillion could reply, Simyon cut loose with an agonized scream.

Quillion feared they were under attack, but Simyon seemed to have forgotten the two mercenaries.

"The deterrent!" Simyon yelled. "I smell it! She's unleashed the deterrent!"

Darrik seemed as confused by this declaration as Quillion and Cole.

"Valeria!" Simyon howled, half crazed and still not making sense. "There are bodies below!" In his madness, he began muttering. "I told her not to engage. I told her a dozen times! Stubborn . . . proud . . . deceitful . . ."

Simyon pushed past them again. For a second, Quillion considered overpowering Darrik. Perhaps he and Cole could cut their losses and escape this place. But even as the idea occurred to him, it was discarded. The red cloaks were near, as were the demons. Quillion did not wish to break the uneasy truce in the presence of so many enemies. Also, to quit now would mean the suffering they had endured would be for nothing. The stout northerner felt he was on the cusp of a realization he could not abandon. Following his instincts, as always, Quillion set off after the frenzied freeman.

Back in the street, on the other side of the building, they found the bodies. Now the odor that Simyon had detected was strong. It was a foreign scent to Quillion, but he had no doubt as to its potency. Even now, significantly after release, the smell made him light-headed and weak.

Two of the bodies were freemen, two were red cloaks. One of the red cloaks had been stabbed in the neck, the other was simply comatose. Simyon ran up to this one. He pulled his sword from its sheath and stabbed the body a dozen times with a ferocity Quillion had rarely observed. Simyon then kneeled to check the two freemen. Shaking his head, he stood.

"Miles and Colton," Simyon said, "both dead. Miles got his throat cut. They've taken her." He pointed at the ground. "Do you see? They dragged her off."

"How many?" Quillion asked.

"Four or five." Simyon put his hands to his head in desperation. "She provoked this! She wants me to attack Brinewater. She gave herself up!"

"That's ridiculous," Darrik replied.

"You don't know her like I do! No one does!"

So that's it, Quillion thought, *he loves her. That explains the erratic behavior.*

Simyon continued, "We have to get her." He stood frozen, questing for a solution, any insane, crazy chance of a hope that he could grasp on to. Quillion recognized his opportunity.

"Send me," he said.

The words cut through Simyon's hysteria and restored a degree of clarity.

"Send you?" he asked, as curious as he was disdainful.

"You've been planning an attack on Brinewater?" Quillion asked. Simyon tensed, but Quillion continued. "How long until you can mobilize?"

Simyon said nothing, his eyes narrowing as he assessed Quillion.

"Send me first," Quillion persisted. "They know me, I can distract them. I can buy you the time you need to initiate an assault."

"You'd like that, wouldn't you?" Simyon replied. "You'd like the chance to warn your friends we are coming."

"Look at me, Simyon." Quillion gestured at his bruises. "Do you think I am the red cloaks' favorite? They've beaten me to within an inch of my life."

"Then why would they listen to you?"

"I can be persuasive. I'm persuading you, aren't I?"

Simyon scowled, but Quillion knew he had scored a point.

"You don't have any time, Simyon. This Valeria, is she the one they know as the archer?"

Simyon nodded slowly, confirming Quillion's educated guess.

"Then they'll have her staked to a pole in the courtyard before the sun sets. Any delay I can create will aid you. Even if they spend time mobilizing a defense, at least they won't be reveling in her torture."

Simyon growled.

"You lose nothing by sending me."

"And what do *you* gain?"

"Your trust and a place among the freemen for Cole and me, or only Cole in the event that I do not return. You'll find him a capable warrior. We don't have the luxury of earning each other's confidence. My instinct tells me you are an ally; my instinct has saved my life before. There is no time."

Simyon's jaw tightened. "If you betray me, your friend will suffer."

Cole said nothing, but his eyes flicked to Quillion.

"I will not betray you."

"Then go."

Quillion didn't need to be told twice. He set off at a jog along the path where the inert body had been dragged.

Chapter 41: Risk vs. Reward

Quillion leaned against the dusty remains of a stone column and retched. Doubt assailed him. Had the moment of clarity passed? Had the *Bliss* or the foul chemical the red cloaks used to corrupt his food altered his perception? The muscles in his stomach strained and he felt a terrible pull against his throat and bowels. A sheen of sweat broke out on his brow. Yet something pushed him on.

The moment has come. It has to be now.

The red cloaks had to fall, and Quillion could perceive the seed of revolution waiting to sprout in the heart of Simyon and his band of freemen. Something yet could be won from the trick Adam Lockhart played when he urged them to seek out this cursed city. The freemen could be forged; they needed only a symbol, something to provide the spark necessary to commit their hearts to war. The archer would be that symbol. Quillion did not fool himself into thinking she remained alive. Captain Jesse did not hesitate when it came to the slaughter of her enemies. Yet even dead, the woman could be useful. Once Simyon saw the broken, tortured body of his love hanging in the courtyard, the leader of the freemen would be open to influence.

Quillion's nausea stabilized. He resumed his march, following the trail clearly marked in the dust before him. He would arrive at Fort Brinewater in the early evening.

Are you mad? She'll kill you!

He snorted at the thought; the time for Captain Jesse's downfall had long since passed. Even she must recognize her current state of vulnerability. The recent loss of so many under her command could not be ignored. Could it?

Doubts rose again but Quillion fought them back. Had she not earned a command? True he had witnessed her make only spiteful and impulsive decisions, but the station she held indicated an inherent capacity for reason. By her own words, incompetence could not rise so high. Quillion hated the masters, but he respected them as well. The world held little tolerance for fools, and those that thrived displayed capacity. Quillion would find her deeply buried sliver of reason and leverage it to her destruction.

Quillion had no intention of dying. Staking the archer would satiate Jesse's bloodlust. At best, he would be able to convince her to hear his counsel; at worst, she'd have him beaten and thrown in the dungeon to save for the next need for public display. Either way, Quillion was confident he could distract Jesse long enough to give Simyon time to mount an assault. Then would come chaos, followed by opportunity—as always

The trail brought Quillion near the narrow alley where the Seneschal-guided troop had been attacked. Bodies lined the street and demons perched on top of them, preening the cloaks and exposed surfaces where the *Bliss* dust had collected. The northerner wrinkled his nose at the sight. Every corpse on the battlefield lay buried beneath a small pack of demons. The pitiful creatures jostled one another for space, their heads moving frantically like piglets wrestling for a sow's teat.

The weaker ones sat propped up against buildings, lifting their arms in gestures of pathetic supplication. They had spent the last of their energy in answering the call of the malicious scent, and they would die here now within arm's reach of their goal.

These rotten, tormented figures were the foundation upon which the world sat.

Forget them, fool! Consider yourself.

Once again, Quillion steeled himself against his internal doubts. Jesse had never disguised her ambition. From the beginning she had marked Quillion as a candidate for example. Before this night was over, he resolved to put an end to her. He looked forward to seeing the look in her eye as she realized the truth of her defeat.

High risk, high reward.

The hours passed and the shadows lengthened as the northerner continued his trek.

A cold breeze sent a shiver down Quillion's spine, and he looked up to see the black gates of Fort Brinewater rising up in the distance. The time had come to put his theory to the test.

As the gates cracked open, Quillion looked past the soldiers who rushed out to detain him, expecting to see the archer's broken body dangling from a pole in the courtyard.

His search was to no avail. There was nothing; the courtyard was empty.

*

Kikkan found the trails easy enough to follow. The battle was over. The zombies or demons had done their work.

Many of the pitiful creatures lay dead in the narrows. Others had managed to scrape up enough *Bliss* dust to achieve a kind of restless sleep state. The ones that were neither dead nor intoxicated had dispersed. That left Kikkan to search for the freemen.

What would they think when they saw him again? Had they intended for him to be killed by the Seneschal? Would they be accepting of the truth?

Kikkan had instructed Janus to trail him out of sight. The thought of having someone he didn't completely trust at his back was discomforting, but Kikkan was not in a position to avoid risks. He knew that someday all the chances he took would catch up with him. He could only dream of a time when threats did not snap forever at his heels.

Kikkan followed a promising set of tracks to a building where five red cloaks had been slaughtered. The demons hovered over the corpses, eating the cloaks and humming to themselves like feral beasts. Kikkan wrinkled his nose in disgust and slipped by the repugnant feeding. The tracks continued through a building, then back down to ground level. Kikkan found the bodies of Miles and Colton, two more he had marched with, two more dead. From there, the paths split; one toward Brinewater, one to somewhere else.

Kikkan picked the latter, shifted his pack, and accelerated to a run.

The day was waning and the air grew colder. The silence of the city unsettled him. Something was happening. The ambiance felt threatening; a predator neared.

Kikkan passed by the buildings, weaving between them, but he did not have far to go. He heard voices up ahead. People were gathering on the surface. It was unlike Simyon to make a spectacle, but Kikkan had little doubt who he had found. Those gathered did not bark at each other, instead there was a kind of muted excitement in their lilting tones. Something essentially . . . human.

"Kikkan!" came a voice, and although there was no order, Kikkan knew the utterance of his name was a command to stop. Stop he did, holding his hands out wide from his body, knowing that the next few minutes would prove delicate. There was some muffled dialogue, then Darrik came running up, followed by Simyon.

"So, you survived the Seneschal," Simyon said.

Kikkan nodded. He looked past Simyon and was surprised to see Cole approaching.

"Hello, Cole," he said, then to Simyon, "So that devil Quillion managed to endear himself to you?"

"He said you marched with him," Simyon replied, measuring Kikkan's response.

"That's true," Kikkan said.

"The red cloaks have taken Valeria. We sent Quillion to delay her execution." At Simyon's next words, Kikkan was surprised to hear the freeman's voice crack with emotion. "Is he honorable?"

Kikkan met Cole's eyes, then turned back to Simyon.

"He is, although I did not recognize it until recently."

Some of the tension that seemed to be eating Simyon eased, but he was still a bundle of energy. He reached forward and clasped Kikkan on the shoulder.

"Will you join us in an attack on Brinewater to rescue the archer?"

"I will," Kikkan said, for the archer had been kind to him; one of the few who had.

"You understand that this task will most likely claim us all?" Simyon continued.

"I do," Kikkan replied, "so it is with all my labors."

Simyon gave Kikkan an apologetic glance. "I'm sorry I've been slow to trust you."

Kikkan nodded. "Do you trust me now?"

"Yes."

"Good," said Kikkan, "for I have brought another asset to our gathering." He turned to the shadows, which were growing steadily longer behind him. "May I present Janus of Edentown."

Cole gasped. Simyon seemed only confused until the tall figure of the Seneschal stepped from the darkness. Instantly, Simyon was a flurry of motion, for he recognized the man from the torture halls of San Aryan. He pulled the gun Quillion had given him from his belt. With a shaking arm, he aimed the barrel at the imposing Seneschal and pulled the trigger as he had seen Quillion do to devastating effect against the red cloaks.

This time, there was no explosion.

This time, the enemy's head did not evaporate into a cloud of crimson fog.

The action turned and the hammer connected with a click, but other than that the weapon was useless.

Janus was startled, but then he smiled, his teeth reflecting white against the backdrop of encroaching darkness.

"I am Janus of Edentown," he declared, "trained by Adam Lockhart. I am not your enemy." He squinted at Simyon. "I recognize you."

Simyon trembled, shaking the mysterious weapon in an attempt to figure out why it had failed. Janus stepped forward and tossed something into the air. The item landed at Simyon's feet. It was a box of tiny cylinders.

"Without bullets, the gun is just a piece of metal," Janus said, his voice taking on an air of exasperation. "I overheard you talking before, and I understand time is of the essence.

I suggest you either load a bullet into that gun and shoot me now, or accept my assistance in your raid. I have the power to render the walls of Fort Brinewater to dust if you'll have me, but the choice is yours."

Simyon gazed at the Seneschal.

A pregnant silence ensued.

*

Men from the gate tackled Quillion to the ground and bound the stout northerner's hands behind his back.

"I'm a red cloak," Quillion declared.

"Why are you out of uniform?" came the reply.

Quillion tried to answer but received a cuff to the side of his head.

After a momentary scuffle, they pulled Quillion to his feet and pushed him through the gates. They marched him with his hands behind his back. The position was awkward and Quillion knew he looked a fool as he was paraded through the courtyard to the jeers of his fellows.

All I need to do is buy time, he thought; *every second is a victory.*

All too soon, Quillion was presented at the door to Captain Jesse's office. The men knocked and waited until Jesse's indecipherable grunt gave them leave to enter.

"Captain," one of the men said, "the deserter has returned."

Quillion ground his teeth at the stupidity. Had not even the recent slaughter unnerved them?

False beliefs hold despite overwhelming evidence and fuse ambition to failure.

Adam Lockhart's words.

The men released Quillion and he was free to stand.

Captain Jesse sat examining some objects. Quillion knew better than to lift his gaze from a submissive bow, but it appeared Jesse was handling an archer's arm bracer.

The moment lingered. The delay played into Quillion's favor.

"Where is your cloak?" Captain Jesse asked.

"The freemen doused our cloaks with a substance that drew the attention of the demons. I had to discard my garment so I could better serve your command."

Jesse snorted.

"To remove your cloak while on patrol is a capital offense."

Quillion made no reply.

Captain Jesse stood and faced the window. Below, a group of men could be seen carrying a staking pole through the front gate.

"I knew you'd be a problem from the moment I first laid eyes on you. There is impertinence in your bearing that cannot be disguised." She turned and walked around the table, coming to stand so close to Quillion that her nose almost touched his. "Even now I see it. Even now in this moment, when you should be trembling with fear and pleading for your miserable life."

"Captain, I did not desert, my troop was attacked. I have valuable information."

Jesse maintained a disinterested expression as she returned to the other side of her desk. "Report, then."

"I am assuming you have the archer in your custody?" Quillion said. "I have learned that she is of great importance to the freemen who attacked us in the narrows. She can be used as leverage, but only if she is kept alive."

Jesse sat. She tapped the surface of her desk with her index finger and stared at the wood.

Quillion fell silent.

"How did you come by this knowledge?" Jesse asked.

"I observed that the archer's capture set off a frenzy among our enemies' ranks."

"What happened to the rest of your troop?"

"Our enemy held an elevated position and slaughtered us with arrows coordinated with a demon attack. Many were killed, although some must have managed to escape and return."

"The Seneschal?"

"I do not know what became of him."

"Private Cole?"

"Struck down."

Jesse laughed, lifting her head to look at Quillion in open mockery. "Of all the sub-human mongrels that have ever stepped through the gates of Brinewater, I believe you must be the most arrogant. Did you really think I would believe you? You've shown nothing but incompetence on the battle-field and insubordination off it."

Quillion paled at the assault but found his voice. "I seek only to serve and to advance within your noble command."

"Advance!" Jesse roared, slamming her hands down on the desk. "There's no advancement for a lowborn outland half-breed such as you. You're inferior! No amount of labor will ever change that. You're barely worth the entertainment that can be gained from watching you dangle on a hanging pole. You are of the ilk that must be cleansed from the world."

Quillion set his jaw. "Captain, your life is at stake."

Jesse's eyes narrowed. "Excuse me?"

"Have you truly failed to perceive the threat?" Quillion said. "Seven red cloaks slaughtered in the market, four in the risers, and today a coordinated attack against an entire troop. We are at war, and losing numbers! Give your loyal men an opportunity to prove their worth!" Quillion studied Jesse's face, hoping he had finally managed to penetrate the prejudice and engage her sense of self-preservation.

Captain Jesse issued a loud snort. "Loyal? Sergeant Keene, enter!"

The name caused the pit of Quillion's stomach to drop. He had not observed Keene during the battle, but truth had never been a vital component of Keene's reports.

The brutish sergeant entered the room. Blood stained his face from a jagged wound across his forehead, but he seemed otherwise fit.

"Sergeant Keene," Jesse said. "Did you witness the actions of this private in the ambush at the narrows?"

"I did."

"And what were those actions?"

Keene did not hesitate. "The private stabbed two red cloaks in the back, then stripped himself of his uniform in an attempt to desert."

What madness was this? Some bending of the truth was to be expected but an outright fabrication...

Quillion glanced at Captain Jesse and recoiled at the transparent grin plastered across her features. Her face reminded him of a petulant child, secure in some artificial sense of victory, while totally oblivious to her impending destruction.

He was struck by a thunderbolt of clarity. A series of mental puzzle pieces wrenched themselves into position revealing a truth beyond the meager vision of his stolen education. The foundation of his thinking had been incorrect, and now the whole of reality seemed a different color.

Throughout his scheming, he'd never imagined Jesse's impulsive mix of pride and arrogance would continue in the face of annihilation. He'd assumed that persona to be an act, a by-product of laziness and boredom. He knew her to be a fool, yes, but he'd never believed her to be a blind fool.

In all his musings he'd failed to conceive there could be a class of people born to such privilege that they had no need to learn or obey the basic principles of survival. He'd believed anyone who rose to a position of mastery over others must posses at least enough competence to make them predictable. Yet here was Captain Jesse defiantly focused on her petty war of spite with Quillion even as a deadly enemy marshaled at her gate. Fleetingly he wondered if she'd be surprised to find out he had actually endeavored to betray her? Or did she take greater delight inflicting punishment for an accusation she believed in her heart to be false?

"Do you have anything to say in your defense?" Jesse asked with a mocking grin.

No, she could not see him as a threat, privy as she was to the truth beyond the veil of lies cultivated within the psyche of the low-born. What monsters they were to look upon a babe and see only a vessel for false wisdom designed to mutilate the child's capacity for navigating life. Quillion now saw the deceptions for what they were, a social covenant maintained by the elite designed to subjugate any man or woman not born to power. The masses were tricked into yielding their youthful strength in exchange for the promise of a vague and distant reward. But the ladder could not be climbed. Captain Jesse did not owe her station to hard work and the demonstration of ability. Those born at the top had sabotaged the rungs that enabled meritorious ascent. Vacant posts were fertile plots corrupted by seeds of incest, and Quillion assumed Captain Jesse to be only one of many.

In all his scrambling to procure the fallen scraps of higher tables, Quillion had been too preoccupied to see the truth. There is no path by which a slave might travel from labor to fortune, and so the masters, to protect their lives of leisure, must make their servants blind. The armor Quillion carried had been forged with a fatal weakness. He could perceive it now, but as the scholar predicted, the realization had come too late.

"Anything Quillion? It's not like you to lose your tongue." Jesse said, she was almost laughing now.

He had fortified himself with reason only to be undone by insanity. He had never conceived incompetence and arrogance might align to so thoroughly defeat him.

"When I returned," Quillion said, resignation entering his voice, "I expected to see the archer hanging in the courtyard."

"We fully intend to stake her, after we get to know her better," Captain Jesse said. "In the meantime, we'll have to make do with you."

Chapter 42: The Martyr

How had it come to this?

To lose to a thing as wretched as Captain Jesse made the torment nearly unbearable.

A horde of shouting beasts closed in around him. Quillion hated them all. Feral creatures devoid of any justification for life. What purpose did they serve but to laugh as they watched the world crumble into destruction by their hand?

They would have their victory now.

The wall of sound they produced seemed to be edged with all the hatred and mockery of the world.

Quillion flashed in and out of full awareness. Keene had thrown the stout northerner against every stone wall and corner as he marched Quillion to a small cell before the courtyard. The northerner had lost even the strength to spit, and blood pooled around his slack lips.

Beyond the door, Quillion could hear voices rise and fall in the courtyard. Declarations were shouted and every one was met with a cheer.

The fools thought they had been spared; too blind to ever comprehend how they sowed the seeds of their own destruction. Most celebrated with joy simply because they would not be the ones tortured that evening.

How he longed to see them all dead!

But that would not happen now.

I have not bought enough time!

The door opened and Quillion was pushed through. Darkness had fallen; torches were raised. Quillion saw only the flash of red cloaks; the bulging muscles of his tormentors; and the black mud as it rushed up to meet him. The dirt ground into his mouth and eyes. He tried to spit, but he lacked the force.

No sooner had he hit the ground than he was jerked again to his feet, only to be struck in the face by an anonymous tormentor.

Quillion collapsed again.

Words were said, but Quillion couldn't comprehend them.

Cheers echoed as if muted by water.

Quillion crawled.

He lifted his head and saw the body of a woman tied to the opposing wall.

That must be the archer. What have they done to her?

The sight of the bruised and battered body filled Quillion's heart with regret.

A hulking form obstructed his vision; another animal wading forward to pester him. The brutalization continued for an indeterminate amount of time. In flashes, Quillion saw faces he recognized, or heard a fleeting fragment of a word, but mostly he knew only disorientation, pain and defeat as he was struck, collapsed, and then made to endure the cycle again.

The laughter was the worst.

Kikkan had been right to answer evil with death. Finesse was self-defeating against such as these. They had to be cut out; there was no chance for redemption.

There was a lapse in the torment, followed by silence.

The mud drawn into his mouth with every breath indicated that Quillion was prone against the ground. In the absence of assaults, he risked cracking an eyelid.

His vision was blurred through swollen eyes and the trickle of blood. Quillion waited for the image to focus, but didn't dare shift his head in fear of the waves of nausea that would surely come.

Despair claimed him. They had won. They were stronger.

In the distance, Quillion made out marching figures. They approached, carrying a stake which they threw down upon him. He didn't move.

"Get up!"

He heard the command repeated twice, followed by a heavy boot driving into his leg.

Quillion wanted only to sleep. He half-expected the raging brutes to mount him in his crippled state. What joy they took from violating weakness.

"Get up!" the command came a third time.

Quillion could not will himself to obey.

"The weakling can't do it," the voice said. The gathering laughed. "Very well, let's stake him here."

The night sky turned red. A demon's face leered before Quillion, yellow fangs flashed. The northerner could no longer separate illusion from reality. Flames erupted along the horizon.

Quillion felt himself being lifted onto the pole. His arms were gathered over his head, one stacked upon the other. More laughter.

A sane man would stop this. A sane man is immune to the seduction of the mob.

But no sane men were present.

Quillion felt the cold metal of a spike pressed into his arm just below his wrist. He heard the noise of the mallet's blow and the vibrations of the rod before he felt the pain of penetration. But when the pain came, it consumed him. He howled, and the crowd cheered.

These aren't people. They are false creatures disguised in human form. I will never mistake them again.

Quillion felt the pole lift into the air.

Breath came hard. The weight of his body tore against his shattered arms. His vision dimmed. He felt himself slipping.

Thunder rumbled in the distance, followed by the pattering of objects on the sand. Quillion waited for the rain to come, but the sound changed again. He thought he heard screams and the clatter of steel.

Am I dreaming?

Am I dead already?

Darkness closed about him, but there was movement below. The red cloaks scattered like rats.

What's happening?

Over the outer wall came a tide. A glorious, cleansing tide to wipe away the refuse and reveal the glittering surface beneath. The tide came with shouts of triumph, and cheers that brought a surge to Quillion's broken spirit.

What . . . ?

Steel blades reflected the flicker of torchlight. Cries continued; cries of victory and terror. Battle raged.

In his delirium, the cleansing wave began to take on the form of familiar figures.

Why, there's Kikkan, laying about with his devastating pipe . . .

There's Cole, cutting a path with his sword . . .

Is that Weasel . . . ?

Is that . . . ?

The images alternated between dream and reality as his consciousness faded. Quillion strained to watch, to make sense, but the pull of oblivion was upon him. He found himself less and less inclined to resist.

Is that the Seneschal Janus fighting? What enticed him to this vision?

Quillion's lips twisted into a smile. The vision couldn't be true and he took the Seneschal's presence to mean he had passed beyond the realm of suffering.

A wave of agony rose up to deprive the northerner of his false calm. Quillion writhed in torment. Every muscle howled in anguish, every nerve-ending withered and burned. Through the trial, his involuntary spirit resisted surrender, manifesting a stubborn compulsion to endure. Branded by brutality, body broken, a spark grew sufficient to ignite the world. Quillion vowed to make his masters lament their efficacy in teaching the depths to which man can descend.

www.ingramcontent.com/pod-product-compliance
Lightning Source LLC
Chambersburg PA
CBHW031332020726
47499CB00005B/1225